Zone War

John Conroe

The Demon Accords:
God Touched
Demon Driven
Brutal Asset
          Black Frost
Duel Nature
Fallen Stars
Executable
Forced Ascent
College Arcane
God Hammer
Rogues
Snake Eyes
Winterfall
Summer Reign
The Demon Accords Compendium, Volume 1
The Demon Accords Compendium Volume 2

Zone War series:

Zone War
Borough of Bones (coming Spring, 2019)

Cover art by Gareth Otton.

Chapter 1

*"And now for today's edition of Zone War. Viewers are warned
that this presentation may include sudden images
of extreme graphic violence, including death. This production is
unscripted and carried live in unedited format for an authentic
viewing experience. Under no circumstances should any viewer
attempt to enter the Manhattan Drone Zone without explicit
authorization by the Department of Zone Defense
Exclusion Authority. All of the salvage and bounty personnel
depicted are duly licensed and trained professionals. There are
no amateurs in Zone War, and Flottercot Productions is not
liable for any injuries or deaths incurred by viewers of this
program. In other words, do not try this yourself."*

Of course I had to cross the living room at that exact moment,
my bowl of ice cream balanced on my work tablet. I had timed
my foray into the kitchen with exacting precision, determined to
be in and out in under two minutes, which was the amount of
time till that blasted show started. The rest of my family was
huddled around the viewing wall in anticipation of the daily
showing of what was currently the most popular reality show in
the world. Not being able to find the ice cream scoop had foiled
my plan.

The screen melted from the skyline background with floating
words to a live feed showing bouncing footage of one of

downtown Manhattan's deserted streets, husks of cars littered about, a stoplight lying on the road. The sun was out and the camera mounted on the outside of the Light Armored Vehicle was broadcasting a clear, high-def picture, even if it was shaky from the vehicle's ride.

Catching the opening scene was my first piece of bad luck. The second was Monique catching sight of me in the corner of her eye. "Hey, AJ's here. You gonna watch it with us this time? Or hide in your room?"

"I'm going to work in my room, little sister, so that we can get paid for what I brought out yesterday," I said.

The *little sister* part was ill-advised on my part, as it was guaranteed to trigger her twin's temper. Gabby whipped around on the couch and glared at me. "Oh, is big brother busy saving the day?"

Fourteen-year-old girls should come with the same kind of hazardous warning labels used for explosives and poisons. I'd rather face the Zone any day than get drawn into a verbal war with my lethal little sisters, who fire off words faster than a Russian Wolf anti-personnel drone fires flechettes.

"Gabby, enough. Ajaya's work is important to this family and you know it. All of our BUIs together aren't enough to support us, even with your father's death benefit," my mother said, shutting down the more volatile of the twins. Then she turned my way. "And you, Ajaya Edward Gurung, how many times have I warned you about arrogance?"

5

"I wasn't being arrogant, Mom. I was making the point that I have other things to do besides watch that crap, especially when I can see it in person any day I want—if I want to take the risk of being near them," I said, moderating my tone.

Behind my mother, the terrible twins both raised their hands and enacted individual ceremonial displays of the middle finger. Monique chose to pull off the imaginary top of her middle finger lipstick and apply a liberal dose to her lips, while Gabrielle blew into her thumb to inflate her own middle digit.

My eyes flicked their way and then back to my mother, whose face had taken on her stoic look. The one where she tries not to crumble for fear of my weekly forays into what was regularly described by the *Zone War* narrator as the most dangerous place on Earth.

And it was. Take the island of Manhattan, release over twenty-five thousand highly advanced Russian, Chinese, and Indian autonomous war drones in a single stunning act of terrorism, and let simmer for ten years. The result was the one borough of New York City that was completely devoid of human inhabitants and whose artificially intelligent denizens aggressively kept it that way.

It was estimated that over three hundred and seventy-two thousand people lost their lives in the first week of the Manhattan Attack. Another twenty-three thousand died during the second week, as rescue operations and military units

6

counterattacked. Only a crazy fast response by US special operations ready reaction teams, in coordination with New York National Guard, FBI, NYPD, and a whole alphabet of other federal groups, kept the drones from escaping into the other four boroughs. The whole world almost died as an enraged America brought the doomsday clock to 11:59:59, saved by uncharacteristic transparency on the part of Russia, India, and China, who all stepped up to provide assistance and data about their drone weapon systems and particularly against the terrorists.

Ten years later, the terrorists who were responsible, the Gaia Group, were completely obliterated, hunted with a chilling ruthlessness by a fiercely unified United States. The borough island, however, was still a no-man's-land. And a rich one at that.

Everyone in Manhattan either fled or died in not much more than a few days' time. One of the wealthiest communities on Earth became empty so fast that countless riches, both literal and information-based, were left lying around for anyone to pick up. Anyone who could get safely past the lethal new owners, that is. Hence *Zone War*, a show that followed five salvage teams as they braved the Zone on a regular basis to kill drones and pull out abandoned riches. The Zone was also the source of my income, the money that kept my family afloat after Wall Street crashed, was abandoned, then relocated piecemeal to backup sites around the East Coast. The massive worldwide recession that followed dwarfed all others before it. Ten years later, the world economy was just now starting to see the sprouts of fiscal recovery. Yes, we all received the Basic

Universal Income checks that were paid out to all Americans, but that wasn't enough to do more than cover bare necessities, as Mom had said.

Zone War was a huge success, a show that followed the flashiest and noisiest salvage teams. And none of them made more noise than Johnson Recovery.

"Oh, Ajaya, there is your girl," Aama said from her spot between my sisters. My father's mother is quite the romantic. Both of my sisters turned and gave me their best smirks. I ignored them, but I couldn't quite bring myself to ignore the monitor. Onscreen, the camera had switched to the face of the LAV driver. The blonde, blue-eyed Scandinavian goddess of the drone hunt, Astrid Johnson.

The youngest member of Johnson Recovery, a.k.a. Team Johnson, Astrid was the principal LAV driver but also filled the role of overwatch sharpshooter when more than two of the team deployed from their armored vehicle. A beautiful, smart, and very tough girl, she was hugely popular across the nation and probably most of the globe, a role model for girls and an object of fantasy for guys of all ages. I've known her since we were both ten.

Only her oldest brother, JJ, was as popular. Tall, muscular, and bold, JJ was the JR point man for ground deployments, and his media nickname was Thor, possibly because of the big sledgehammer he used to break into buildings, possibly because of his blond good looks. Women sure seemed to dig him.

You had to give him his due. Even with full body armor, he took enormous risks every time he stepped foot on Manhattan soil, mostly due to his father's preferred approach to things—drive fast and loud, shoot everything in sight, and then haul ass back out at extreme speed. Right on cue, the camera view switched to show JJ crouching with his father, Brad, just behind the driver's seat.

Brad Johnson, or Colonel Brad Johnson, was ex-US Army. He'd started his career in tanks, then moved into a Stryker Brigade Combat Team, and never looked back. He and the rest of his family were in Manhattan, visiting an old military friend, on the night the drones were released. They escaped, as did their host family. Drone Night was a life-changing event for anyone who survived it and Brad Johnson was as effected as anyone—maybe more so. Within a year, Brad had quit the military and the Johnsons had relocated to Brooklyn. Brad started Zone salvage work, even as the military was still permanently blockading the island. He started work with his military friend, an ex-British SAS sniper named Baburam Gurung—my father. Eventually they had a falling out over work methods and went their separate ways.

I turned away from the show and walked out of the room, down the hall, and into my bedroom, which is also my office. Time to make some money.

Chapter 2

"Status?" I asked.

"Current bids on items one through ten, twelve, and fourteen are all below reserve level," my personal AI reported. *"Items eleven, thirteen, and fifteen have been purchased for the Buy Now price."*

"Time left on remaining items?"

"Fourteen hours and seven minutes."

There are almost as many ways to make money in the Zone as there are ways to die. Almost. The most common is salvage. The New York State court system ruled that anything found and recovered inside the exclusion zone was the property of the finder. Federal Circuit court cases backed that decision. Finders keepers was the law of the Zone. And Manhattan was chock full of stuff to find: from cash, gems, jewelry, art, furniture, fashion items and electronics, to corporate secrets and proprietary information on stand-alone computer systems, all abandoned in the Attack.

The Johnson family had proven to be experts at monetizing the Zone. Initially, Brad and my father had brought out cash that they recovered from stores and banks. Nowadays, the JR team just went in hell bent for leather, raided an art gallery, jeweler's, or even an haute fashion store, and bulled their way back out. Only licensed recovery agents were allowed onto the island, but the Johnsons also acted as guides, highly paid ones, for rich people who wanted to experience shooting a Chinese Raptor drone or firing a .50 caliber anti-material rifle into a Tiger ground unit. Then there were the massive studio fees paid to the on-air talent that made *Zone War* the top show on the globe. Yes, the other teams contributed to the popularity, but the attractive Scandinavian war family was top draw. If you don't believe me, just count the ads you see some or all of them in. Hocking everything from the latest workout clothes to Astrid's own line of makeup for combat, to JJ's signature basketball shoes.

As wealthy as they had become, the JR Team's approach to salvage left a lot to be desired, especially if you wanted a really tricky recovery, like, say, corporate intellectual property left on the twenty-second floor of a downtown high rise. Their bull-in-a-china shop approach stirred up every drone in a half-mile radius, leaving them with just a handful of minutes to extract their valuables before the sheer numbers would overwhelm even their heavily armored vehicles.

That's where I came in. Gurung Extraction had a sterling reputation for bringing back hard-to-recover items. That's because I'm stealthy AF. Slip in and slip out. Part training by my sniper dad and part tech magic of my own design. The things I was selling on the Zone-ite auction site were just extra, mostly jewelry, that I found along my way. We also had the beginnings of a pretty good family bank account going, the result of stashing any and all cash picked up during my Zone travels.

That was going to pay the twins' way through college. But the real money came from specific recovery missions.

"You have three new queries for services."

"Summarize, please." For some reason, I was always polite with AI. Most people weren't. It just seemed right somehow.

"One is a request for choice items of sports memorabilia housed in a private collection in the Upper West Side, the second for recovery of legal papers from a personal residence, and the third is a corporate query for proprietary software in a Wall Street trading office."

"Triage, please."

"The corporate request is the only one that meets or exceeds your risk-reward minimum offer. The sports request is not remotely rewarding enough, and the stated offer for the legal papers is far below the corporate query. Additionally, there is a time-adjusted bonus for the recovery of the computer records."

"Display."

The one blank wall in my room lit up with the email including two financial numbers, the main offer and the bonus, each of which were large enough to make me set my ice cream aside. Somebody really wanted their algorithms. Which immediately begged the question as to why now—ten years later? Actually reading the email all the way through answered that question, or at least provided an answer.

"—Zone recovery rates of success have not been deemed sufficient until now to attempt salvage," I read out loud.

"Somebody's been paying attention to Gurung Extraction," I mused. The corporate name on the email was something called the Zeus Global Finance Corporation.

"Correct. ISP addresses assigned to Zeus Global Finance began viewing the Gurung Extraction website two weeks ago. Additional bot searches on the web have left sufficient evidence to indicate a relatively deep review of Gurung assignments to date."

I thought about the offer, then reread the few details of the extraction that were listed.

"Did Zeus Global have an office on Wall Street?"

"Negative. However, the Zeus website lists two corporate executive officers who were employed by a different firm, now defunct, that did have offices near Wall Street ten years ago."

The wall view changed to list the two officers as the Chief Investment Officer and Chief Financial Officer, complete with pictures, as well as a side-by-side map of lower Manhattan with a building highlighted in yellow, located on Broadway about a block from Wall Street.

"Add in known salvage team activity for today's date and tomorrow," I instructed.

The map on the wall suddenly showed three new highlights in red, green, and blue respectively. There were currently five teams on *Zone Wars*, and one of the government's stipulations regarding the show was complete disclosure of each team's daily location plans. Independent salvage people, like myself, did not have to disclose any information other than designating our chosen Zone entry point and our intended egress site. Proposed trip duration was also collected, but that was just so the Zone Defense people could alert our primary contacts if we went overdue. That was it. Nobody would be coming in after us if we didn't come out on our own.

During its four years of production, *Zone War* had followed a total of twelve teams. Seven of them had either died or quit the business during that time. The actual number of salvage people lost in the Zone was currently at one hundred and sixty-two. The survival rate was so low that the production company only occasionally picked new teams and only from people with several years of experience.

Myself, I had close to eight years of experience, most of it with my father. After Brad and JJ Johnson, I was probably the most experienced salvager out there. Flottercot Productions had approached me exactly three times to be on the show, once a year for three years running, but much to the dismay of my sisters, I had turned them down all three times. No way was I allowing a drone camera to follow me around, giving away all my secrets, and there wasn't a camera team anywhere that could survive accompanying me, even if I was to ever give permission. I personally doubted any of them were stupid enough to try. My longevity in the world's deadliest job was directly due to my highly personalized approach and my very customized technology.

"Inform the sender that I agree to attempt the extraction. Strike any guarantee clauses and disclosure amendments," I instructed my AI.

"Done," it replied.

"Okay, now we need to get down to planning."

My father was huge on planning. Massive time was spent on every aspect of a recovery before we ever set foot in the Zone, no detail too small. I could quote every drone's specifications forward and backward by the time I was twelve. Nowadays, two years after his death, I have an exhaustive data bank of information built up in my AI's drives. My planning is still just as thorough, just generally a whole lot faster.

First we reviewed current satellite footage of the building's neighborhood on Broadway, then pulled blueprints on the building itself from the NYC Department of Buildings database. The laptop in question was thought to be on the seventeenth floor, which was gonna be a bitch. Better than the thirty-seventh floor, which the building had, but still, dragging myself, my stealth suit, and my gear up seventeen flights of stairs was gonna suck—hard.

"Suggest carrying cutting torch, bolt cutters, and titanium pry bar. The state of the building is completely unknown. No record of other recoveries occurring at that address."

Great. My AI was right, of course. Getting in and out of multi-story buildings could, and often did, require serious abilities to break and enter. All of my gear was miniaturized, but my pack weight and the resulting suck factor went up with every ounce.

"I'll go through the Brooklyn Battery Tunnel entrance," I decided.

"Concur. That will place you far from the Chelsea Pier entrance. Johnson Recovery and Egorov Salvage are both scheduled for entrance to the Zone at that point tomorrow. Diversion rate is estimated to be sixty-four-point-eight percent."

Diversion rate was my own proprietary measure, calculated by my AI using satellite footage, *Zone War* production crew drone counts, and my own drone counts measured at the same time, if I happened to be in the Zone. I got the idea watching one of the few full episodes I had ever sat through. At some point during the episode, I realized that someone or some AI on the studio team kept a running tally of observed drones at the bottom of the screen. The producers used it to raise the viewing tension, as the number would race higher the longer a team was in the Zone and the more noise they made. I, myself, kept a running count of any and all combat units that I observed during my forays, along with the time observed.

After egress, I would give that information, along with details on which models and makes I had seen, to my AI.

Twenty-five thousand was the estimated number of drones released in the Attack, an entire ship's hold's worth. Since that time, thousands had been killed or damaged in the course of the passing years and the active action of the salvage crews. The US government paid a hefty bounty for every unit that could be confirmed destroyed, with varying payouts depending on the sophistication and danger each unit posed. Also, Air Force Render drones hunted the high altitudes, preying on any visible drones, and marksman units on barricade duty sniped as many drones as they could see.

There were a couple of mothership drones that had onboard 3D printers that could make small replacement drones, but otherwise the number was estimated to be dwindling, perhaps as low as fifteen thousand drones remaining. Unfortunately, the most lethal and sophisticated units that were the best at killing humans were also best at avoiding their own destruction.

The bounty for an Indian Tiger hunter-killer was north of two hundred thousand dollars, and forget about one of the three remaining Chinese Spider CThree units thought to be at large. Each Command, Control, and Communication master drone could orchestrate up to three hundred lesser drones at a time. They had been the most highly advanced units in the Chinese arsenal at the time of the Attack, equipped with real, progressive machine-learning software that was capable of rewriting itself to adapt to the battlefield.

One Spider had been destroyed at the end of the second week of the Manhattan Attack. That single unit had coordinated battle drones that killed an estimated two hundred thirty soldiers, cops, and federal agents. The fact that three such units were still unaccounted for was likely the main reason the military hadn't gone back into Manhattan in force.

So the bounty on a Spider CThree was approaching a million dollars. Cheap, if you ask me. You might wonder if we didn't have more advanced drones now, ten years later, that could go in and fight the battles without human lives being lost. We do, and it didn't work. The CThrees kept learning, kept adapting, kept growing. They beat the more advanced drones sent against them. In fact, the information in their CPUs, the software that they wrote and rewrote over ten years, would be worth, in my estimation, closer to a billion dollars. Every army on Earth would pay up for it.

Some people wonder if any of the CThrees are still active, still functioning. I can personally vouch for two. Scariest moment of my life. Eighteen months ago, in the north end of Central Park. I use the Park often, as the drones tend to stay in the more urban areas. Not because they don't function well in the park, but because the park is full of deer and coyotes and a small number of animals that escaped the Central Park Zoo. Combat drones are designed and programmed for killing humans. They ignore animals. But having that many warm bodies clouding their thermal senses is confusing to most drones, costly in processing power. So they tend to stay out of the Park. Which makes the Park one of my favorite places.

Anyway, I was skirting though the woods and came upon the edge of the old softball fields. It was a really nice, sunny summer day and I sensed motion out on the overgrown field.

Dad's lessons kept me deep in the shadows, peeking over a small hummock of rock and dirt, my low thermal signature camouflage hood over my head. Through my monocular, I saw a veritable army of drones, motionless, solar collectors spread out for maximum charging value. Right in the middle of four tank killers, seven Tigers, about twenty Russian Wolves, and a veritable flock of various flying units were two CThrees sitting in the open, charging batteries like the rest. The CThrees look like their nickname—Spiders—black-painted, armored spiders, each the size of a sofa loveseat, except these Spiders have seven legs, not eight.

The horde stayed that way for an hour, then suddenly the entire battle group of drones activated all at once and flew, crawled, or rolled off to the east, leaving me in a pile of sweat and maybe a little urine. Maybe more than a little.

I bring out dead drones fairly regularly, but mostly just small ones, or I yank the CPUs and ID plates from bigger ones. I don't have a heavy, electro-powered hybrid LAV to haul my catches, so my paid kills are kinda low. My actual tagged kill numbers are a different story. The Zone is my real office and salvage my work—and work is good. Tomorrow, I'd head into the Manhattan Drone Zone.

Chapter 3

I inserted the next day, calling for an Ublyft car to transport me and my gear to the Brooklyn-Battery Tunnel. Self-drivers aren't allowed in the tunnel, only military or salvage company vehicles, and they have to be manually driven ones at that.

Catching a ride with a Zone military driver that I knew, I tried going over my plan as I rode. Fat chance. My driver turned out to be quite a Chatty Cathy.

"Yo Gunga Din, whatcha got going today?" Corporal Links asked. I had quoted the final line of the old Kipling poem once to him and since that day, he'd called me Gunga Din. Ignorant bastard didn't even know that the fictional Gunga was Indian while I'm Nepali-American.

"You know, just thought I'd go skipping around Wall Street and find some old stock certificates I can forge my name on," I said.

"You can do that?" he asked, brows raised, looking at me and not the road.

"Nobody has used certificates in decades," I said, shaking my head and pointing at the left-hand tunnel wall that we were about to slam into.

"Oh, not spilling your real deal, huh?" he said, swerving back to center. "You don't trust me," he stated, now pissy.

"Confidentiality agreements in my contracts. My clients don't want me giving out any of their secrets," I said, which was true. I wouldn't have told him anyway—op sec—operational security. Dad was huge on that one. Any mission information you gave out would travel faster than a bullet and could be just as deadly.

Links kept silent, not speaking for the rest of the trip, which was fine with me.

We arrived at the Zone Checkpoint-Battery Park, which actually lies under the park in what used to be the old Battery Underpass. Links let me off before taking his load of supplies to the Zone Quartermaster. I thanked him but he just gave me a nod and drove away. I know for a fact that a lot of the Zone guards collect under the table money from reporters about any juicy salvage gossip, and Corporal Links was definitely one of them. The fact that I didn't give away much of anything informational was a sore point for him, like I was shorting him his additional pay. Nevermind that it was part and parcel of my Zone protocol, and one that helped keep me alive. Soldiers, like all people, talk, and often by phone. Drones can hear phones. 'Nuff said.

"Ah, Mr. Gurung, what brings you to our little slice of Heaven here in the Battery?" the entrance sergeant asked, holding out his hand for my pack.

"You know, Sergeant Alonso, just looking for my personal pot o' gold. Heard the rainbow came down on the other side of those steel doors," I said as I carefully watched him give my gear a casual, but professional, once over. Weapons, ammo, first aid, breaking and entering gear, distraction devices, booby trap gear, food and water, but no commo gear and no batteries. That was the rule unless you were going in as part of a team, and then only on an armored vehicle. Even the military special forces units that used the Zone for training went commo free.

Most Manhattanites lost their lives during the Attack because they lacked all the right instincts. Modern humans were both totally reliant on electronics and so self-absorbed by them that they missed the danger cues all around them. They completely failed to react usefully to the drone threat, or once they realized it, called their own doom down upon themselves with those same phones. I've seen hundreds of bodies of people who died looking at their cell phones, which everyone seemed to have back then, before personal AIs.

Many people died because they ran over each other, blocked up escape routes, or simply froze in place. People often failed each other as the veneer of civilization was ripped away and it became every man or woman for themselves. The majority of people tried to shelter in place. Then they called for help on those damned phones. Instead of rescue, they called the drones right to them. Even when the military tried overflights with speakers announcing to any survivors to leave their phones and attempt escape on their own, most still tried to call for help.

Combat drones were built by humans to kill humans, and they built them very well. Almost every model in the invasion group had the capacity to detect and track electromagnetic signals. Most could find ways into buildings, open doors, or hack electronic locks and alarms. And drones generally work in swarms or at least pairs. One would bang on the door while a flier would drop down and shoot you through the window.

So we weren't supposed to bring electronic stuff in. Weapons galore, no problem. Personal comp and commo, no way. As if I needed to. I had a city of stuff that I had been combing for eight years, and I certainly knew enough to avoid electronics, even electronic sights on my weapons.

"Just your personal side arm and your rifle, which you aren't even carrying?" Alonso asked.

"Yup, and I don't usually need either of them," I said truthfully. Picking a fight with machines built for war was a really, really fast way to meet your maker. My weapons were either last ditch, as in the case of my Ruger Wesson Five-Seven pistol, or for harvesting particularly juicy drones, which was the purpose of my heavy caliber, suppressed rifle.

"How the hell do you do it, kid?" Alonso wondered. I'd heard the same question a thousand times before. I shrugged, collecting my gear and stepping up to the entrance line.

"He's clear," Alonso yelled, giving the door operator a wave.

I heard another voice then, one I instantly recognized.

"Hey look, the weasel's slinking away." I turned and met the eyes of Martin Johnson, second born and middle child of the Johnson clan. He held a tablet out toward Alonso, the kind of thing the *Zone Wars* teams used to file plans with the Zone Authority. But the massive steel door had begun to open and I turned away from the middle Johnson and walked into the clean room chamber.

Just what I needed. Instant distraction at the worst possible moment, as all of my attention should be focused on the Zone outside the next door. There was a flatscreen mounted on the wall next to the outer door that showed three separate camera views and a diagram listing electromagnetic scan results. Nothing on screen, and the scan was clear of dots representing drones. Normal. Drones didn't hang out near the entrances we use because the auto cannons and laser weapons mounted above them tended to make short work of killer machines. No, the dangerous ground would be the area just outside of the guns' kill zones.

I hit the outer door control (the one for the smaller, human-sized door, not the big vehicle door) and waited for it to cycle open, taking at least that time to consider Martin's presence. Astrid, I had always liked, while JJ was six years older than me and had been a bit of a hero of mine when I was a kid. Martin, though, was always an asshole. Middle child with attention issues and more than a bit of Narcissism. Couldn't compete with Astrid's beauty or his older, bigger brother's handsome sex appeal, so he was bitter and petty to all those he could be... which had often been me back in the day.

Nowadays, our interactions were rare but usually consisted of trading insults. But more important than his being a giant douche was the fact that his presence meant that there must have been a change of plans regarding Johnson Recovery's intended incursion for the day. And that wasn't good for me. The very last place I needed or wanted to be was anywhere near the clusterfuck that was JR in action. My area of operation would be knee-deep in drones for the rest of the day once they began slamming their way around the Zone.

The door opened enough for me to slip out and that's just what I did, putting my retrospection on Team Johnson on hold for the moment and instead concentrating on my surroundings. Behind me, the door reversed and closed almost silently. When Team Johnson came through, they'd use the giant vehicle doors and make all kinds of racket. I had better be far, far away by then.

Like any driving tunnel in a city, the road rose up at an angle to meet the surface streets, concrete retaining walls rising up on either side. Ahead of me, the center of the road was open, husks of abandoned cars shoved against either retaining wall.

I crouched, listening, smelling, and watching, my only motion the act of pulling up the hood on my stealth suit.

Let's talk about stealth suits for a moment. Mine is pretty good, maybe not state of the art, like active soldiers are issued, but still pretty good. It better be, 'cause it cost like crazy.

The outer layer is optically reactive, like a chameleon's skin, changing colors to blend in with the immediate environment. In fact, it was closely copied from nature, using nano-chemistry instead of electronics to provide the best camouflage available short of a Potter cloak. *Those*, which I leave you to guess why they are so named, used electro-optics to bend light around an object and thus hide it perfectly. Worked great for humans but not so well with drones. The electromagnetic signature was low but still detectable by drone sensors. Stealth suits had no such problem. The energy for the chemical changes in a stealth suit came from the wearer's own body heat, which had the secondary effect of reducing the wearer's thermal signature. Additional thermal reduction came from the internal cooling system, activated by muscle movement to circulate coolant throughout the suit. Accumulated heat was stored in insulated heat sinks in the soles of the boots that were attached to the suit.

Overall, the thermal effectiveness depended a great deal upon the weather and environment you found yourself in. Cold weather, rain storms, puddles of water, or actual streams were my best friends because of the small ports that I could dial open in the soles of the boots, allowing a really rapid dispersion of heat. Dry, hot summer weather was harder. Not impossible, but it really took a whole different approach to move about the Zone in the dog days of July and August.

Stealth suits also had a charcoal layer to absorb odors and biological telltales that could also alert drones. Additionally, there was a thin layer of Kevlar just under the optical layer to stop some of the shrapnel-tracking tags that some drones used, and it could even slow down flechettes. Not armor like JJ Johnson wears, but way better than regular clothing.

I moved down the open road slowly and carefully, head swiveling as I opened up *all* of my senses, feeling the breeze and getting into my own zone... in the Zone. No pun intended.

I stayed tight up to the left side retaining wall. I've noticed a tendency of drones to cluster on the left side of passageways, roads, and hallways, although not all do it. I don't know if that's deliberate programming or not. I think it is. There is a perception that people tend to turn right or stay right more than left (not sure if that's actually a true thing), and I think the programmers plugged that into their algorithms. It doesn't really matter if it's true human nature or not, as long as I can use that trait to my advantage. If drones were hanging in and on the high rises to my left, then the defiladed area against the left wall was dead space that couldn't be engaged from the left side. I used the smashed cars to give me cover from the right.

The next part was tricky. I was still in view of the Zone Authority cameras but getting really close to the end of the entrance's kill zone, the part where the retaining walls were down to a meter in height, the tunnel exit ramp almost level with the street. I was going to be extremely exposed in short order and so I had to execute a bit of misdirection to keep my observers from learning my secrets, all while using those very same secrets to stay alive.

From a pocket on my stealth suit came a little spring-loaded device. It had started life as a mini flare launcher but was now modified to toss a little sonic package a distance of twenty-five meters. I did exactly that, lobbing the screamer over the wall and onto an open sidewalk, where it began to belt out a tone that would probably make me cringe if my human ears could have heard it. Pitched just above dog whistle range, it was actually a series of sound bursts in a complex pattern.

I know what you're thinking. Ajaya, you lazy bastard! Are you so weak you can't even throw a five-gram object? Nah, I just don't want to make a big, giant, attention-getting arm motion and maybe get laced with a couple of dozen flechettes, drilled through the skull by a laser, or blown up by a mini bomblet.

The sonic screamer activated a bit off to my side, so I hunkered down between the last wrecked car on the tunnel ramp and half

26

a meter of retaining wall. Nothing to do now but wait, possibly anywhere from five minutes to maybe twenty or twenty-five.

The car next to me was a Kia, both windows on my side shattered, probably by kinetic fire from one of the bigger land drones during the first days of the Attack. Most of the big units came ashore armed with full loads of ammo for their auto guns. Most, especially the Chinese Ground Raptors and the Indian Leopard units, had pretty complex ammunition usage programs that maximized the economical deployment of limited and irreplaceable rounds. During the initial attack, these units used automatic weapons fire, but most switched to single shot mode when they dropped to seventy-five percent of munitions load out. From there, the drone would calculate to optimize the effectiveness of their weapons use. Ten years later, these drones had almost all exhausted their ammo supplies. Only flechette shooters, which could fabricate raw ammo from any available wire stock, and laser armed units were still capable of ranged fire. The empty gun shooters were still dangerous, adaptive combat programming allowing them to rearm with close-quarters weapons like fire axes or anything that could bludgeon or cut. They also could use human firearms, which was one reason my father, myself, and every salvage person I knew policed up any stray weapons we came across.

A piece of fabric fluttered in the shattered car window, a tattered scrap of faded pinkish material that once might have been silk. It took a second before I realized it was the tip of a scarf. I felt no inclination to look into the car and see the scarf's wearer.

You probably wonder about smell, but ten years after the Attack, most bodies are now just weathered bone, which is where Kade and Kyle Bonnen had taken the inspiration for their team name: the Bone Shakers.

I sometimes find remains that have been completely desiccated, like an Egyptian mummy, usually in the upper floors of a high rise building where sunlight and intact windows worked to dry the body like jerky in an oven, but most of the dead are just bones.

My sonic screamer attracted just one drone, a long-bodied Russian Wolf, its green camouflage paint chipped and scraped but its motions still an eerie approximation of a real dog. I doubted it was alone. Usually an aerial UAV works with a land-based UGV, especially out here in the open. But my homemade screamers are pitched so high that they mostly fail to trip the human-based parameters that drones hunted by. There are always exceptions, as the Wolf was demonstrating.

A shadow shot across the road, cars, and buildings, a flier moving fast across the open sky. I looked up, but it had gone by too quick for me to see much more than a blur. Still, it was enough. My wait was over.

Keeping one eye on the Wolf, I put an actual, antique dog whistle to my lips and gave a short, quick blast. The Wolf lifted its coffee-can-sized metal head and turned visual sensor panels in my direction. The screamer kept screaming and I refrained from any more whistles, movements, or even deep breaths. The hound lifted one metal foot as if to investigate, but then its head abruptly tilted up, taking in an object that dropped from the sky like a meteor.

US Air Force Render drones own the high altitudes over Manhattan, but the undisputed master of the low-altitude urban airspace in the Zone was without question the Russian Berkut—the Death Eagle. The Berkut was a sophisticated flying transformer, whose shape could shift from a round hovering ball to a sleek, streamlined fighter-shaped missile that could drop on its prey at four hundred kilometers per hour and either skewer it on its spear-shaped front nose or shoot it with its 9mm x 21mm firearm.

The arrow-shaped object shot toward the ground like a bullet, then suddenly pulled up, the V wings shifting and collapsing as the segmented body rolled up like a grapefruit-sized carbon-fiber pill bug, the whole thing hovering on four powerful turbo fans.

The Wolf paused, silently communing with the Berkut, then turning and moving off to the north. The Berkut spun around slowly in place, scanning the area. It suddenly tilted two of its four hover fans and shot my way. Two seconds later, it was right in front me, gun barrel in my face.

"Hello Rikki Tikki," I said softly, so the retreating hound wouldn't hear.

Chapter 4

At the sound of my voice, LED lights lit up across the front of the deadly drone and a soft ticking sound came from its speakers. My clenched stomach relaxed. Part of me always expects it to shoot me dead. *"Voice recognition complete. Facial recognition complete. Hello AJ,"* it said in a quiet, slightly tinny British voice. I had wanted to change that to a Nepali-accented voice, but there was only so much reprogramming I could do without messing up Rikki Tikki's best features.

Oh and yes, I know about Kipling. I hate much of what he wrote, as did my father. We also loved some of what he wrote. Both feelings are possible with one writer. "All things come with both good and bad, Ajaya," my father used to say. "It is up to us to find and polish the good and push away the bad."

Rikki hovered, waiting.

"Target is 55 Broadway," I said, keeping my voice just above a whisper.

"Currently seven drone units between this location and target. Sensor override ninety-six percent likely to succeed. Distance point-four-eight kilometers."

Rikki Tikki is my ace in the hole. A reprogrammed drone whose upgraded processor was sophisticated and powerful enough to override the base programming of many of the drones still in the Zone. At least, within ranges that were up close and personal.

I rose from my crouch, the hovering killer drone now leading me through the Zone to my target destination like a pet dog. Eat that, Johnson Recovery.

I caught Rikki when my father died. I'd been obsessed with the drones since the night my family evacuated Manhattan, with me carrying Monique and Astrid carrying Gabby. I helped my father study the units that inhabited the Zone and even got my hands on some of the units that he and Brad Johnson brought out in the early years. The Berkuts fascinated me as much as the Spiders scared me. They were designed to hunt soldiers and law enforcement. Silent, swift, and armed with a powerful nine millimeter weapon whose steel-cored bullets were created to defeat body armor. I almost destroyed Rikki—came mere micro seconds from pounding his fantastically engineered frame into scrap. My father's words stopped me. Now Rikki helped me provide for the family. And survive the Zone.

My high school had a drone technicians college credit course, offered through a local community college, and I got hooked. The two-year degree from the same college gave me the tools I eventually used when I captured Rikki. Core code rewrite of the CPU, upgrade a bunch of components here and there, tweak the batteries and capacitors, repair the damage that happened during his *capture,* and *voila...* my own drone escort. Perhaps I'm oversimplifying everything I did, especially the software work. Maybe, but that's part of my secret. An escort that could still talk to every other drone in the Zone and convince most of them that the human target their sensors reported in Rikki's proximity was an anomaly. A sensor phantom, erroneous data to be overridden by the Berkut's much closer sensors and more powerful processor.

We moved at a pretty good pace, still as stealthy as possible. Rikki's subterfuge depends on me giving as little concrete evidence as possible. Every bit of my stealth suit technology and sniper stalking skill is required, but the complete knowledge Rikki has of the drones around us allowed me to move faster for bursts, between the drones. When we got close to a patrolling or stationary drone, I had to really be careful, and that's when our pace slowed way down.

Mostly we looped around the deadly machines, but at times that was impossible and we had to pass close to them. In the two years I've had Rikki, the sensor suppression gig has failed only a handful of times. Those episodes resulted in sudden gunfire, me with my full-auto, suppressed Five-Seven and Rikki with his internal nine millimeter. Rikki would then report to the greater drone net that the human intruder was killed at the cost of one drone. So far it had worked, but I avoided those situations like plague. Gunfights with drones are terrifying. They have machine-quick reaction times and computer-corrected aim. My only chance is overwhelming firepower from both myself and my guardian Berkut. That and the fact that most drones are either ammo depleted or shoot lightweight flechettes or underpowered lasers.

As you might imagine, Rikki's ammo hoppers are the only regularly refilled magazines in the Zone. I scavenged, hand loaded, and mail ordered the odd Russian ammo wherever and whenever I could to keep him topped up with both full power and subsonic rounds. My pack was always inspected upon entering the Zone, but no one ever looked at the odd-caliber rounds I was packing. Ammo was ammo and frankly, the huge .338 Lapua armor-piercing rounds my rifle ate usually got the most attention.

55 Broadway was only half a klick from Battery Park. Back in the day, it would have taken less than ten minutes to walk there. Now it took an hour *and* ten minutes. Still not bad, but then the thirty-seven-story office building was looming over me, taunting me with the knowledge that I had seventeen floors to climb with a full pack that went over twenty-five kilos even though much of my gear was aluminum, plastic, or titanium. Nothing to it but to do it.

Rikki scanned the building lobby through the two revolving doors. No drones. Lots of skeletons, but no drones. One of the lobby spinning doors was jammed open by the skeleton of a man in a security uniform. I stepped over him, foot coming down carefully so as not to snap any bones. That would be disrespectful—and noisy. Noisy is bad.

Moving deeper into the building, I looked everywhere. What looked like four more skeletons were spread in pieces all across the floor. Just based on that, I would have guessed dogs, but the big piles of dried dog shit absolutely confirmed it.

For the first five years after Drone Night, dogs were a huge issue. Left behind by panicking New Yorkers and ignored by the drones, dogs were everywhere. And they really only had one ready food source to work with. For a time, they were well fed. But as that primary food supply disappeared down the throats of rats, roaches, ants, foxes, more roaches, cats, raccoons, skunks, vultures, crows, ravens, and the dogs themselves, man's abandoned best friend grew hungry. Feral and hungry, with a taste for their former masters. I've shot more dogs than anyone should ever have to. Some days, Dad and I would have to post up on the edge of the Zone and cull a pack with suppressed NYPD M4 carbines liberated from empty police stations. I hated those days. In those early years, the packs often kept us from getting more than a few blocks into the Zone. Worse, the drones learned to pay attention when a pack was following us. Only proximity to the containment wall and its automatic anti-drone guns kept us alive some days.

I like dogs, a lot, but I'll be honest. After seeing packs of thirty or forty feral mutts tear apart a Central Park deer, then follow our scent trail because they were still starving, well, let's just say I have a trust issue. And it's not the dogs' fault. Abandoned and surviving as best as they could, they became what nature always intended.

There are a lot fewer now. The easy food lying in the streets is gone, and New York winters are still harsh, so only the strongest have survived. Which means they're much better hunters and killers than the early packs, just fewer and more spread out. It's one of the major reasons I spray my boots with fox piss. In case you're wondering, I buy the commercial stuff like regular hunters. I wouldn't have a clue on how to harvest it myself. The global recession brought sustenance hunting back in a big way, as people found old ways to feed their families, and these days, the overpopulations of suburban deer are a thing of the past.

One of the eight elevators had its door jammed open on a briefcase and what looked like a femur. The others were shut, but of course, there was no power in the building. City Maintenance shut the whole borough off when satellite and Air Force drone surveillance showed the terrorist drones tapping into the power grid to recharge.

So it was the stairwell and seventeen stories of stairs. My father always insisted on constant physical conditioning. But at least I was smarter these days. "Rikki, scout," I said, pointing up.

My drone rose up the stairwell, disappearing from view for seven or eight minutes, then returning to report no collapsed stairs or blocked doors, and most importantly, no drones. That meant I could leave much of my breaking and entering gear behind. I could bring one titanium pry bar, small acetylene cutter, lockpicks, water, snacks, escape and evasion gear, and, of course, my rifle. Eight kilos of sniper rifle and ammo is a lot, but you never know what you'll see when you're seventeen stories high. My MSR always went with me.

The Remington MSR might be a bit old-school for current snipers, but it was still a solid piece of ordinance. And entirely without any easily detected power sources, unlike a modern 11 millimeter electromagnetic Gauss rifle. There is also the not-insignificant fact that it was free. I found it absolutely mind-boggling that a weapon system that had cost well over $16,000 ten years ago was now mine, again courtesy of the NYPD, for free. I had two of them, at least that anyone knew of. Inside the Zone, I had stockpiles of guns, gear, and explosives like to outfit a small army, cached all over the island. But outside the Zone, I had just my DoD-issued Ruger Wesson and my two personal MSRs, all of which had to be kept at the local precinct near our apartment, checked out for each and every Zone incursion.

My pack was lighter but still not light and I started the climb, step by step, one foot in front of the other, Rikki alternating between hovering or clinging to my pack to save power.

I'll skip a replay. Suffice to say, it sucked. But it also wasn't filled with sudden death and heart-wrenching terror. No AI killing machines.

The seventeenth floor had six financial offices on it. The one I was looking for was Rocon Financial Associates, and of course it was located on the opposite side of the building. I took my time, checking each office for surprises, of both the happy and the scary kind. My stealth suit was unzipped and pulled down to cool off my sweating torso. There was only so much the internal coolers could handle. Turns out they couldn't cool much after floor four.

I found bodies in three offices, being careful not to disturb them in any way. Family photos, memorabilia, and advertising swag were everywhere, on every desk. Before I went too much further, I made sure that Rikki was parked by the windows at the southeast corner of the floor, carbon nano-fiber wings spread to collect the sun on their photovoltaic surfaces.

When I finally got to Rocon, it took fifteen minutes to scope out the office and find a total of sixteen laptops. Another five minutes identified my target. Zeus Global had provided the make, model, and serial number so I could be absolutely certain of recovery even without any way to power the PC up. Bingo.

I would never try to turn on any piece of electronics here in Manhattan. Bringing it to life inside the Zone would result in an automatic query for Wi-Fi or Bluetooth, or both. Might as well stand on the roof and wave a flag.

It wasn't even mid-morning and my job was well over half done. Now to go down seventeen floors, sneak half a kilometer to Battery Park, and home free, baby. Shit, I'd probably beat the twins home before they were done with school. They didn't even know I had gone in today.

I wrapped the laptop in bubble wrap, slipped it into a Faraday net, and then packed the bundle deep in my pack. My rifle came out of the carry sling built into my pack, leaving my back a net six kilos lighter. Holding the MSR in my arms would be easier going down, and I always carried my rifle for at least part of every ingress and egress, if only to keep my arms conditioned to its weight. Mission accomplished, I went to collect Rikki.

He was still in the windows, but his wings were folded into ball form and he was facing out, visual and auditory sensors aimed at something outside and far below. Dull sounds reached my ears as I moved closer.

The southeast windows looked down at Broadway south of my position, and what I saw made my stomach clench, all thoughts of a fast egress gone in the blink of an eye.

A war was raging on the city street way down below. A white and orange Johnson Recovery light armored vehicle was poking out of a side street just a few buildings down, and it appeared to be somehow stuck, all while a veritable assault force of drones fired on it from every direction. Flying units swarmed around the LAV, not appearing to do anything, but in reality I knew they would be burning every sensor or armored window with invisible laser beams. On the ground, there were three or maybe four Wolf drones waiting to spray bursts of electromagnetically accelerated flechettes at any hatch or door stupid enough to open. But the real danger came from the Russian tank killers facing off with the LAV.

I pulled my Zeiss binoculars from inside my stealth suit and zoomed in. A thick cable was caught under the front axle of the LAV, which had eight wheels, in effect lifting the front of the heavy vehicle almost two feet off the ground. I scanned the length of the cable and found a Russian heavy tank killer on each end, each robot reversing to tighten the cable even as one fired its heavy caliber machine-gun at the LAV while the other TK lit it up with its hundred-kilowatt high energy fiber optic laser. One TK was on the south side of Morris, the other on the north.

Johnson Recovery had fallen into a trap, and that meant only one thing. Swinging my binocs around the fight in ever-widening circles, I found what I was looking for. There, further down Broadway, right at the back of Bowling Green Park, high atop the US Customs house, was the seven-legged, black armored form of a Spider CThree, clinging to the roof. My little circle of vision swung back to the LAV, right to the armored front windshield. I found a blonde head, wearing laser-resistant goggles, swiveling everywhere, arms spinning the wheel as the LAV surged forward and back. Astrid Johnson.

The Johnsons were fighting back, the GAU-17, M-134 minigun on the roof of the LAV hosing the laser tank killer while two gun barrels, a .50 sniper rifle and the 11 millimeter electromag that JJ favored fired at the machine-gun-mounted robot tank. The minigun used 7.62 rounds, individually not sufficient to threaten the mini-tank's armor, but when fired in an angry stream of up to six thousand rounds a minute, it could chew up even hardened steel.

But their time was running out. The TK with the standard gun was too close to fire either of its two anti-tank missiles, being well inside arming distance, and that heavy machine-gun would eventually cut through the LAV's side armor. Those massive rounds would then begin to ricochet around the interior. An image of Astrid cut down by heavy bullets popped unbidden into my head.

My mind kicked into gear. Had she not been there, I'm not sure if I would have helped. Not proud of that, but there it is. Instead, I started moving, even as my suddenly hyper-active brain laid out all the steps I needed to take.

"Rikki, airplane mode." Turn off the IFF responders and remove him from the net. I didn't trust my software against a Spider's raw computing power. My own Berkut might be turned against me in a New York second.

"Airplane mode engaged."

"Designate tank killers as units North and South. Range both units, range Spider on Customs house," I instructed as I started shoving furniture around. Two standing desks were just the right height to fit side by side, creating a raised shooting platform maybe six feet back from the south window. I screwed the Titan ACC suppressor onto the MSR, unfolded the bipod, and laid out two mags of ammo.

Then I split my pack into two pieces. A small daypack holding the recovered laptop went back on my body, and the tool bag propped open the glass entry door to Rocon Financial. From the tool bag, I pulled out the mini acetylene canister and a red plastic jar of powder. Inside the jar was a second, smaller jar that held another powder. When I mixed the two powders, they went from inert to an activated binary explosive that was susceptible to high velocity impacts. I taped the now volatile mixture to the acetylene, leaving the bomb out in the middle of the doorway, my hands shaking with adrenaline.

Next, I used my titanium pry bar to split apart the elevator doors and jam them open. My fast descenders clamped smoothly onto the elevator cable.

Racing back to the standing desks, I climbed up, lay down prone, and snugged the big rifle to my shoulder. I slid my hood-mounted hearing plugs into each ear. Satisfied, I inserted the first big mag of five cartridges into the gun and cycled the bolt.

"Range to Spider?"

"Two-hundred ninety-one meters."

"Range to TK South?" The southern tank killer was the one with the 12.7mm machine-gun and, from what I could see, only two remaining anti-tank missiles of its original four. The northern unit with the laser had empty rocket tubes and I decided it was the lesser of the two evils.

"Eighty meters."

Both tanks were really close range for a sniper rifle. Even the Spider wasn't all that far. The angle of declination on the Spider wasn't all that big a deal either, so rather than get Rikki's more precise calculations; I decided to shoot by eye. The TK units were almost straight down. Dad might be rolling in his grave, but time was of the essence here. The missiles were likely too close to achieve arming distance, but that could change.

"Three-round burst on south window on my mark. Triangular pattern, twenty centimeter spread."

"Affirmative." Rikki was hovering over my shoulder.

The first round up the pipe of the big MSR was a subsonic 'cause I needed the quiet for at least the first shot. It was followed by four full-power, armor-piercing rounds. Sound wouldn't matter after the glass hit the ground, and I would need the extra power.

The crosshairs settled over the black armored form of the Spider, hovering over one black electro-optical sensor. The subsonic round might just glance off its armor at this angle, but a shot through the eye should break its concentration, so to speak.

"Three, two, one, mark." I started my squeeze at the *two* and the gun bucked against my shoulder just as Rikki burst fired three suppressed rounds, Spiderwebbing the plate glass before my bullet left the muzzle. A small part of my brain considered that I hadn't thought of high-rise buildings having anti-shatter glass. But the .338 bullet and, probably more important, the massive muzzle blast of my rifle blew out most of the glass, solving the problem for me. I had maybe a bit under four seconds before the glass hit the ground, alerting the combatants to my location.

Time slowed down as I cycled the bolt, seeing the Spider's left ocular lens explode, before shifting crosshairs down to the heavy machine-gun turret on the tracked tank killer.

TKs have heavy armor. My .338 wasn't gonna penetrate that, but the gun-mounted aiming module was fair game. The heavy armor-piercing round smashed the robot's gun sight all to crap but I was already running the bolt and aiming for the top rocket. My number three round smashed through the missile tube a third of the way from the back, my fourth shot hitting the lower rocket in almost the same spot. Nothing happened, but that was my goal. Try launching those missiles now, motherfucker.

The Spider was gone, having vanished like a phantom, and the gun turret on the TK spun toward my building, heavy machine-gun rounds blindly smashing the floors below me. I focused on my last round, taking a breath and locking the crosshairs a smidge over my target. My gun bucked, the cable connector on the front of the laser-equipped TK snapped, dropping the LAV's front end to the ground. The cap blew off the end of the top missile tube on the other TK, the launch charge shoving the rocket partway out of the tube before the flight charge ignited, a blow torch of flame jetting out the bullet hole in its side. The missile failed, spinning end over end into the air, like a Chinese firework.

Time sped back up to normal and things happened quick. The LAV engine roared, the cable still caught in its front axle. The other six tires spun, sending the twelve-ton LAV back down Morris Street. The cable tightened and yanked on the smaller eight-ton TK, spinning it around like a fish on a line. The front of the LAV disappeared but I could see minigun tracer rounds lighting up the little robot tank as it got dragged around the corner and down the road.

That's all I had time to see. I rolled off the desks, ejected the spent mag, and inserted the other one as I ran for the elevator, Rikki keeping pace.

"Target red plastic jar in doorway," I ordered as I slung the big rifle and grabbed the descenders, sliding my feet into the fabric loops. A whirring noise by the windows caught my attention. Six flying drones swarmed through the opening as I stepped off the edge, instantly starting to fall.

"Fire one round on Mark, then follow. Three, two, one... Mark!"

I loosened the descenders, dropping two meters as the world above me roared and flashed orange flame.

Chapter 5

I fell forever.

Okay, that's maybe a bit dramatic. I didn't fall; I slid at what felt like a crazy speed as debris rained down on my head and shoulders. Then something bigger hit the side of my head, followed instantly by my legs jamming onto an object that filled the elevator shaft. I fell backward, my slung rifle whacking my elbow with its steel barrel, a hard object slamming into my lower back.

It took me a good five or six seconds to bring my wits back on line. I was on top of the elevator car. Rikki was on top of me. His lights were dead, his spherical hover form likely the heavy object that had glanced off my skull. Dust and sheet rock and other shit trickled down from above, but nothing moved overhead. High, high above, I could see the light and smoke in the open doorway, but down here it was pretty dark.

"Chora, you must always take stock before you decide on a course of action. Think, my boy—think of what you have, what you need, where you want to go, and how best to get there." My father's voice echoed in my head as if he were still with me, still alive. I think perhaps I shall always hear him so. I hope so.

I started to move but pain shot through my right ankle, ripping a short, sharp "Shit!" out of my mouth before I could stop myself. Freezing in place, listening for movement. Nothing. A pocket of my stealth suit yielded a chemical light tube. When I unwrapped it, I found it was already starting to glow, the inner glass tube of activating chemicals broken when I fell. Shaking it brought a soft green light to my little world.

We were at the bottom of the shaft, the elevator car parked at the basement level, at least according to the words stenciled on the elevator shaft. I say we, but Rikki was dead, or offline at the very least. With ginger movements, I pulled myself over to the trapdoor at the top of the car, dragging Rikki with me. It wouldn't open, not till I *convinced* it with my kukri, using the big knife like a pry bar. The chem light dropped neatly down, showing me it was empty, which was a good thing. Never know where a body could be lying or a drone waiting.

I tied a piece of parachute cord to Rikki, my rifle, and the last part of my pack, the part that contained my payday salvage. Lowering the whole bundle and then dropping the end of the cord was easy. Getting my body ready to drop on my one good leg was harder. I shimmied and shifted till my feet were through, then my hips, stomach, and finally shoulders and head. Hanging from my hands, I was only a couple of feet above the floor of the car. I dropped. Left foot hit first, but I fell to the right and my bad foot came down automatically. The pain was enough to make my vision narrow and darken, spots swimming before my eyes.

No swearing this time but mostly because my jaw had been clenched hard enough to crack a tooth (which I didn't—lucky me), but damn.

When I could see (and breathe) again, I decided the elevator car was a good place for some first aid. Medical supplies were always distributed about my body, something Dad had taught me. Wound clotting bandages and tampons (which make great bullet hole stoppers—not that they helped my dad all that much) in more than one pocket, ibuprofen and stronger pain killers in a shirt pocket, and an elastic bandage in yet a third pocket. I wrapped the ankle right over my boot. The skin was already swollen and I was afraid of taking my boot off, only to not get it back on. Three ibuprofen were dry swallowed and then I turned to my rifle. Dad was gonna be rolling over for sure. But nothing for it. I wrapped a regular gauze bandage over the muzzle of the MSR, then put duct tape over that to hold it all in place. Now I had a $16,000 precision crutch for hobbling about. Super.

My kukri slid between the doors and they pried apart pretty easy, considering that they'd been shut for ten years. I tossed the chem light out and pulled back, my Five-Seven in my right hand even though the butt of the rifle-crutch was in that same armpit. Nothing. Just empty basement.

Now, how to get out?

The building wasn't real old, but old enough that when fiber optic lines came along, it was retrofitted. And the fiber optics took up much less space than the original copper wires did. The result was a utility pipe that ran out under the street, sixty or seventy centimeters in diameter, with a much smaller fiber optic tube only taking up a portion of that little tunnel.

It took forever. First I had to stack boxes and stuff to climb up to the utility tube, then haul up my drone, rifle, and pack. Then scoot through the tunnel on my stomach, my only light a pale green chem stick.

Stale dry air, my light reaching just a few feet forward before the wan green glow faded to black, dust and dirt in my face.

I'm not claustrophobic, not after all the years of worming through openings and windows, basements and tunnels. That's how I got Dad to take me with him in the first place. A locked and barred jewelry shop on the West Side. He couldn't get the doors open enough to get through and our bills were piling up. I begged and begged and he finally relented. Big fight that night between Mom and Dad. But in the morning, I went with him and when I torqued myself through that narrow gap, I came face to face with the object that was jamming the door. The owner's bones. My fear of the skeleton wasn't as strong as my fear of failing Dad, so I sucked in my scream and scrambled around it. Then I looted that store like a professional. After that, he started to bring me into the Zone from time to time, mostly when he needed a pint-sized infiltrator.

But that damned utility tube went on and on. My leg was killing me and I had no idea what I would find at the other end. If it was blocked or dead-ended, I was screwed. And of course there could be rats. Really large, human-flesh-fed rats. If I got blocked, I'd have to crawl backward and shove my gear with my feet. If there were rats, well, I'd just die right there. So yes, it was nerve-racking. I kept telling myself that at least Astrid should have made it out. That helped... a little.

But the end of the tube brought me to a bigger tunnel. One of the newer ones, dug when the whole fiber optic craze hit Wall Street, the need for faster and faster links to bring more and more money. Nowhere was the adage that time is money more true than the old Wall Street or the new Hoboken Exchanges.

Now able to stand up and completely uncertain how much time had passed, I hobbled uptown, despite the fact that it would take me further from my closest Zone exit point. No way was I getting out of the Zone today. I'd have to camp out for the night and see what I could do to help my fallen companion.

Chapter 6

My father set up bolt holes all over the island, a practice that I've continued to expand on. Most are below ground level, as meters of dirt and concrete do wonders for masking sound and electrical activity.

My nearest one was west of Broadway, just a couple of blocks away, but it seemed like miles. I came up from underground via a utility manhole cover, then started the journey, which took hours. It was all old-school stuff, what with Rikki down and out. Slow, stealthy movements, staying low, sniper crawling under cars, buses, delivery trucks, which thankfully had been abandoned where they stood, in long lines of deadlocked traffic. There was lots of ongoing construction at the time of the Attack, so the scaffolding protecting the sidewalks is everywhere, and I love it. Invisibility from UAVs. Sometimes a Crab will hang on the outer frame of a sidewalk scaffold, but mostly they were clear. When I had to crawl, it was actually less painful than hobbling would have been. But it sucked.

From there, it was belly worming all the way, crossing between vehicles only when I was sure the skies were clear and the streets were empty. And they mostly weren't—empty, that is. I counted eleven aerial units and four ground drones during my three-block trip. That's way more activity than normal. Thanks, *Zone War* and Johnson Recovery. The result was that it was even slower going than getting out of that fiber optic tunnel. Crawl, stop, listen, look, drag, listen, look, wait, repeat. Occasionally stand up under a scaffold tunnel.

But at least the sun was out and fresh air blew across my face. Most of my cover was vehicle-related, and most lined up nearly end to end. There were some gaps, however, and those were dangerous. The worst was a ten-meter gap between a city bus and a UPS delivery truck. I looked, I listened. Hell, I even smelled the air for oil or the smell of electric motors. Nothing.

So I started across. Inch by slow inch. Smack dab in the middle of the open street and that's when I hear it. A whirring—soft—so soft. Most people wouldn't notice it. Most would die right there. But my father had been a thorough teacher. I froze.

There were seventeen models of flying drone released into Manhattan. Most were armed, and all of them could call for deadlier backup if needed. That's not counting some of the parasitic microdrones that a few of the land drones could launch.

The one above me was the smallest and quietist of the aerials. An Indian Kite. Eight inches in diameter with six small, ultraquiet turbo fans. The Kite was unarmed; it worked with other aerial UAVs and land UGVs, primarily with Indian Tigers. Which meant an eight-foot-long mechanical killing machine was likely somewhere nearby.

Tiger drones don't have any standoff weapons—no guns or lasers. They were built for close-quarters butchery only. And they had way more weapons than their namesakes. Side mounted body blades that scissored together, scythe-like claws for ripping, spring-loaded broad-bladed spears that shot out from their shoulders, and razors lining their mouths. Their designers created them to fall upon an enemy and shred them to bloody ruin in micro-seconds. So fast, enormously strong, they had inflicted the worst nightmares on the American psyche. Personally, I sniped them every single time I could.

Now I was lying on my stomach, listening to the aerial eyes and ears of a Tiger hovering just above me. Frozen, I listened to it buzz softly over the road, stopping just behind me. Then the sound dropped closer to the ground. It was right there, over my pack, my rifle and... Rikki. Of course—it was curious about the motionless Berkut. Rikki probably still had some power somewhere, and the Kite would easily be able to detect it. So it would likely send for... rocks suddenly tumbled, seven or eight meters away. Then the scraping of steel on stone, closer.

Me on my stomach, rifle behind me on my pack, and a freaking Tiger bot coming to investigate a stunned Berkut.

The sun was out and both the street and my stealth suit were close to the same temperature, so I had that going. But my heartbeat would be unmistakable if it got close enough to poke at Rikki.

I have little pieces of mirror sewn into the wristbands of my suit, just tiny little bits of highly polished metal. I use them to look ahead without lifting my head, because crawling is something I do a lot of. Currently, my right hand was by my face, which was turned so that my left cheek was pressed to the ground. The view in the bit of mirror was almost straight ahead. I twisted the wrist a millimeter. A monster came into view. The fucking Tiger was right there. Striped, like its namesake, only in gray and black, it prowled closer, big head with black ocular band swiveling left and right. It would pass right by me on its way to Rikki. I was dead. My Five-Seven was only a slim possibility, but those light-armor-piercing 5.7 millimeter bullets were never gonna do much to a hundred and eighty kilo monster of steel, scandium, titanium, and carbon fiber.

A stone bounced on pavement, fifteen meters or so down the road. The Tiger snapped around and the Kite immediately buzzed across the intervening space. I twisted the mirror in that direction and found the little recon drone hovering over a small chunk of red brick, right in the middle of the road. Suddenly, another piece landed almost next to the first, almost hitting the Kite. The drone whipped around at the same time that I moved my wrist. In my tiny, tiny view of life, the corner of a building came into sight, an odd shape disrupting its straight lines. It took me three heartbeats to recognize that shape. Half a human face, one black eye watching and black hair hanging, silver metal on her cheek. Then it was gone and the Kite shot after it. A grey and black streak flew through my line of sight, the Tiger leaping fifteen meters with a flick of its servos, skidding on rubble as it tried to corner around the building. Then it too was gone. A person? Here? In the Zone? Throwing rocks at fucking Tiger bots?

Three more heartbeats to listen and then I fast crawled under a city bus, then out alongside a Toyota sedan, then rolled under a panel van, out the other side and into the shadows of a tow truck, the corner sign telling me I was now on Rector Street. Almost safe. My brain settled a bit and the image of that face popped unbidden into my head along with another thought— female. Somehow, a young girl had just saved my life.

My nearest hide was in the basement of a bar and grill on Rector Street, inside the old keg cooler. It took me twenty-six more minutes to get a hundred meters till I was at the door. This one was smaller than many of my others, but I could have cared less when I finally thumped down the staircase behind the bar and was able to latch the heavy metal refrigerator door behind me.

Battery-powered light was a major upgrade from my long-depleted chem stick, and thanks to upgrades in battery tech in the years just before Drone Night, I had lots of power, shielded by the metal refrigerator walls.

After drinking at least a liter of water and shoving a couple of long-term-survival food bars down my throat, I got up the courage to unwrap my ankle, unlace the boot, and try to wrestle it off. I had to stop and down some stronger painkillers before I could get the boot off.

It still sucked, but when I finally got it free, I popped some first aid instant freeze packs and re-wrapped the ankle with the chillers right under the bandage. Then I placed a call home.

Radio, cell, or satellite calls will get you killed super quick. Using an old-fashioned landline low-voltage rig will dial right out, at least right out to a computerized answering system in Brooklyn that in turn sends a text to my mother's AI. It's a one-way system, with no way for me to get a response or answer from home. But at least it would tell them that I was alive, safe, and prepping for egress. If Rikki was up and running, I could have just had him send a burst transmission. Four letters in a text to my family's AIs. TTFN. *Ta-ta-for-now*. A phrase from my sisters' favorite childhood book series.

Too bad it couldn't go both ways because I would have loved to ask some questions. By now, they would have all seen the replay of today's episode, and the long, lonesome crawl to my safe site had left me plenty of time to wonder about things that had nothing to do with young, exotic, female faces peering around corners.

Like why Johnson Recovery would shift to Battery Park all of a sudden, and why they would insert so early in the day. Prime time for the show was early afternoon, and it was a rare thing for any of the show's salvage teams to deviate from the production schedule. In fact, despite all their vaunted bravery and bravado, Team Johnson toed the producer's line, being as Brad really liked those fat Flottercot checks. The stuff they went after nowadays had caused me to scratch my head on multiple occasions. Simple smash and grabs, stuff that looked flashy on screen, like ramming the LAV through the windows and glass doors of a Fifth Avenue Prada or Louis Vuitton and auctioning the *rescued* goods after autographing it for added value. Or the time the JR rig was outbound and screeched to a sudden halt outside a cigar shop so that JJ could grab a couple of boxes of ancient high-end cigars that the three Johnson men smoked in the open top hatches, puffing away like hotshots. Idiots.

Something weird was going down, and it had almost killed them. The Spider had them dead to rights, which also begged the question about how it knew they were coming. I had walked right past that area and none of those units had been there. Rikki would have warned me.

Speaking of Rikki, I gave him a once over. Nothing seemed broken, which was a shock. His carbon fiber exterior protected his internals pretty well, but the fan blades were plastic and prone to breaking. At home, I make extras on my 3D printer and pack them as part of my Rikki repair kit.

But nothing external looked damaged. Blasts are fairly common in a war zone and the Russian designers had built Rikki with that in mind. There is a safety program that will trigger if a Berkut's accelerometer detects wildly excessive cross-vector bursts of speed. The drone will pill-bug up for protection, then the CPU gets shut off. According to the helpful specs provided by the Russians after thousands of their kill machines ended up in downtown Manhattan, the idea is that the drone will go into stasis. When next the sun comes out and powers up the solar film coating the whole back of the Berkut, it will come back online.

Down in my basement lair, I had to improvise, hooking him up to a battery-powered recharger, then changing the batteries every hour or so. Good time to clean my rifle.

No sleep till the rifle is clean. Those were my rules growing up. Take care of the weapon and it will take care of you. Rikki was one of my primary weapons, so I think Dad would agree that taking care of him was as important as the Remington.

Dragging my rifle around behind me all day hadn't done it any favors, but other than scratches on its exterior, it was okay. My body must have cushioned its fall down the elevator shaft. I cleaned it, oiled it, reloaded the mags, and put the suppressor back in my pack.

Then I lay back and thought about the shots. And Astrid's face in the windshield of the LAV. And the face peering around the corner... and the horrible speed of the Tiger as it too went around the corner.

A hum woke me sometime later. Rikki was hovering in front of me, gun pointed right at my face. It was unloaded but the titanium spear point above the barrel was still deadly.

"Hello Ajaya," my drone said. Odd. He's never called me Ajaya. I programmed him for AJ, but his files, of course, include my full name.

"Status?"

"Airplane mode engaged. Number three prop functioning at impaired level. Sensors nominal. Weapon system depleted."

"Transform and disengage hover function," I said.

Rikki's protective ball shape opened out, his eight primary segments unrolling, then snicking smoothly into his flight shape. Rikki looks like the love child of an old Northrup Grumman B-2 Spirit stealth bomber and the even older Lockheed F-117 Nighthawk attack aircraft. His wings can tuck in tight when speed is required, and his gun barrel looks like a stubby mouth under a titanium beak. Two of his fans move into the wings to provide mainly hover and lift, but also propulsion if he tilts them, while the other two turbofans slide to the back to provide linear propulsion, both forward and back.

His top is all black, for better solar charging and also so that he is hard to see from above. His underside is a mottled blue and white, which helps hide him from ground observers. Rikki can lift straight up, then go either forward *or* backward, sideways, barrel loop, or spin end over end in some crazy wild maneuvers that no human-flown plane could or had ever managed.

With his wings fully extended, he can float on city thermals for hours without using hardly any power. If a target is sighted below or a Render drone appears above, he can fold wings, tilt his wing fans toward the back, and arrow for the ground at speeds approaching four hundred kilometers per hour.

My Berkut has plenty of scars, both old and new. There are two bullet gouges on him, one on the top of his left wing and one crossing his underside. Then there is a patched hole on his nose, where the cockpit would be on a human-flown aircraft. The scar is covered with a sticker of a beautiful woman, like the airplane nose art that crewmen used to decorate their war planes with. I did it in an odd moment one night, when I was camping out in one of my better-equipped lairs near the east side of Central Park. It was a modern sticker, of a current celebrity, and I almost immediately regretted doing it. But the adhesive was really strong and let's face it, no one was ever going to see my Berkut. It would, however, be embarrassing on a life-ending scale if *she* ever saw it.

The sticker did help me to forget how Rikki got those scars, and that was something. The bullet gouges were mine. But my dad's last shot had cored the drone that had killed him. That's what the sticker covered. I had congratulated Dad even as I plugged his bullet wound with one tampon in the front of his torso and another in the back, where the bullet had exited. All in all, a survivable wound. Then I had raised a foot to stomp the Berkut and he had stopped me.

"Ajaya, we have never captured a Berkut intact. Think, son. If we could repair it? If *you* could repair it?" he had said.

He died twenty minutes later. It took me two days to carry his body out of the Zone. The worst two days of my life. But we don't leave anyone behind. That's what he taught me.

The autopsy had revealed a fragment of his rib, blasted apart by the armor-piercing bullet, had lacerated his abdominal aorta, just nicked it a little. Just enough. The internal bleeding had gone unnoticed... by me.

Two weeks later, I went back in and found the Berkut where I had left it. I almost destroyed it that moment, and then again when I took it to a safe house. Instead, after staring at it for hours, I pulled the CPU and took it home. Three months later, I came back, reinstalled the CPU—rebuilt with upgraded features—then fixed the drone's damaged parts, tied the thing down, and rebooted it with the muzzle of my Five-Seven pressed against the open CPU compartment. The drone had recognized me, as it was programmed to recognize anyone in my family and a few others, ticking loudly to itself as it did. I named it Rikki Tikki two missions later, after *my* favorite childhood story. Dad had told me that story every night he put me to bed, at least between his Afghan missions. He held off exposing me to the rest of Kipling's work till I was older. Take the good with the bad, as he said. Rikki was definitely bad mixed with good.

"Disengage airplane mode," I said.

"*Airplane mode off. Unable to connect to network.*"

The beer cooler's walls acted like a Faraday cage, blocking all signals, which was really good. I tinkered with his faulty fan blade, eventually replacing it with a 3D printed spare. Then I checked the time. Wee early morning. O dark hundred hours. A good time to move.

All of the combat drones in the Zone used solar power to recharge, although some could harvest power from the electrical grid if it was up. The hours just before dawn were the point where they remained the most dormant. A few hours after dark, they might still patrol or at least stay alert, but in the cold, dark hours of morning, they would be mostly quiescent. Ten years was long past all of their designed lifespans, yet many were still going, but they were having some issues. Battery life was a biggie.

I got my foot back into my boot but couldn't lace it. Instead, I wrapped it with duct tape with a couple pieces of the leg of a bar stool taped in to act like a splint. My rifle, stock folded, went back in the pack sling next to the bubble-wrapped PC, and I made a cane from a piece of sturdy stair railing, also from the bar. With Rikki near full charge from a dozen exhausted batteries, we headed out.

We made it back to Battery Park just as the sun came up. No Kites, no Tigers, and no human faces.

I put Rikki into standby mode, sending him up into the skies above to await my next contact, be it sonic, reflected laser, or in cases where we are really far apart, I will sometimes dig out a cached police radio and rubber band the mike open, leaving it far enough away to avoid the other drones that inevitably arrive.

My drone disappeared up into the sky and I shuffled into the auto-cannon protected space in front of the Battery tunnel entrance.

The man-sized door let me into the security space, then cycled shut behind me.

"Welcome back, Mr. Gurung. Put your weapons in the bin and then kneel on the white X, hands behind your head," a voice said over the speaker.

Alarm bells rang in my head as I stood stunned. Never in the history of the Zone have I heard of a salvage specialist being treated this way.

"Now, Mr. Gurung. Let's avoid the gas if we can, shall we?"

Chapter 7

I complied, in a daze, but not wanting to explore whatever the gas thing was. As soon as I had painfully lowered myself to a kneeling position and placed both hands behind my head, the inner door swung open. Four Zone Defense security types entered with M-43 electro mag assault rifles aimed square on yours truly.

With swift efficiency, they zip-tied my hands behind my back. Two grabbed my arms, hauling me to my feet and through the opened door, while the other two grabbed my weapons and pack. Within seconds, I was sandwiched between two burly soldiers in back of a Mobile Utility Vehicle, which was basically a fancy electric golf cart with multiple rows of seats.

The other two hopped in front and we took off, traveling past the Zone entrance, past the ready response team, and deeper into the admin part of the facility.

My guards stared straight ahead and didn't say a single word. Myself, I just kept quiet, my normal wiseass wit having fled my head at this unexpected turn of events.

A few minutes later, after passing several armed checkpoints, we arrived in big brass country, as noted by the desks of clerical types manning AI workstations. My over-muscled escort hauled me out of the vehicle and passed the now staring administrators, down a hallway, and then hooked a right into a stark, utilitarian conference room.

I was unceremoniously placed in a chair sitting in the middle of the room while my weapons were unloaded and laid out on a table on one wall, followed by the contents of my pack.

Each guard then took up a corner of the room, all facing me. Ten long minutes later, the door opened and four new men walked in.

I recognized the first man as General Davis, current commander of Zone Defense. That was easy, as his picture was on the wall of every Zone entrance around Manhattan. That and his uniform, which was a pretty good giveaway. Two of the other men wore dark suits that screamed government agents. The fourth man, I recognized instantly. Well, not his identity, but I recognized that he was a special ops kind of guy. How? He had the same look as my father and the guys my father had worked with before he left the British military. Hard physique, hard face, hard eyes, all screaming unyielding soldier. He was smaller than the four guards who had dragged me in here, but my money was on him against any two of them in a fight, and maybe all four at once.

"Mr. Gurung," General Davis said, his own eyes pretty granite-like themselves in the hard planes of his dark-skinned face.

"General Davis," I said. My earlier shock had worn off and my father's voice had risen up in my mind during the ten-minute wait.

He frowned, glancing at one of the two men in suits. The fourth man, the spec ops guy, was over at the table, inspecting my gear.

"We don't normally meet with salvagers in this manner," the general went on.

"We've never met at all, sir. I have met your two predecessors, just not you. Sir," I said. Dad always said that officers liked to hear a lot of *sirs*. Seemed like a good idea in light of my current situation.

"I was referring to your bindings," he said, one eyebrow now raised. He had two stars on his shoulders, so he was a major general, but other than that, I didn't know anything about the man.

"Yes, sir. This seems new. Maybe a change in protocol that I missed in my emails?" I asked, unable to stop the wiseass now that I was calmer.

The spec ops soldier had my MSR in his hands and was inspecting the opened action, even sniffing it.

General Davis paused, face blank but eyes hardening—even harder. "Ajaya Edward Gurung. You hold the distinction of having the most solo excursions into the Zone, *and* being the only current certified solo salvager on record."

"Mike Dumas is a solo..." I trailed off as the general shook his head.

"Missing for five days and presumed dead," he said. "He lasted thirty months. You're in, what? Your eighth year?"

I nodded, still processing the news.

"How is that, Ajaya? How is it that a young man of your short years has survived and even prospered entering the Zone on a regular basis, on foot and lightly armed?"

I've always wondered if the brass had wondered. My father had thought we'd be called upon to explain our techniques, maybe even teach them.

"Well sir, my dad taught me well. Plus a healthy dose of luck, sir," I said.

The spec ops guy snorted, his back to me as he studied the condition of my kukri.

"Oh, yes. Where are my manners?" General Davis said, which was funny because my dad always said that high-ranking officers had fewer manners but always talked about them. "Ajaya, this is Mr. White and Mr. Black from the… federal government. And the curious fellow digging through your gear is Major Yoshida."

White was dark skinned, Black was white, and Yoshida was mixed ethnicity, but likely mostly of Japanese ancestry.

Mr. Black leaned back against the table where my gear was and glanced sideways at Yoshida.

"Major, how many times have you been into the Zone?" he asked.

"Seven," was the immediate answer. Yoshida had my multi-tool out and was opening it into pliers.

"Is it as tough as they say?" Mr. Black asked in a friendly, conversational tone. He was watching me.

Yoshida snorted again. "The first time, we made it three blocks before one of my guys got wounded. Second time, four blocks. The third trip, we barely got one block in before our Chief Petty Officer's head exploded. Never even saw the drone that did it. Fourth and fifth times, we made it to Central Park and back out. Sixth time, I went in to help pull out another team, or what was left of it. Two out of six."

We waited for a second, then Black shifted his feet, impatient. "And the seventh?"

"We crossed the whole island, west to east. I made it all the way to the water and was picked up by boat," the major said. "I was the only survivor—out of a six-man team." He looked around at each of us, then walked behind me and snipped my cable ties with my own multi-tool.

I pulled my arms forward and massaged my wrists. Black was staring at me. "You went into the Zone when you were not quite a teenager. You've gone in so many times that I'm afraid we don't have an accurate count. Something about the confusion of the early years," he said.

His partner, White, moved around in front of me, his left eye glowing red as he read something on his iContact. "You've entered and exited from every access point we have. Thirty-eight recorded overnights in the Zone. The last eighteen months, you've gone in at least once a week, every week," he said. "It's like the damned drones give you permission."

There it was. My father used to say that one of our greatest threats was falling victim to our own success. I had thought he meant complacency, but he had explained he was worried that others would notice our accomplishments, and not in a good way.

"Did you know we asked your father to train soldiers in his techniques? Four times, we asked. He declined. Said he didn't want to be responsible for their deaths. Yet he brought you, his only son, into the most dangerous place on Earth. Why?"

I struggled with my thoughts. "He needed my help. Our family needed the money and no one would hire an Indian-looking ex-soldier after the Attack, at least for the first couple years. By then, we were a team and we did pretty well. He said I was a natural."

All four just stared at me, dead silent, faces like granite. My father had told me to never offer information. Keep your mouth shut. Answer yes and no. Don't embellish, and always, always wait out the pauses.

White waved his left hand at the wall and the whole white surface lit up with a projected image. Satellite—looking down on the Zone from above. It zoomed, moving up close, going from the edge of space to a single city street. The resolution was frighteningly sharp, clear enough to read a Pepsi bottle lying in the gutter. Something moved on the open street. A blurry spot—a set of wavy lines like heat distortion. Roundish shaped, at least from above—same color as the street. It moved in short, slow, random motions. Forward, then suddenly sideways, forward again but half as far. Then at a diagonal, twice as far before freezing in place.

It was me. That's how I move in the Zone. A shape flew past me, turned and came back, delta wings folding and twisting into a ball.

"That's you. The drone—is a Russian Berkut. The soldier monitoring this feed thought you were dead. Imagine his surprise when it hovered in front of you, then moved out in front to scout. A fucking Berkut," White said, his voice only rising at the last bit.

"You working for the drones, son?" General Davis asked.

Time for one of those short answers. "No, sir."

"Then what the hell is that?" the general asked.

"It works for me. Sir."

"A Russian Berkut works for you?" Black asked, incredulous. "The deadliest UAV in the Zone?"

"Yes," I said.

Yoshida chuckled. Black looked at him sharply.

"You don't get a sir... Agent Black. But the general does," the major said. "Funny kid."

"A funny kid who somehow suborned one of the deadliest killers in the Zone," White said.

"Yeah, true," Yoshida said, suddenly moving in front of me and squatting down to stare into my eyes.
"You know how many of my people might still be alive if you had shared this little secret?"

"You're the first person to ask—me," I said. "I didn't know you had asked my dad. Nobody ever came to me."

"We thought you'd get killed quick without your dad. Seems you upped the game but didn't think to share it," Black said.

"Right. Do you hear yourself? *We thought you'd get killed quick.* We're just gonna sit back and watch you die. Oh? But you didn't, you selfish bastard. How dare you? Now share everything! Nobody shares Zone secrets. The *Zone War* teams all have their secrets, the other salvage people all guard their little kingdoms, and Zone Defense never tells us anything. You people don't offer *us* any help, either, Major. You just make us sign an acknowledgement that we're going in at our own risk," I said. The video was still up on the wall and the string of numbers across the bottom suddenly started to make sense. Part of the string was likely location—longitude and latitude. But that part right there... a date.

"You took this video six months ago. Why are you interrogating me only just now?" I asked. "What changed?"

The two agents exchanged a look. "Nothing—nothing at all," White said with a sigh.

"You familiar with the Zone drone specs, kid?" Black asked. "What am I saying? Baburam Gurung's kid must know the manuals forward and backward. Riddle me this, hotshot. What single specification has turned out to be wrong on every drone in the Zone?"

That one came easy. "Unit lifespan," I said. "They talk about it on that *show* all the time."

"Bingo. Give the kid a treat," Black said, looking at Yoshida. The major reached into my pile of stuff and pulled out a protein ration bar, tossing it my way.

Enlightenment hit me as I caught the bar. "Manhattan was supposed to be reclaimed by now," I said. "The drones should have worn out by now."

"Yes, and the powers that be want it back," White said.

"Is that why *Zone War* was allowed to start? To speed up the end of the drones, or was it to distract the public from the fact the drones were still going?"

"Why not both?" White said, both palms up in a shrug.

"But you guys are DoD right? Like Defense Intelligence guys or something? You only care about national defense," I said, testing some sudden insight.

"Whoa there, kid. Where'd you get all that?" Black asked, leaning forward.

"A hunch. Why else are you suddenly busting my balls? Because the drones all changed their behaviors and are functioning way longer than anyone predicted," I guessed again.

"What do you mean *changed behavior*?" White asked, moving up next to his partner.

"You know... shortened patrol patterns to reduce wear and tear, decreased night activity because batteries and capacitors are beginning to short cycle, Wolf drones chewing up coat hangers to produce flechettes for themselves and other drones. Things like that. Power sharing, staying out of animal-rich areas like the Park or the subway tunnels."

"You've seen that? The coat hanger thing?" Yoshida suddenly asked.

"Yeah, most drones are less prevalent inside buildings than they used to be, but the Wolves will scavenge for wire products, particularly coat hangers. I use them as bait."

"Bait?" Black asked.

"For traps. I set traplines," I said. "Doesn't everyone?"

"No kid. No, they don't," White said, shaking his head.

"Where? Where do you set them?" Yoshida pressed.

"All over. Gyms are good 'cause you can use the smith racks with heavy weights on the bars. Catch Wolves and even Tigers under two hundred kilos, they don't usually get away. They can lift that easy, but if you get them at the neck, it's like a mouse trap. Also, auto repair places are great 'cause the Wolves go there looking for metal and there's lots of machinery to rig up in different ways. You have to be creative and change things up because the ones that get trapped transmit the details to the rest."

"What else have you seen, kid?" Black asked.

It hit like a ton of bricks. "Oh, the trap that the drones set for Johnson Recovery. The Spider and all that," I said.

"Spider? What Spider?" General Davis asked, suddenly interested.

"The Spider on the Custom House roof," I said. "You don't think tank killers set up *that* ambush by themselves, do you?"

"You saw it?" the general asked.

"Saw it and shot it. Didn't kill it, though," I said.

"You shot four times, and all of those were aimed at the TKs," Yoshida said. There was a question in there, I think.

White moved his hand and then waved it at the wall and new footage showed up. Taken directly from *Zone War* cameras, likely exterior hull cameras on the LAV. It showed the machine-gun on the northern TK suddenly lurch as the weapon sighting module on top burst into pieces. The image froze and a red circle appeared on a building in the background, specifically, a window on a mid-level floor—my window.

"I fired *five* times. The first shot was a sub-sonic round on the Spider. Suppressed. Angle was bad for armor so I shot its ocular band. The other four shots were all full power AP 'cause the cat was outta the bag."

"Wait. You deliberately fired a low-powered round at a Spider? Why, for God's sake?" Black asked, incredulous.

"I needed to disrupt the Spider's control of the situation, but I also needed the extra time to get off the other four shots. Full power would alert the aerial drones instantly," I explained.

"Killing the Spider would have likely given the Johnsons the edge they needed. Instead, you gave up close to a million dollars!" Black said.

"But that didn't happen, did it?" Yoshida interjected. "The TKs kept fighting even after he took out targeting and rockets. If he hadn't shot the cable, they might have died."

"You don't even like the Johnsons?" White asked. "It says so in your file."

I didn't answer that one. I gotta file that says who I like? General Davis answered for me, a second later.

"He doesn't like *most* of the Johnsons," he said.

"Ah, the girl," White said, nodding thoughtfully. "Kinda outta your league, kid. Doesn't she date some professional athlete?"

"Nah, that was last month. She's with some musician now, I think," Black said.

Ewww. Forty-something creeper agent was stalking Astrid.

"He's known her since they were in middle school," Davis said.

All four of them looked at me for a moment.

"Okay, so you fired *five* shots, then the building exploded," White said, running the footage forward till flame blossomed out of four windows on the seventeenth floor.

"Just Tannerite and a small amount of acetylene. I had to slow down the UAVs that came my way."

"You blew up your own sniper hide?" Yoshida asked, eyebrows raised. "Where were you?"

"In the elevator shaft, or rather, falling down it. Cable descenders," I said.

"How'd you set off the bomb?" Yoshida asked.

"I had Ri- I had the Berkut shoot it," I said, deciding they didn't need to know I named the damned thing.

"You deliberately set up this whole shoot-and-explode thing?" Davis asked.

"I had like five seconds to come up with it. I was up there, getting that notebook computer for a client," I said, nodding at the bubble-wrapped PC. "I had no idea Team Johnson would roll in behind me, and in the morning no less. What's up with that, by the way? Is the show no longer really live?"

"Take us through it, kid. Start at the beginning," Black said, ignoring my question, which was probably answer enough.

I spent the next thirty minutes detailing the whole thing, answering their questions and repeating my story at least four times. I did not mention the face I saw, the person who deliberately distracted a Tiger unit so that I could live. Mostly because I was having trouble believing it myself.

"Ajaya, I'm suspending your permit to go into the Zone," General Davis said, ending the interview.

"What? Till when?" I asked.

"We'll see. We have to review this information. It's disturbing, you understand, to learn about this pet drone of yours," the general said.

"Is that it or is it dependent on my teaching you guys how to do it?" I asked. They were so holding my access hostage.

"Hmmm, interesting question. We get back to you on that?" Black said.

"When?" I asked.

"When we're good and ready," Black said and then walked out, followed by Davis and White. Yoshida motioned me up and over to my gear. He started to hand me stuff and I began to pack it under his watchful eyes.

"You are a hell of a sniper, Ajaya," he said after a few moments.

"Not really a sniper. Never served in the military or anything. Dad was the sniper," I said.

"You *are* sniper, through and through. Five shots in what? Six or seven seconds. Improvising a shooting platform, escape route, and covering explosion, then exfiltrating an enemy-rich environment with a wounded leg? That's a sniper, Ajaya," he said with a grin. Then he clapped me on the shoulder and headed for the door. "Have a nice day."

Chapter 8

It took another hour and ten minutes to get a self-driver and get back to Brooklyn, or at least our little beat-down section of it. Then I hobbled into the neighborhood precinct and checked in my firearms with the desk sergeant. I must have looked particularly bad because a lot of the cops were giving me funny looks and it's not like I haven't been in there a bazillion times.

Weapons load lighter (but not wiped out 'cause I was raised Gurkha and *always* have my kukri), I limped the three blocks to our apartment building.

When Manhattan became no-man's-land, the wealthy spread into the other boroughs, with many of them ending up in Brooklyn. We'd had to move four times in ten years because of rising rents. After Drone Night, the US and world economies dropped into recession, as I've mentioned before. But the rich were still rich, and they could afford to pay way more than the rest of us. My dad and Brad Johnson plowed most of their combined monies into the recovery business, even the newly salvaged money, because used armored vehicles cost like crazy. They pulled out just enough to keep our families going. Our living arrangements reflected that reality. Astrid and her family used to live down the hall from our first apartment. Now they live in Cobble freaking Hill.

After a couple of years came the breakup, as my mom used to call it. Originally, my father would infiltrate the Zone and then set up overwatch before Brad and JJ came barreling in in an armored vehicle to smash and grab. Dad shot a ton of drones that brought in a ton of bounties while the other two essentially looted. But the bigger, higher-bounty drones became less numerous after the first couple of years and Brad started to feel that my father's sniper skills weren't contributing as much as he and his son were. He adjusted the company structure without my dad knowing and suddenly just cut us out. Dad was a great sniper, not a great businessman.

We had to rebuild, which we did once I joined my father on incursions. We even stepped up to a nicer place. Then dad died and our income dried up again. So we moved to this place. When I started going back in, and particularly once I had Rikki, our money started flowing again. But this time, Mom and I agreed that we would build up our reserves and emergency funds to a level that would leave us independent if we fell on hard times again. Like today.

The front of the building was normal, except for a big, shiny new Tesla SUV parked in front. Unusual. On any given day, you'd see lots of Kias, Chinese FAWs and DFMs, Hyundais, even a couple of older Hondas. Only one Tesla. Hmm.

The elevator was actually working today, so my ankle was thankful as I rode up to the third floor. The door recognized me and unlocked as I approached.

"Mom, I'm home," was my typical announcement but today I immediately heard voices in the living room so I stayed quiet, dropped my pack, and snuck up on the archway.

I peeked around the corner and almost dropped my jaw to the floor. Trinity Flottercot, daughter of media mogul Chester Flottercot, and, more importantly, executive producer of *Zone War*, sat in the easy chair that I often claim. My mother and Aama were on the love seat, and bracketed between Gabby and Monique on the couch was... Astrid. I haven't seen her in our apartment in years.

"Ajaya, I thought I heard the door," my mother said. She's hard as hell to sneak up on. Something to do with being married to a sniper, I suppose.

"Ah, hi, Mom. Girls, Aama. Hi, Trinity. Hi, Astrid," I said, eyes flicking past the producer to the star, then back to Mom. The smile that bloomed on Astrid's face did something funny to my insides.

"We've been waiting for you," Mom said, frowning. That frown was because I was late and had worried her. Thank the government, Ma.

"Oh, I had to move slower than normal," I said, unable to keep myself from glancing at Astrid. The freaking twins were sandwiching her and smiling like Cheshire cats. They *love* Astrid. Part hero worship and part family memories. In fifth grade, at the beginning of all that middle school shit that all kids go through, one of them had bragged about knowing her. It was near the beginning of *Zone War* and the show was already a hit. The other kids had mocked them mercilessly, calling them liars and other vile teenager shit, right up until the day Astrid came to the school with my mother to pick up the girls. Shit stopped then.

Astrid was a dutiful Johnson, but she had some rebel in her and had kept in low-key, quiet contact with my mother. Anything more would bring the wrath of Brad and Martin down on her head. She had probably paid for that one single school visit, but it had cemented my sisters' reverence like nothing else could.

My mom glanced down at my legs and spotted the duct tape and wood stool splint. "What did you do?" she demanded as she launched from her seat, Aama right behind her. "Here, sit down," she said, pointing to the love seat.

"Ma, I'm filthy," I said, backing away a bit. Not my best look, I'm sure. Covered in dirt, powdered sheet rock, soot from the fire, dust, and unidentifiable shit from the tunnels. My stealth suit didn't have to copy the ground because I was basically wearing it.

Aama brought a kitchen table chair with a solid wood seat, solving the problem. Mom all but forced me into it and then crouched down to look at my leg.

"Just a sprain, Ma," I said.

"And just how did you sprain it, Ajaya?" Mom asked.

Across the room, Astrid looked concerned but Trinity's eyes were popping like she was going crazy. The truth was she was probably jonesing for a camera to record all of this. Footage, footage, footage.

Trinity is about thirty, I think. Maybe mid-thirties. Only child of Chester Flottercot. Crazy good at finding trendy shows, with her penultimate production being *Zone War*. She's always scared me a little. Her body is super fit, like she moonlights as a fitness guru, but her face is too severe, too sharp in its features to be on the other side of the camera. People use the terms *foxy* and *vixen* for hot women, but Trinity's pointed chin and triangular face is very foxlike and I don't find it attractive at all. Killer bod, though. I've met her maybe seven or eight times. Dressed in black, fitted designer jeans and some kind of black fashion t-shirt, her figure would turn heads. Walking next to Astrid, she might go unnoticed.

My childhood friend looked absolutely amazing. Knee-high boots with those stretchy-type jeans tucked in and a white blouse that was showing enough cleavage to erase a third of my IQ. Blonde hair loose and flowing over her shoulders, framing her face and those amazing blue eyes.

"Well?" Mom asked.

"Fell down an elevator shaft," my mouth answered before my distracted brain could shut it down.

"You what?"

Shit. Now focusing on my mother, I nonetheless picked up the others leaning forward in the outside edges of my vision.

"Not really, Ma. It was a controlled descent... mostly."

"Ajaya Gurung, are you telling me that when that floor exploded, you got blown down an elevator shaft?" Mom asked in her most dangerous, quietest voice.

"How did you know about the explosion?" I asked, attempting distraction.

Trinity snorted. I glanced at her. "Please. Over two billion episode views and climbing," she said.

"Oh." Mom was still waiting. "I was already in the shaft when the bomb went off. I just descended a little fast and some stuff bounced off my head and then I kind of slammed into the elevator car... a bit."

"Just your head? Then nothing to worry about, Mom," Gabby said, laughing at my predicament. I gave her an unimpressed raised eyebrow and then glanced back at Mom. Oh, need more damage control.

"Really, Mom, it went as well as can be expected. I'm fine. My ankle is a little shacked but otherwise no wounds or bleeding or anything."

"Language, Ajaya," she said.

"Mom, *shacked* is just slang," Monique protested. I could count on the twins to back me if it came to freedom of expression. They were all about expressing.

"Short for shacking up, a euphemism for fornication, young lady, and not a word I want thrown about this house, got it?"

Barbara Gurung, linguist. Words mattered, especially when you spoke English, French, Spanish, Italian, Russian, and Nepali. That's how she met Dad. Translating for the UN. Oh, and don't even start about the first names—Barbara and Baburam. Heard it all before. Get over it.

Aama had pulled her ever-present Karda, the little utility knife appearing from somewhere in her clothing, and was systematically cutting off the duct tape. Mom peeled as Aama cut. I might have sucked in a breath when they pulled the boot off.

"God, AJ, your feet stink!" Gabby said, making a face.

Great. I glanced at Astrid. She smiled and crossed her eyes, tilting her head like the odor was killing her. I laughed. She could always make me laugh. But still.

"Mom, maybe I should just go shower first. Much as it pains me to say it, Gabby's probably right," I said.

Mom ignored me, peeling off the sock. Now it was her turn to draw a sharp breath. My ankle was pretty swollen, black and blue bruising starting to darken up all around it.

Astrid popped up off the couch. "That calls for ice. I'll get it," she said, heading for the kitchen. Always jumping in to help. Aama went with her. I heard them talking in the kitchen but couldn't, for the life of me, make out their words.

"So, ah, Trinity. What brings you two out to our slice of heaven?" I asked nervously as Monique went and opened the living room window.

"Oh, I don't know, Ajaya... maybe just the biggest single show in the history of the world," she said with a vulpine smile.

"Well, it was a pretty nasty trap," I said. Monique now had my boot held at arm's length and was taking it out of the room.

I heard a light laugh behind me. "Honestly Monique, that's nothing. Martin's worse than that at his best and forget about JJ's feet. Whew!" Astrid said. She came around in front and squatted down, placing a towel-wrapped bag of ice against my ankle.

"Ah, geez Astrid, I can do that," I said, nervous to have her suddenly in my apartment and kneeling at my smelly, grime-encrusted feet.

"AJ, you fell down an elevator shaft protecting us. The absolute least I can do is put ice on your ankle," she said, twisting her body into a cross-legged sitting position that appeared to be way more comfortable. It also left me looking down at her and, more distractingly, her blouse, the one with the top three buttons undone. Eyes behave, dammit!

"How did you know it was me?" I asked, glancing from Astrid to Trinity, which helped with the whole distracting view thing.

"Please! Four rapid-fire magnum shots from a high rise in like six seconds? Who else would it be?" Astrid answered, giving me her patented *don't be stupid* look. That one had been directed my way virtually every day of middle school and the first two years of high school, before she got yanked out to be home tutored.

"It was five," I said, because I always have to correct her when she's giving me that sass.

"Five what? Shots?" Astrid asked, expression of disbelief telling me she thought I was pulling her leg. Not that I had a history of doing that or anything.

"First one was subsonic and suppressed enough that the falling glass covered it," I said.

"Why and what?" Trinity demanded, almost coming out of her chair. Somehow I understood her and then I understood that my mouth had gotten away from me again.

"Because I needed the extra moment and I needed to drive away the Spider," I said, much quieter.

"Spider?" Trinity and Astrid said simultaneously.

"A Spider CThree? You shot at a Spider CThree?" Trinity asked, scary intense.

"Yeah. It was on the Custom House. It set the trap. I shot its ocular lenses and it took off while I shot up the TK and the cable."

"You could have killed it," Astrid said. It was actually a question.

"No dear, he couldn't. He needed every microsecond to fire all those shots and almost didn't make it out before those aerial units would have been on him," Mom said matter-of-factly.

"Just how much coverage did you get?" I asked Trinity. They all knew a whole lot about my shooting.

"The outer hull cameras went mostly unscathed. The live shots were crazy confusing but we immediately edited and replayed it. It's been consuming the news ever since. Four networks wanted Astrid to be on camera today, but we sent JJ instead. We needed to be here," Trinity said, smiling again.

"How many other people figured it out? Nobody really knows about me," I said.

"They do now. Your name got mentioned on live air as the LAV was pulling out. The Johnson family certainly recognized your shooting," Trinity explained.

"And you're here to..." I asked.

"To thank you, AJ. Thank you for saving my family and me," Astrid said quickly before Trinity could answer.

"Anytime, Trid," I said. "Anytime."

She smiled at my use of my old nickname for her. It was mostly that unless she pissed me off. Then I just called her *Ass*.

"That's *Astrid's* reason for being here. I tagged along because I want you to reconsider coming on the show," Trinity said. "I'll beg if I have to."

I became the center of a whole lot of eyes, watching my reaction. Three times before, I had shut her down. I stalled.

"Why were you guys even there? And so early?"

Astrid turned to Trinity, letting her handle the question. "We got a lead on some stuff that was supposedly at the Stock Exchange. Seemed like a quick in and out," Trinity said.

Lots of really good comebacks to that one popped into my head. I squashed them ruthlessly, on account of, you know, my mom and grandma.

"You still got that exemption to bring non-licensed people into the Zone?" I asked. Mom frowned, the twins looked surprised, and Trinity's gaze sharpened even further. Astrid looked confused.

"Yes, of course. Why?" Trinity asked.

"Yeah, why?" Mom asked.

I sighed and ran a hand through my hair. "'Cause General Davis yanked my license to enter the Zone. They're on to me and I think they're trying to force me to teach their men what, ah, I do," I said, looking at my mom.

"What do you mean *on to you*?" Trinity asked.

I didn't answer, instead watching Mom. She knew all about Rikki, had, in fact, had been the first to tell me it was okay to use the weapon that killed her husband in order to provide for his family.

"Did you recover your salvage or wasn't there enough time?" she asked.

"It's out in the hallway," I said. Mom was my partner, at least as far as information and money went. She knew all the details of every recovery. She knew that while this payment would be a good one, it wasn't enough to give us independence. She gave me a slight nod.

"What's your thought?" I turned to Trinity, who was watching our byplay with absolute fascination.

"I thought we'd interview you about what happened. About everything you did up there in that building. About what you do that no one else seems able to do. But you're wondering about going in like the guided hunters, right?" Trinity asked, a greedy light coming into her eyes.

"Just an idea. Brad wouldn't likely go for it," I said, glancing at Astrid, whose eyes were pretty wide.

"Oh—I don't know about that. He can be reasonable. What would your role be? Observer?" Trinity said, smiling like she had me in her crosshairs.

"I'd roll out of the LAV partway in and set up overwatch. Like my dad used to."

That caused a frown to replace the smile. "That didn't work out so well last time, according to my sources," Trinity said, glancing at Astrid.

"Yeah, the big baddies started to hold back a bit. It became just the little ones. Not as much threat," I said with my own smile. "Not as much bounty."

The frown got deeper. "And now is different?"

"Oh yeah. Lots different. The Spiders have come out to play."

"We only have your word on that. You didn't actually kill one for proof."

"How many times have the drones set traps for salvage crews?" I asked. " And please don't tell me that a cable across the road isn't a trap."

The answer was none and she knew it. She sat, staring at me, wheels turning.

"Not sure that's enough proof," she finally said.

"Okay."

"Okay? Okay what?" she asked, glancing at my mom, who just stood, arms crossed, face expressionless.

"Okay. You asked, I offered. I can wait. Got a payday from the recovery in the hall. Let's see what happens the next time one of your crews goes in. Probably hear from General Davis in a week anyway. Maybe it's time to work as an instructor." I shrugged.

"Yeah, well, it's not gonna be me driving," Astrid said to Trinity. "If AJ says there's Spiders setting traps, then there's Spiders setting traps." She glanced at me and gave me a nod. I nodded back, an indescribable feeling in my chest that she believed me.

Trinity looked dangerously thoughtful. "Would you still consider the interview?"

"Does it pay? Got bills to pay, mouthy debutantes to feed," I said. Behind Trinity's back I saw Gabby start to raise her middle finger but Mom's head swiveled to her and she had to abort mission.

"Oh, it will pay. Let me get back to you on all this. Either this evening or tomorrow morning. Agreed?"

"Agreed," I said.

Chapter 9

She got back to me before dinner. Both women were gone by the time I got done showering and cleaning up. My AI announced the email as I sat in my favorite chair, leg up, a bowl of Aama's dal and a plate of her famous momos in my lap, feeding my face.

Everybody was around, Mom working from home, Aama cooking, and the twins making up homework that one of their friends brought over. Mom lets them stay home from school if I don't come out of the Zone the previous day. Even if I send in an all okay message, they still won't be any use in school. We pick on each other mercilessly, but they already lost Dad to the Zone. Losing their big brother is a real worry.

My AI announced the email and I told it to read the quote. The number was kind of ridiculous.

"Is that shacking for real?" Monique asked.

Mom was so shocked, she didn't even notice the language.

"Wow. Who knew television paid so well," I said. That much money would do wonders for our family's FU fund and buy a lot of time for me to get my license back.

"When are you delivering the recovery?" Mom asked.

"I told them tomorrow, mid-morning. They wanted it today but I said I needed rest. Supposed to meet at a coffee place a couple of blocks from here."

Mom raised her eyebrow.

"I'll get a ride if my ankle's still sha—messed up,"I said, getting a single motherly nod in reply.

"You gonna do it, AJ? The interview?" Monique asked hopefully.

"That much money, how could I not."

My mom looked conflicted but she didn't say a word. That single interview was worth as much as my last four trips into the Zone combined. More, even.

The next morning, I had the place to myself. The girls were at school, Mom was out meeting with her boss from the translation company she worked for these days, and Aama was at the market.

"*So* Zone War *has announced an upcoming interview with the sharpshooter. What do you think about that, Jeremy?*"

"*I think, Lynn, that I'll be glued to the screen for that interview— like most of the world. As we've already discussed, there have been rumors for years of people that entered the Zone on foot, but to actually have one intercede to help the Johnsons and then to escape the drones... well, that story is gonna be intense.*"

"*The shooter is named Ajaya Gurung,*" Lynn said, my high school senior yearbook photo popping up on the wall screen behind and between the two talking heads. "*We know this because of this piece here—*"

Anyone who had ever watched the *Zone War* show would immediately recognize the inside of the Johnson Recovery armored vehicle, which was apparently in motion.

"Who? Who the hell was that?" Martin Johnson asked. He looked like he might barf.

"Has to be Ajaya, Mart. You said yourself that you saw him enter a couple of hours before we did. Plus, who else shoots like that," JJ said, frowning.

"He doesn't like us enough to help," Martin protested, still looking like he could spew at any moment.

Brad moved behind him, up toward the driver's section, where the back of a blonde female head could be seen. Brad looked pissy, or maybe just extra pissy. Hard to tell.

"Correction. He doesn't like most of us. There's one of us that he likes a great deal, aye little sister?" JJ said.

Astrid gave him a real quick glare over her shoulder, then went back to concentrating on her driving.

"That was pretty sophisticated shooting, JJ," Brad Johnson said, frowning.

"Do you remember Vermont, Dad? He was what? Nine? He cleared the range you set up faster than anyone, including his own father," JJ said. *"Pissed me off big time, but you said it yourself. He's a natural. Got a gift."*

"That was shooting .22 rifles, JJ," Brad said. *"Big difference."*

"And he's now twenty, same as Astrid. And we know he shoots .338. Those were heavy rounds to do that much damage. No way was that a 7.62."

The camera pulled back as the video segment froze.

"So they know him. And it makes sense. Brad Johnson's first salvage company was called Johnson Gurung. His partner was Baburam Gurung, ex-British special forces whose specialty was... sniping. Baburam was killed in the Zone two years ago, his body brought out by his only son, Ajaya. Which makes him one of the few people whose body was ever retrieved from the Zone," Lynn, the blonde news anchor, said. *"But let's talk about that shooting. As our consulting expert, Jeremy, talk to us about the shots."*

A holographic image of lower Manhattan popped up on the table between them, zooming down to Broadway with a frozen image of the Johnson LAV caught on the cable between the two tank killers.

"Lynn, we've recreated this from the camera footage of the episode itself, plus the enhanced video that the Zone War *production staff put out immediately after the live show ended. Here you see the LAV caught on a heavy steel cable between two Russian Tank Killer units. The aerial units are all just approximations, as the action was too fast to be sure of their movements, so just ignore them. The real danger in this situation was always the heavy machine-gun and, to a much lesser degree, the high-output laser."*

"Why, Jeremy? Why not the anti-tank missiles on that one tank killer?"

"The laser would have to burn through the ablative armor on the Johnsons' LAV, so it wouldn't be an issue, at least not for a long time. And missiles always need to travel a certain distance before going live. Arming distance, in military vernacular. On anti-armor systems, it is typically somewhere around sixty-five meters. As you can see here, the TKs are both only twenty meters or so away. But here's the interesting thing, Lynn. Should the LAV driver, Astrid Johnson, get free from the cable

and pull back, she'll only create distance, distance that the tank killer will use when it launches its two remaining missiles."

"That's... that's terrifying. What would they do? How could they have escaped?"

"Well, all that they could do would be to attempt to damage the missiles with their mini-gun before they could be launched at the LAV. So here's the fascinating part about that overwatch shooting. The sniper takes out the aiming module on the TK heavy machine-gun, instantly degrading its ability to damage the LAV. Then he punches holes in both missile engines, effectively removing that threat, before finally making a shot on that one eight-millimeter cable almost straight down. He did all four shots in a little over six seconds, then had to deal with his own problem, incoming aerial assault drones. Talk about combat pressure."

"But the floor he was on blew up?"

"Well it certainly blew out, that's for sure. See all the windows blasting out? And here you can actually see two of the drones getting blown back out of the building." The hologram zeroed in on the seventeenth floor and zoomed enough to pick out individual drones being thrown backward.

"Back up and freeze video at beginning," I ordered my AI. "Copy holograph and rotate for head down view."

A separate window opened up next to the broadcast and showed me a satellite-type view of the same holograph. "Calculate camera angles from production units secured to the LAV hull."

A set of red lines showed where the cameras could and couldn't see.

"Place a red X on the Spider's position on the Customs building per my notes." A bright red marker showed the seven-legged horror's position. No camera angle was close enough to pick it up. The Spider had picked a perfect blind spot for its vantage point.

"Save to new file, titled *spider*. Play broadcast from last point."

"So this shows us the bomb had plenty of blast and pressure but that power wasn't directed at damaging the building but more likely at the drones."

"The sniper set a trap for the drones? How'd he escape?"

"That's the billion dollar question, Lynn, one I'm dying to find out. My guess... stairwell or maybe inside an elevator car, or perhaps another room on the back side of the floor, but he'd have to be awfully fast to get that far away. Olympic sprinter fast, at least."

"Jeremy, Congressman Numer has made a statement to the effect that this episode is exactly why salvage should be discontinued and his Zone Reclamation bill be pushed through Congress. What do you think?"

"Lynn, having served our country as an infantry officer with actual combat experience, I would say that the congressman has no idea what he's asking, or if he does, then he places zero value on human life. His bill would send active military units into the Zone to fight street by street to eliminate the remaining fifteen thousand estimated functional drones. Urban combat is hell. Urban combat against drones of that quality is a bloodbath. Could our military do it? Yes, but at the cost of how many lives? Personally, the reason we didn't go in right after Drone Night is still just as valid now as then."

"But what about all those people who lost property and wealth, just leaving it to be salvaged by anyone who goes in? And if you remember, the other part was the drones were supposed to have an active life of five years. Ten years later, they're still killing people."

"Do I really have to answer that? Either hire someone to go get the stuff you think is so important or go in yourself. Me, I did three tours for Uncle Sam. I wouldn't go into the Zone in a tank with aerial support. You saw what I saw. That was an out-and-out trap. Everybody knows someone who died on Drone Night, lost property, or both. Nah, I'd hire this Ajaya to go get it. He's been successful like no one else."

"How, Jeremy? How can anyone be so successful in that environment?"

"You'd have to ask him, Lynn. I, for one, can't wait to find out what he says,"

The footage froze itself. *"Thirty-five minutes until scheduled meeting with Zeus Global Finance, Ajaya,"* my AI dutifully reminded me.

"Status of email account?"

"Nine thousand, seventy-two emails. Fifty-three percent new salvage requests, twenty-seven percent requesting human remains retrieval or identification, eight percent what might be classified as fan mail, six percent potential hate mail, three percent random dialogue, and three percent spam-slash-phishing."

Who knew sniper footage made great advertising material?

"You are still responding that we are not taking any new cases at this time?"

"Correct."

"Please continue on that path. I'm heading to my meeting." I paused at my next thought. "Also start a private web search for any and all mention of live person sightings in the Zone over the last ten years. Any and all rumors of people actually living in the Zone. Name file *Ghost*."

Chapter 10

The coffee shop was just a couple of blocks and my ankle seemed better, but I humored Mom and ordered an Ublyft self-driver. The car was outside by the time I got out of our building and I arrived only four minutes late. Not bad for Brooklyn.

Honest Bean coffee was doing a brisk business, with a line at the counter five deep. Two men sitting at a table facing the door spotted me instantly, one of them lifting a hand to wave me over. Several other people took notice of me as well, recognition flaring on faces that I was certain I had never met.

"Ajaya, I'm Calvin Shussman and this is Josh Devasagayam," the shorter one said. Blond hair, pale skin, ice blue eyes that seemed cold and calculating despite his smile. His partner was taller but still a few centimeters shorter than my own hundred eighty-eight centimeters, with skin as brown as my own and dark brown eyes. He seemed excited and maybe a little nervous.

Shussman was the CFO of Zeus Global and back in the day had apparently worked for Rocon Financial. "Show me the unit," he said. It was an out-and-out command. Not really digging that tone.

I raised one eyebrow at him.

"I need to verify it before I will authorize payment," he said, not at all repentant.

Moving at my own speed, which in this case was snail slow, I opened my backpack and pulled out the bubble-wrapped PC. Shussman reached for it but I held it back while I snicked open my folding knife and cut the tape holding the bubble wrap closed. I shut the knife and handed him the PC, holding his eyes as I did so.

The man was confident but I had seen a flicker cross his face when I opened my blade. His hands flipped the notebook computer over and he checked the serial number carefully. Then he looked at the big Rocon sticker on the front and the two IT department stickers on the underside. Finally he nodded and handed the unit to Josh.

Eagerly accepting the notebook unit, Josh lifted his left hand and I spotted a reader glove over the back of his hand, hooked to his index, middle, and ring fingers. He waved it over the PC and frowned. That's right, you bastards. Not gonna let you scan the drive and pull the goods without paying.

"Not getting anything," he said, now his turn to flip it over. He opened the battery compartment and found it empty.

"You've verified the PC. My payment please," I said to Shussman.

"We haven't verified the data."

"Not my problem. You hired me to retrieve *this* unit from *that* building. Done. What's on it is your issue. Battery is back in the Zone. I don't move electronics around that might give off an EM signal."

"That battery was ten years old," Shussman protested. "There's no way it had power left."

"Oh, you're an expert on the Zone?" I asked, my right hand snatching the PC from Josh before he could react. "I'll just take back my property and be on my way."

"That's our property!" Shussman said. People turned to look at our table.

"Anything I retrieve from the Zone is mine until I transfer ownership. State law. Tested up through the Supreme Court. This is the PC you wanted, so pay me and it's yours."

He studied me coldly for a moment but then nodded, a bit sullenly. He touched the hearing unit behind his ear to activate his AI. His right eye lit red as he flicked fingers in the air in front of himself. The red light died about the same time my own AI spoke through *my* own earpiece.

"Payment received, Ajaya."

I handed the PC back to Josh and stood up. "Right. Have a nice day, gentlemen."

Turning to leave, I came face to face with staring blue eyes. A boy, maybe ten, almost right in my face... but lower.

"You're him! You're the one who saved the Johnsons!" he said, very loudly. Really loudly. Loud enough to stop most of the activity around the shop. Now everyone was staring at me and fingers were reaching up to touch the side of eyes or ears as contact lenses began to take pictures.

"Who? Never heard of them, kid," I said, moving past him. His mother was frowning at me instead of him. Come on, lady. Teach your kid manners.

I made it out the door, sliding through a group of four who were entering. They stopped, bewildered, by all the people staring their way with eye cams clicking, but I was outside now. Hobbling down the street, I faded into the masses.

Four blocks later, a break was desperately needed. My ankle was killing me so I slipped into a sports-bar-type restaurant and got myself a table. Never did get any coffee at the meet. Definitely time for a mid-morning nosh.

Sixteen wall projections and at least and half of them were showing *Zone War.* Again with the morning show? The banner at the bottom of the screen said it was Drone Destroyers and they were entering the East Side over the Queensboro Bridge. Trinity had found a team stupid enough to go in.

"When did it start?" I asked my waitress, who was middle-aged and looked bored with everything.

The show had been consistent with its afternoon scheduling, for the most part, but there had been exceptions. Sudden changes that pretty much shut down work and sometimes even schools, right at any hour of the day. Just the day though, never the night, no one went in after dark. Nighttime was reserved for replays of the earlier daytime episode.

"A few minutes ago," she said with a shrug, then her eyes narrowed at me a bit but she said nothing else as I ordered a three-egg ham and spinach omelet and coffee, with bacon on the side.

The coffee came immediately, so I sipped it and watched the show. Heading back across the room, my waitress put in my order and started talking with another waitress, this one younger. They both glanced my way. Great.

On screen, Mike Destin was at the wheel of the heavily modified Oshkosh Joint Light Tactical Vehicle that was named the Drone Des-Troyer, while his partner, Connor Troyer was manning the remote weapons turret. Get it—Des-troyer? Clever, right? Oh well, the show was popular because of the action, not the brains of the teams involved.

Drone Destroyers always seemed to be trying to catch up to the others. The show, if you don't know, lists the weekly salvage profits recovered by each team and ranks the teams by gross total. Team Johnson, a.k.a Johnson Recovery, was always on top. Bone Shakers usually was second and sometimes put real pressure on Brad Johnson, while Team Rumble (a.k.a. Egorov) and the badass ladies of Team Up Town Girls mixed it up well for third and fourth with occasional jumps to second. Drone Destroyers was almost always dead last. Poor Mike and Connor ended up doing stupider and stupider salvage missions in an effort to move off the bottom. But the fans liked them because they were such good old boys. At least, that's how they came across, humble at times, brag talking a bit here and there, but they always had the worst luck, never quite executed the plan. Every once in a while they'd make a small score, enough to catch up on their repair bills, maintenance costs, stuff like that.

The road was mostly cleared, at least the main entry points, as various teams had run heavy vehicles in, clearing abandoned vehicles out the way. In an early episode, Team Johnson had armored up an old city garbage truck, welded a snowplow blade to the front, and used it to slam cars and trucks off the Madison Avenue Bridge. From that point on, all the teams, and there were more than five in the first season, copied their actions, clearing other entry points with heavy equipment with makeshift armor.

So Mike was driving and Connor had the weapons turret spinning, looking for drones, thermal and electromagnetic scanners seeking signals.

They cleared the bridge easy, but then entries weren't usually the problem. Deeper into the city was usually the issue, although the Johnsons barely made it a few blocks before their trap got sprung.

They turned down onto 59th, going the wrong way, but who cares, right? *Deadlocked* had a whole new meaning in today's Manhattan.

Then they went the wrong way down 3rd Ave, passed right by 58th, and took a right on 57th street, headed west.

The waitress brought my omelet, setting a smaller side plate with extra bacon next to it.

"What's their target?" I asked her.

She was eyeing me, super curious-like. She shrugged. "Hey, Mitch? What's today's target?" she asked the guy watching from behind the bar. He occasionally polished a glass or two.

"Trump Tower," he said.

"Really? Thought the Up Town Girls hit that a few months ago?" I asked.

"They did, but they got bum rushed out by a combined unit of Cranes, Wolves, and a mess of aerials. Still lots of swag to grab," the guy, Mitch, said.

"You're him," my waitress said, still staring at me. "The shooter guy who saved Team Johnson, right?"

"What? Don't know what you're talking about," I said. Stupid. Okay, so I'm not always fast with words.

She smiled in a knowing way. "Yeah? Guy like you that knows all 'bout the show, don't know about the biggest episode of all. Pull my other leg, honey."

"Shit!" Mitch the bartender said loudly. We looked away from our awkward eye lock and at him, then at the screen he was focused on.

Team Destroyer had come to a screeching halt, the path forward completely blocked side to side by a city bus across the street. It was one of those big double buses with the accordion middle. An armored car on the sidewalk was jammed against a building wall and the front of the bus, while some kind of delivery truck was holding down the same spot at the other end.

*"Where the *bleep* did that *bleeping* thing come from?"* Mike said on camera, face going white against the collar of his dark gray combat shirt.

"It wasn't there two hours ago when we checked the satellite footage," Connor said, voice rising. *"Turn around. Quick... turn us the *bleep* around, Mikey."*

The screen split, showing both team members' faces while simultaneously showing exterior shots ahead and behind them. It was a jumbled rush of images as Mike expertly put the big vehicle through a tight multi-point turn. He got it around and both their faces brightened as the way ahead showed a clear street.

"Go man, go," Connor yelled, pumping his left fist, his right still locked on the gun controls.

Mike accelerated forward, expression tight with concentration. The brightly lit street ahead of them suddenly darkened and something huge slammed into the road—tons of machinery and metal crushing cars and lampposts. Debris flew in all directions.

*"*Bleeeeeeeep*!"* Connor yelled as both men stared in shock. They turned to each other, then, almost as one, turned to the

gun sight monitor. Connor moved his hand and the gun up top tilted back and up, the in-vehicle production camera zooming in on the monitor. Blue sky with a dot in the middle. The dot grew, doubling in size, then quadrupling, then recognizable as a giant double fan, tower-top HVAC unit. And then it hit.

The screen feeds all died simultaneously and an instant later, the show logo popped up to replace the picture. Four seconds after that, an ad for a nano heart disease treatment filled the screen.

The restaurant was dead silent, every person locked on the stupid ad.

"Incoming call, AJ. General Davis," my AI said in my ear.

"I'll take the general's call," I said, eyes locking with the waitress's.

Chapter 11

They picked me up out front, a new black government sedan, a driver, who was a corporal, and a staff sergeant. Neither said a word, just moved us efficiently through traffic as they headed for the Queensboro Bridge.

Forty minutes later, we got through to the checkpoint on the Brooklyn side of the bridge and crossed on to Roosevelt Island, where Zone Defense HQ was housed.

After Drone Night, the military worked frantically to quarantine the island. One of the greatest engineering feats in the history of the world. Setting up walls, steel netting, and knocking down buildings as fast as possible. In the rush to evacuate, Cornell had abandoned its Tech campus on Roosevelt Island, rightfully thinking that having college kiddies so close to the Zone might be bad for enrollment. The government bought the campus from the university and turned it into Zone command. The hospital at the north end of the island remained in operation, even after the horrific numbers of wounded had finally finished treatment and been sent home.

So I was met at the steps of one of the old university buildings by another sergeant, name tagged as Nico, who led me deeper into the building.

My palm and retina were scanned four times through just as many checkpoints until Sergeant Nico led me into an auditorium where a cluster of officers studied video on a giant screen while flunkies swarmed around them like bees servicing a fat, bloated queen. The walls of the room had massive recruiting posters, loaded with badass images of army tech and weapons systems.

Davis was at the center, along with at least two colonels, five majors, including Yoshida, and more lieutenants than I could count, 'cause they kept moving and scurrying and butt kissing. There were civilians as well, including Agents White and Black, as well as some folks who looked like attorneys and a big, white-haired, older white guy who I happened to recognize as Chester Flottercot himself.

A tall major with darker skin than my own held the floor and most of the brass's attention. The big screen held several simultaneous live images of the JTLV, smashed with tons of debris on top. Other images were focused on the tops of nearby towers. The major pointed at one.

"Render UAV footage shows the rooftop HVAC units came from these buildings just east of Trump Tower. As you can see in this close-up, the metal infrastructure holding the cooling units has been systematically cut with lasers. The amount of time and power needed to do that is still being calculated, but initial estimates are enormous. It must have been done much, much earlier: days, weeks, perhaps months ago. Then we don't know how the drones pushed them off the roof. Each unit weighed in excess of ten tons and had to be moved eight to ten meters to the edge of the roof," he said.

"Wolf drones could do that easy," I said to Sergeant Nico as he led me down the stairs to the front of the auditorium.

"What was that, young man?" a nearby lawyer looking dude in an expensive suit asked, loudly enough that everyone turned to look. "What did you say? You have something to add?" the suit continued.

General Davis locked eyes with me and nodded.

"I said Wolf drones could do that easy. Same way they moved the bus and armored car," I said, raising my voice.

"How is that done, Ajaya?" Major Yoshida asked, interested.

"Each Wolf drone is basically a four-legged hydraulic jack. They can fold themselves down to less than a foot in height and press more than a half-ton each. Tigers can do even more although they can't get quite so low. Put twenty or thirty Wolves and Tigers under one of those units and they could pick it up and walk it over," I said.

"How would they tilt it over the edge?" a colonel asked.

"They can stack on top of each other."

"You've seen this, Ajaya?" General Davis asked.

"Yes. I've seen them move cars and trucks that way. I've seen as many as three stack up to lift a beam that I had used trap a Tiger."

"You're the sniper's boy, right?" the same colonel asked.

"Everybody, this is Ajaya Gurung. His father was SAS, four tours in Afghanistan as a sniper. Co-founded Johnson Gurung with Brad Johnson. Went independent eight years ago. Killed by drone fire two years ago. Ajaya has followed his footsteps since, what? Age twelve?" Davis asked.

"Yes, sir."

"As you all know, Ajaya's shooting saved the Johnsons from a trap two days ago. He has more time in the Zone than anyone else alive," Davis explained.

"But General, this is unprecedented behavior. Extreme problem solving and planning, far beyond anything we've seen before," a skinny guy in a white shirt and khakis said.

"The Spiders are learning," I said. "Just like the Chinese military created them to."

The room went silent.

"Spiders?" a voice asked. I turned and looked. It was Chester Flottercot himself, the big man of Hollywood.

"It's unproven, Chester," Davis said.

Flottercot opened his mouth to say something. Another voice spoke first.

"General! One of our Renders is being lased," a soldier wearing VR goggles and Translation gloves said. I thought she might be a Render pilot.

Everyone looked at the screen and could see one of the sub feeds flashing to whiteout sporadically.

"There sir, down low by the street," another pilot said. One of the feeds focused on the JTLV showed a small drone flying low over the street, its laser aperture focused up at the other Render.

"You have Artemis micro-missiles on board?" Davis asked the second pilot, who nodded.

"General, I don't think you should shoot," I found myself saying.

He eyed me with an unhappy frown. "Shoot it down."

The pilot touched an invisible control with her gloved finger, the laser drone took off sideways right at the nearest building, and a white streak shot from the Render.

The little drone flew into a broken widow in the building, the missile followed, and a split-second later, the front of the building blew out. Then a decent section of the front of the building slid down into the street, burying the JTLV even further.

I had a flashback. Five months ago. Deep in the Zone. Watching from a twenty-first floor hide on a particularly sunny day as Wolf UGVs moved into and out of a building across the street from me. Must have seen six visible at a time and since some were streaming in and some were streaming out, I figured there were a whole lot more inside the building. The ones coming out were covered in sheetrock dust and concrete debris. They would recharge in the sun, then head back in when others came out. That was on Fifth Avenue, south of 57th, but it now made sense.

"General, I think there's a pretty good possibility that the drones have been destabilizing structures all over Manhattan," I said.

"Creating kill zones?" Yoshida asked.

"That's mildly terrifying," Agent Black said to his partner, but loud enough to hear.

The major who had been lecturing was leaning over the shoulder of the female pilot whose Render had been lased. He was watching the big screen as he gave her instructions, which she conveyed to the Render. The footage zoomed in on the top of another tower.

"Sir," the major said, standing upright. "These other cooling units look like they've been cut free from their supports. Not moved, but ready to be."

Davis was quiet for a second. "Effective immediately, ground transportation into the Zone is suspended. Render units will begin a survey of high rise rooftops for signs of similar damage."

"What about my people?" Flottercot asked.

"Major Yoshida?" Davis asked. I noticed that Yoshida's combat uniform was slightly different than the others. Subtle differences in the color of the urban camo and different shoulder patches.

"Only option is aerial assault, sir," Yoshida said.

"Another trap. Sir," I said. Everyone looked at me. "It's the old *wound the soldier and shoot the rescuers* ploy. Sniper trick."

At the same time I said all that, I was wondering about Zone Defense planning a rescue mission. Never before had anyone attempted to save a team from the show. Something had changed.

"What if you come with us? With your... trick?" Yoshida asked.

On screen, the building had mostly stopped crumbling, just some falling dust, pebbles, and debris. Connor and Mike were okay dudes. I'd met them once, not that they knew anything about me other than that I went in on foot. The show had sent them in, knowing about the likelihood of a trap.

Shit. That waitress had been right—I knew way too much about the show. Knew Mike and his wife had just had a baby girl. She'd be growing up without her daddy. Yeah, fuck that.

"They're waiting for us to use air," I said.

"Yeah? What are they going to do? Drop another HVAC unit on us?" Yoshida asked, curious.

"Gonna engage us with Cranes. Snipe at us from every building. Get us all looking up. Then probably come at us from underground. Up under our bellies. Also try to hack any of our autonomous assets. Use them against us," I said, the ideas just coming to me.

"Shit. That's... that's pretty slick," the other major said.

"What do you recommend?" Yoshida said.

I thought some more, then turned to look back up the stairway at the big recruiting posters. "Well, you military types need to work out the details, but if it were me, I'd set off the trap, snatch the bait, and trap the trapper," I said, pointing at one of the posters.

Yoshida followed my finger, then smiled an evil smile. "Similar to what I was thinking, but explain."

So I did.

Chapter 12

I complain about Zone bureaucracy a lot, but there are times when the military impresses the shit right out of me.

An hour and a half later found me in a ready room, getting buckled into the best body armor the US military complex had ever created. Special forces powered armor was one of those ill-kept government secrets that always pop up. Enough information had bubbled to the surface over the last five years to move the idea from conspiracy theory to openly accepted idea, but still real shy on details. Lots of eyewitnesses, some grainy and poorly lit video, but no real pictures or explanation.

Now I was being buckled into shit that Robert Heinlein would have creamed his jeans over.

Nano synthetic muscles under multi-laminate nano-scale reactive armor. I almost crapped myself when Yoshida told me the full details of the plan I had kick started.

Now a soldier, a woman named Akachi, was helping me into armor that she had casually mentioned cost thirty million dollars a suit.

"This is a training suit. Turned down so that you don't hurt yourself. Do not try to do what you see us do," she said, turning on the armor's back power unit. Akachi was seriously tough, hard black eyes, muscular arms flexing under skin darker than my own, a scar over her right eyebrow. I could tell she was conflicted, mostly 'cause she mumbled to herself.

"Taking a newbie into combat, what's he thinking," she'd said as she first measured me with a laser unit that I guessed sent my particulars right into the suit of armor standing by itself next to me.

"You the one shot up the tank killers?" she asked me a second later.

"Yes ma'am," I said. She'd had me put on a spider silk undersuit first, a clingy second skin that could stop most handgun bullets on its own. So basically I was feeling naked.

"Some of the nicest shooting I've ever seen," she said. I smiled and thanked her. Then she frowned. "But we don't sit still, lying around like a lump. We *move*. Shoot and scoot. You think you can do that?"

"Yes," was all I said. Didn't know jack shit about powered armor or special operations or any of that. But I can shoot—in any and all situations. Dad made sure of that.

"Major said you aren't checked out on an M-43 or M-45 e-mag rifle. Said to give you a FN SCAR medium. You good with a SCAR?"

"Yes ma'am. That's perfect, ma'am."

"Don't you give me that *ma'am* shit. I'm a sergeant; I work for a living. Call me Sergeant Rift or, if your civilian brain can't handle that, I suppose you can call me Akachi."

"Yes, Sergeant Rift," I said.

She flicked a finger in midair and the top half of the suit rose up on cables, leaving the hip and leg unit standing empty. "Alright. Now step into the lower housing. Once you get in, you gotta put your dingle dangle in the urine entrapment pocket so that *when,* not if, you piss yourself, it doesn't run all down inside *my* expensive training hardware, got it?"

I nodded, not trusting my voice. My legs slid easily down into the cushioned interior and then my ass, hips, and groin were similarly encased. Reaching into the suit, face flaming hot, I did as instructed while she ignored me to prep the upper unit. Something she did made the torso armor segment open, expanding the opening above me.

"Done? You sure? Be hard as hell to make any adjustments after we lock you in."

"I'm sure, Sergeant." Damn, my face was burning up

She eyed me like I might be lying, then shrugged. "Hands up."

I put my arms up and looked up into the bottom of the upper half. Her finger twitched in midair and the upper slid down over my arms, head, chest, and stomach. Then she touched a spot on the armor and it clicked, slid, and folded back together like an old-time accordion. I know 'cause I've found more than one in the Zone.

No helmet or faceplate, but I wasn't gonna ask. Better to have her question my fitness for this trip than open up my yap and remove all doubt.

"Okay, spend the next fifteen minutes moving around. Make sure it feels natural. The suit shouldn't feel heavy. If it's tuned right, it should feel like you got plastic costume armor on, not two hundred pounds of ballistic laminate. How's it feel?"

I moved, slowly, then shifted almost immediately to normal speed. "It feels like slightly bulky motorcycle leathers," I said.

"Good, keep moving though. It's gotta be natural and you don't have any time for training," she said. I started to do squats and leg lifts.

Sergeant Rift casually pulled off her combat uniform, revealing a skintight set of black silks that hugged muscular feminine curves in a decidedly distracting way.

"Don't be staring at my ass, sniper boy. Just square yourself away," she said without turning around. How the hell had she known?

"Na... no, Sergeant," I mumbled, turning back toward the doorway, doing knee raises and then trying to run in place. Luckily that's the direction I was facing when Yoshida came in, already in armor, two men right behind him, one short, the other massive.

"He ready to roll out, Sergeant Rift?" Yoshida asked, eyeing my suit.

"Good to go, sir. Didn't issue no SCAR though," she said, already lowering the upper section of her suit onto herself. Her armor had boob bumps. Not sure what I expected, but there they were.

"Estevez, get young Gurung a weapon and ammo loadout," Yoshida said.

"Yes sir." Estevez was a corporal, short but wide, same hard eyes as the others. He moved to a locked steel door and leaned into a retina scanner.

Yoshida moved up close, the other, much bigger guy right behind him.

"As I'm *absolutely certain* Sergeant Rift explained, your suit won't have the extra abilities of ours," he said, checking over my armor.

Behind me, Rift snorted.

"Yes sir. No time to learn how to use super strength. It'll be weird enough wearing armor, let alone trying to use abilities I know nothing about. Also glad I'm not gonna be toting a weapon I've never checked out on. A SCAR is perfect though," I said.

Estevez came out of the armory with a short black rifle and a cluster of black magazines.

The big guy, whose armored chest nameplate read *T. Thompson*, took the mags from the smaller corporal and started sliding them into molded holders built into my suit. Four across the waist, two on my right thigh, one on each bicep. He handed me the last one without a word and stepped back. I glanced at he cartridge rim, *.300 ACC Blackout* stamped in the metal, arcing around the primer pocket. Old cartridge but solid performance out to about three hundred meters.

Estevez moved up and clicked the weapon sling onto magnetic attachment points on my suit's shoulders, letting the light rifle hang diagonally across my body in patrol fashion.

"Don't load till one of us tells you to, got it?" Yoshida asked.

"Affirmative, Major," I said, clearing the action, eyeballing the chamber, then adjusting the stock to fit my arms and armor. The e-sight came on anytime I lifted the gun to my shoulder. Not used to that, 'cause anything electronic will get you dead in the Zone. There was a molded mag holder on the stock, and I put the one I had been holding into it.

Yoshida studied me closely. "Here's the deal. You already know the basics 'cause it was your idea in the first place," he started. The other three glanced up at that sentence, then exchanged a look. Yoshida didn't move his head but I knew he'd caught the exchange. "So we fly in, shoot the shit outta any drones we see, drop our little surprises, hook onto the JTLV, and haul it outta there. Your job, and the whole reason *I* want you with us, is to use all those years of Zone experience and look for surprises. You are to sound off loud and clear if anything, anything at all, tweaks your gut, clear?"

"Affirmative, Major."

"Your ace in the hole gonna be around?" he asked me.

"Depends on if I call him, Major," I said, trying to figure out what he wanted. "That much commotion, though, and he might already be there. Likely is," I said.

"It won't attack us?"

"No, Major."

"You're not in the army, kid. You don't have to Major me all the time," he said.

"Hard to break my father's training, sir," I said, wincing at the involuntary *sir*.

"I read up on your old man. A real hard soldier, wasn't he? SAS Colour Sergeant. Decorated out the ass. Sniper's sniper. Honest to God Gurkha soldier."

"Yes sir," I said, uncomfortable for reasons I couldn't put my finger on.

"When did he start training you?"

"Basically the cradle, sir. Kinda the Gurkha way."

He nodded, still not looking at the three other soldiers but I suddenly realized all of that was for their benefit. Give me some street credit or something.

"So you stay out of our way, don't do what we do, but put all your instinct and knowledge into helping me keep my people safe. You'll hang near Thompson here. He's our heavy weapons guy and if you think something can benefit from application of his Cerberus, you bring it to his attention, clear?"

Thompson was coming out of the arsenal, a massive three-barrel weapon held easily in one hand.

"Affirmative," I said, managing to catch the *sir* before it could leave my mouth. He clapped me on the shoulder, rocking my heavy armor a bit, then turned to discuss weapons with Estevez.

Thompson, who wore sergeant's chevrons on his armor's shoulder, motioned me over to his side as he began going over his Cerberus.

I knew a little about the weapon, but like the armor, there was more myth and legend than detail on the Internet about it.

Three weapons in one. Stacked munition 40 millimeter grenade launcher, 20 millimeter electro mag Gauss gun, and some kind of energy weapon that no one knew the details of.

"Major says you got a pet drone?" he asked as he opened breeches, checked magazines, and replaced energy packs.

"Yes, Sergeant. A Berkut," I said, eyes focused on the massive weapon.

"A fucking Berkut?" Sergeant Rift asked from just behind my shoulder. "You telling us you got a fucking Russian Berkut Death fucking Eagle on a leash?"

"Yes, ma-, er, Sergeant."

"That thing points my way and I'll blast its ass," she said.

"Rikki won't attack humans. Probably won't even see him unless it all goes to shit. Then he'll be shooting drones, not soldiers."

That reminded me that I needed some of my own stuff before we went in. I moved over to the locker Rift had assigned me and dug out my backpack with clumsy armor-gloved hands. I *always* carry some basic stuff with me. I found three thirty-round blocks of Rikki's 9x21mm ammo and my kukri.

More soldiers were coming in, all of them already armored and armed. I got a lot of curious glances, frowns, and headshakes. I couldn't figure out how to store the ammo or the knife and the new soldiers looked disgusted.

"You got collapsible pouches here and here. Leave the sheath off the knife and it'll stick to the magnetic tool point here," Rift said, suddenly right beside me. "What you gonna cut with that knife anyway?"

"I always have it with me. Kinda a family thing," I said.

"Gonna try and cut a drone, newbie?" a soldier I hadn't met asked. Another female, shorter than Rift, but still tough-looking. Pretty face though. Short black hair and brown eyes. Hard to guess her ethnicity.

A tall, lean guy was right behind her, sneering.

"It's made of differentially hardened D2 tool steel. I've taken the head right off a Crane before," I said.

Both looked at me like I might be lying.

"AJ here is the sniper that shot up those TKs and saved Johnson ass," Rift said.

"Made it through the blast?" the female soldier asked. Her nameplate on her boob bump said K. Jossom. Her rank tabs said corporal.

"I set it off. I was in the elevator shaft when it blew."

"In the shaft or falling down it, kid?" Major Yoshida asked, moving past us.

"Controlled descent, Major. Barely," I said.

He snorted and kept going to the other side of the ready room.

Jossom and her partner, who was B. Boyle, also a corporal, were looking at me a little differently. Like judgement had been revised and pulled back for review.

"That ammo for your bird?" Rift asked. "Thought it wasn't gonna be needed."

"I like having and not needing over needing and not having."

"Bird?" Boyle asked.

"Fucking pet Death Eagle," Rift said, enjoying herself.

"Bullshit," Boyle said, looking at me in a challenging way.

"Just don't shoot any Berkut you see loitering about," I said.

"You *don't* see a Berkut until it's too damn late," Jossom said, head tilted like she was still waiting for the joke to be on her.

"Exactly. So if you *do* see one... it's mine."

"Time to saddle up," Thompson said, looming over me.

"Roger that," I said, following as he moved toward another doorway.

Chapter 13

We went in style—a huge Quad tilt-rotor, big enough for a hundred people, kind of cavernous with just eighteen of us. I sat across from Yoshida, sandwiched between Thompson and Rift. No real window to see out of so I occupied myself with my AI, its mobile unit having fit nicely in yet another hidden storage compartment in my armor.

"Status of file *Ghost?*"

"Initial results indicated 2,139 hits meeting basic criteria. Filtered for credibility of observer as well as key words indicating person, female, and young resulted in one hundred two possibilities. Further filtering for just the last six years narrowed results to forty-seven."

I had added some parameters before getting to Roosevelt Island and now seemed like a good time to check in on the project. See just how crazy I was. My AI had added an additional set of its own, discarding the sightings from the two years immediately after Drone Night.

"Rolling view of sighting summaries," I murmured. Immediately my eye contact went live, a list of sightings screening past.

"Freeze. Open top item."

The one that grabbed me was a newspaper article talking about ghosts in the Zone. Kinda close to the title I chose for the file, so maybe that's what caught my eye.

The reporter wrote about crazy sightings by Zone Defense personnel, things tourists thought they saw when flying perimeter helicopter tours, and stories from salvage operators.

All kinds of crap, from walking skeletons to glowing apparitions to women in white dresses. Two parts of the story caught my attention. The first was a former Zone Defense auto-gun technician who was replacing a barrel on a weapons system one evening in the spring, two years ago, when he saw a slight, humanoid figure picking its way around the corner of a building. Thing was, the guy was working lower Zone, not far from Wall Street. Also, it was early evening, in June, when daylight is lasting longer and longer.

The second story was told right after, kind of a supporting piece. Previous team on *Zone War,* City Slammers, now retired, had been deep in a fighting retreat, working their way toward the Brooklyn Bridge, when the turret gunner on the old Russian BMP had seen a face peering out of a first-floor window at him. A female, young, and... wearing something silvery on her face.

The gunner, Pasha Gachev, was still alive and living in Brooklyn, as of the time of the article, two and a half years ago. Maybe I could look him up—if I survived the next few hours.

I looked through the rest but there was nothing as good as that one article, so I cancelled the list. My vision cleared and I found myself eye to eye with Corporal Jossom, who was studying me like a bug under a magnifier.

"Ghost?" she asked.

"Just some research I'm doing."

"We're flying into the fucking Zone and you're doing research?" she asked, eyebrow raised.

I shrugged. "Got all you hardasses to watch over me, big ole Quad and like twenty Renders escorting. Not much to worry about till we get there. Plus, you know, cool armor and shit," I said.

"How you know my ass is hard?" she asked, quirking a brow.

"'Cause he studied the shit out mine and assumed we're all the same. Know what they say about ass-umptions, right, kid?" Rift asked.

"If you can't make them about asses, you can't make them at all, now can you, Sarge?" I shot back.

Rift's eyes opened wide.

"Oh shit, newbie," Boyle said, a nasty smile on his face, like I had just stepped into something.

"No, he's right," Thompson rumbled, which dropped Boyle's jaw open, snapped Jossom's head around, and earned him an incredulous look from Rift. "And *I* know about asses," he said, then leaned back and closed his eyes. I got the feeling Thompson didn't talk much and that this outburst was unusual.

Jossom looked at Rift and mouthed, *"What the fuck?"*

Rift shrugged, then turned my way and tapped a spot on each of my shoulders. My armor made mechanical noises and I felt something rise up around the back of my head, then a transparent face guard slid down over my face. All around me, soldiers were activating helmets that segmented out of the back of their armor, reminding me of Rikki when he transforms from ball to delta-shaped terror. A heads-up display lit up inside my helmet, feeding me information on every soldier I looked at, direction, air temp, altitude, and a whole bunch of other information I didn't really need.

"Look sharp, people," Yoshida said from the rear of the aircraft. Our forward flight was slowing. One of the tilt-rotor's crew hit a button and the big ramp at the back opened. A high-pitched, fast thrum sounded suddenly from multiple points around us. Thompson held me back at the end of the queue that formed at Yoshida's words. I found myself right next to one of the few windows on the aircraft and looked outside.

Automatic e-mag guns on exterior pods of the tilt-rotor were firing streams of magnetically accelerated carbide bullets at what seemed like over a hundred assorted drones in building windows, on rooftops, the ground, and in the air. We were hovering downward, the pile of rubble and HVAC equipment that marked the Destroyer's JTLV just becoming visible.

"Come on. You're with me," Thompson rumbled. Ahead of us, the line of armored operators had already diminished to half, and another one jumped lightly out the back as the big Quad turned a tight circle.

Boyle went out, then Jossom, who turned and gave me a snappy little mock salute as she dropped casually off the edge. She wasn't on a rope; there was no parachute; she just jumped.

The plane continued to turn and people continued to drop and then we were last, just us and the crew chief. Said chief hit another control and twin ropes shot down out of the upper aircraft hatch, forcibly ejected from what I could now see were launchers.

"Grab a line and step off the ramp. You aren't trained for jumping and your suit isn't set for that. So we rappel. Your suit will control the descent," Thompson said, grabbing a line and holding it out to me. I reached out to snag it with my left hand but was startled when my glove automatically clamped down on it without my direction or control. Somehow the suit recognized the cable on its own.

"Step off now," Thompson said, a determined and reluctant look in his eye. I did as he said without hesitation and saw his expression change to surprise. Then I was falling down the line. Well, descending down the line. It was actually slower than my epic elevator shaft adventure, my left fist opening and closing on its own to keep me at a steady speed.

I had time to look up and see Thompson just a couple of meters above me, then looked down to see the street and the ring of armored combat soldiers who were shooting every drone in sight, my HUD showing me who each armored figure was and what model drones were trying to kill them. The ground rose up suddenly and I was landing, the suit automatically absorbing the impact by bending our legs. Much better than the elevator shaft.

The whine and crack of supersonic e-mag rounds whipping out at ridiculous speeds and the lighter snap of flechettes coming back surrounded me.

My gun was up and aiming but Yoshida's soldiers were handling the attackers smoothly. Above and around us, Cranes and Wolves were poking their heads over roofs and window ledges to fire streams of hypersonic three, four, and five-centimeter-long wire flechettes. Most were getting hosed by the Quad guns and the troopers on the ground. But high speed wire was pinging off the ground all around us and occasionally off my armor.

Four troopers, led by Estevez, were on the mound of rubble that was the JTLV, digging out the massive rooftop cable attachment points and connecting heavy-duty snap rings to them.

Other troopers were moving in teams of two, one soldier firing while the other emplaced coffee-can-sized cylinders on the open street to either side of the JTLV.

When the Gaia group announced responsibility for the Manhattan Attack, the United States moved to a war footing not seen since WWII.

Even the 9-11 response was muted compared to this. Military enrollment shot through the roof and new weapons streamed out of government and defense contractor labs. The option of hiding out from US fury in mountainous tunnels went extinct along with the terrorists.

The poster I had pointed to in the auditorium was a scene depicting a soldier emplacing the very same M-982 anti-tunnel, shaped-charge, plasma mines that Yoshida's teams were laying out. They were nicknamed Mole Traps.

I remember seeing a news story on them. The top of the cylinder has a readout that showed a ground radar scan of the earth below the mine. Tunnels were easy to pick out. Once you found one, you set the mine in place, hit the anchor button to fire four piton-tipped legs into the ground, and let it adjust itself.

When next someone or something traversed the tunnel, boom, a jet of sun-hot plasma, along with cannon-force-accelerated stone and dirt, would cut across the entire tunnel. No more moles.

Yoshida's people were emplacing them in clusters over the subway and utility tunnels below the street.

This was going too smoothly. I looked around at the buildings on either side. Then I looked back at the most obvious target, the Quad. A lot of the buildings were straight-sided, flat-walled edifices climbing into the sky. But some were stepped, like the difference between South American pyramids and Egyptian

120

pyramids: the base wider than the next layer, which was wider than the one above it, and so on.

Each stepped layer created flat, elevated sniper hides, perfect positions to shoot down on an enemy. But from down where we were, you couldn't tell, and the Quad was now so low, it had no observation ability either. Plus, the big aircraft's gun pods couldn't elevate that far up.

Thompson and I were on the south side of the street. I didn't like a building on the north side that was set up like a big square wedding cake. Lots of shooting sites on that sucker.

I patted Thompson on the arm, taking his attention from a constant scanning swivel. Pointing at the building, I said, "I don't like that one. I want to get up there before any big nasty does."

"Major said to follow your gut," he said. "Now follow me."

He slung the big Cerberus and jogged across the street, me on his heels. Right up to the building's side and then he just started to jam his feet and hands into the material of the wall. Concrete hard siding just caved in like snow when his suit punched it. He climbed it like a ladder. He wasn't much taller than me, but he was a lot bigger, so it was easy to step into the holes he made and follow him up the side.

SCAR banging around on my back, I climbed as fast as I could. The suit helped, but his was helping him more. He quickly pulled away, reaching the first level at least twenty seconds before I did. My right hand just hit the edge of the roof when I heard the hard whining snarl of his 20mm e-mag barrel going off and as I stumbled to my feet, I saw a drone I'd never seen before. Recognized it instantly, but there's never, to my knowledge, been a sighting of one in the Zone.

Putin's Sabre, an eight-legged walking rail gun that fired 30mm chunks of depleted uranium at speeds almost fast enough to leave the Earth's gravitational field. A combat artillery drone that was reserved for real, open country warfare. Where the fuck had that thing been hiding for the last ten years?

One round from one of those autonomous artillery units would swat the Quad from the sky like a mosquito. A second rail barrel caught my eye. There were *two* of them on the roof level above us.

Thompson's round hit the thing in the lower back end, spinning it sideways. The second one instantly scuttled backward, hiding from our view.

"Shoot the rail gun or breach if you can," I suggested. He did both, his next round tearing apart the rail barrel right where it met the chamber of the weapon.

"We gotta get that other one—" I started to say but he just snorted and fired the grenade barrel. The big fat weapon stuttered like a jammed 3D printer. Four fat grenades lofted over the edge of the building, exploding so close together, it sounded like a one huge blast.

I ducked down and crouched as chunks of drone and pieces of building rained down on us. The level above us, and the ones above that, looked suddenly unstable.

"I'll check the roof. You stay here," he said, then ran and jumped, landing halfway to the top, arms and legs swarming so fast, I knew he had held back on the previous climb. Three seconds later, he was standing among the ruins of the Sabres.

"Building clear," he said over the suit comm.

"Stay on overwatch," Yoshida's voice came instantly. "Ajaya, you come back down here. Use the built-in descender in your left arm vambrace."

I was still right on the edge of the building and at his words, a targeting reticle appeared in my HUD. The red dot inside a green circle swung down and locked onto the roof in front of me. On the level above me, Thompson held out his left arm, pointed down.

I copied him and as soon as my palm was pointed at the same spot as the reticle, I felt a vibration and a line so thin, it was like fishing line shot out of my forearm, blasting deep into the roof.

"It will hold. It would hold you, me, and two others all day long," Thompson said, still watching me in between his visual sweeps.

I backed up, the line feeding out automatically, then put my heels on the edge.

"Descend," a voice said in my ear.

With a mental shrug, I leaned back and the damned thing slowly powered out enough super strong cable to let me swing perpendicular to the wall, feet standing on the side of the building.

"On belay," the suit AI said.

"On rappel," came my automatic reply. Then I bent my legs into a crouch and jumped off. The suit automatically fed out just enough line that I made a perfect bound down the side of the wall. Seven more jumps and I was on the ground. The line up top somehow released and zipped back into my forearm like an automatic dog leash.

"Cool," I said. Then the street mines went off in successive waves and all hell broke loose.

Chapter 14

Both sections of street on either side of us disappeared in a cloud of debris and superheated gases. When it began to clear, I could see the road surface had collapsed into huge manmade sinkholes. A sound overhead brought my attention upward, the world around me falling into shade, as if a storm cloud had rolled in.

Hundreds of aerial drones filled the sky, all of them coming straight for us. The Spider was triggering its trap.

"Grenades," Yoshida's voice said in my ears and ten arms flexed almost simultaneously. Round objects shot upward at inhuman speeds, the grenades thrown harder and higher than any pitcher could ever hope to match.

They went off like fireworks, staggered across the sky, the concussions pounding my suit with physical force.

Then it began to rain—bits and pieces of metal, carbon fiber, and plastic. Flechettes bounced off my armor and my facemask darkened on its own.

I found myself looking upward through the weapon sight on my SCAR, and when the first intact drone appeared, my gun fired, almost by itself. Then I acquired another target, and another.

Three Raptors came in a cluster. I shot two. The third exploded on its own, the bottom blasting out like it had been shot from above.

A shadow dropped to the earth, a second UAV exploding as the delta shape shot past.

"Rikki," I said before I realized my words were more likely heard by the soldiers than by my drone. I was still shooting drones out of the air, the mental counter in my head telling me my magazine was half gone.

But Rikki already knew where I was, pulling up out of his dive so hard and fast that anything organic would have been crushed by the g-forces. *"Ajaya, I am your six,"* sounded in my ear. I felt him hovering behind me.

Above us, I spotted something new: Hairspray units, a dozen or more, coming overhead. Cylindrical, just like the cans of hairspray or bug spray they were nicknamed after, with a single big rotor on top, they were the bomber units of the Zone. Inside each canister were ten to twelve golf-ball-sized bombs, each with enough power to completely destroy a car. Suddenly I had a new target. I missed my first two shots, but my third resulted in a spectacular explosion that immediately triggered five more just like it. The shock waves drove even the armored soldiers to the ground, but it really cleared most of the air for a moment. Then another wave of UAVs came over the rooftops.

I spun, slowly, counterclockwise, shooting drones as fast as I could acquire them in my sights. Behind me, the flat boom of Rikki's 9mm beat a counterpoint to my firing. Part of me was aware of the sharp crack of M-45 e-mag rounds breaking the sound barrier, the occasional Hairspray bomb going off, and my faceplate showing red figures dancing all around me, but I ignored them. I was in my zone. My shooting zone, the space in my head and awareness where the world is simply targets and firing solutions to be solved.

My magazine went empty exactly as my internal count reached zero, my left hand pulling a fresh mag while my right thumb dumped the empty from the rifle.

"Rounds dropping to six, five, four, three, two, one," Rikki's voice said, my left hand grabbing one of his three ammo packs and tossing it up into the air behind me. I didn't look, couldn't spare a glance, but I *knew* the agile Berkut would execute an incredible aeronautic spin, flip, or twist to eject his empty ammunition carousel while snagging the full one in midflight.

A plastic box-like object bounced off the ground by my feet, confirming his actions.

"UAV count down to three. Incoming Wolf at your four."

I spun right, toward my four o'clock, and put three thirty caliber rounds into the head and neck of the Wolf UGV that was bounding my way. Into an ocular lens, the open-mouth mandible, and the flex steel mesh neck that couldn't stop rifle rounds. Three flat reports above and behind me announced the demise of the UAVs.

"Tigers approaching soldiers K. Jossom and B. Boyle at the seven."

I twisted at the waist and acquired the lead Tiger of the pair that was leaping in thirty-meter bounds. The knowledge of the weak points in its side armor almost screamed in my mind as my reticle found each, rifle swing through led by gut estimation, as each trigger press released a copper and steel missile. Three out of five shots found the mechanical killer, even as my feet heel-and-toed me closer to the targeted pair of armored operators.

The second Tiger was too fast to acquire until it crashed into Boyle, knocking him to the ground, his own fall pushing his partner off stride and into a stumble. The Tiger's side blades snapped out and down to cut into the prone human as hooked claws ripped at laminate armor.

I crouched, only five meters away, shooting into its heavily armored side, trusting that the range was so short, my bullets would penetrate.

Jossom was still rolling to her feet as my gun clicked empty. I dropped the gun on its sling, grabbed the kukri in my suit glove, and smashed it down into the mesh neck of the robot.

I might not have been dialed up to full armored combat power, but there was definitely something extra in the swing, the hardened tool-steel blade shearing through the steel chain link neck armor and through the jointed neck axle. The toothy head fell to one side, my booted foot kicked it over, and then K. Jossom fired a hypersonic carbide M-45 round through the length of its body, effectively spalling the internals through and out the tubular body of the bot.

Boyle sat up, his armor slashed through with rents that showed the black of his silks. But no blood. He limped, the synthetic muscles of his left leg slashed completely through in several places.

"Pull it in," Yoshida said in my ear, sounding like he was just a meter away. "Our ride is leaving."

The Quad had cables linked to all four corners of the JTLV and was pulling it out of the debris and rubble. Yoshida's operators were rising up on more ropes at the open back of the giant tilt-rotor, four at a time.

We moved into line and when the time came, I copied Jossom and Boyle, reaching up to grab a cable with my left hand, the glove automatically locking down with a vise-like grip. Then we were lifted into the air, Rikki in ball form hovering up in front of us, gun pointed outward.

"Bring it with you, Ajaya," Yoshida ordered. I would have ignored him and sent Rikki away but I feared his double agent drone cover was now completely blown. I had no doubt that a Spider CThree had been directing that trap and Rikki would now be marked.

"Stay with me, Rikki." He hovered backward until he was almost against my armored chest and I grabbed him with my right arm.

Then we were aboard the Quad and underway.

Chapter 15

Rikki sat at my feet, ammo carousel open and empty, my own SCAR now in the care of Estevez. Yoshida sat across from me, staring at us both. He wasn't the only one.

"Did you see that freaking thing?" Rift asked Thompson.

"I saw them both. Back to back. It was a thing of beauty," the big sergeant answered.

"You programmed all that?" Yoshida asked after a quick glance at Thompson and Rift.

"No," I answered. "That was... new. But we work together all the time, and like all the drones, Rikki learns and adapts on his own. We've been in gunfights with other drones before, just not so many at once."

"Rikki?" Jossom asked. She had been staring at us a lot.

"Rikki Tikki Tavi. Rudyard Kipling?" I clarified.

"The mongoose that killed the cobra," Estevez said, snapping his fingers. "I always liked that story."

"But it's a Death Eagle, not a ground bot?" Rift asked.

I shrugged. "More about personality than looks."

"Personality? Drones?" Jossom, whose first name I had learned was Kayla, asked.

"Oh they all got 'em. Learning machines, remember? No two have exactly the same experiences, and thus they learn to be different. Subtle stuff among the less sophisticated, but pretty pronounced with the high-level ones."

"And the Berkut is the highest of the UAVs," Yoshida said, nodding as he thought about it.

"Hey, I know that sticker. That's Astrid Johnson from Team Johnson," Boyle said suddenly, pointing at Rikki's nose cone. He'd been pretty quiet, but like his partner, his eyes hadn't left us.

"What?" Jossom said, leaning close. "Damned if it isn't." She wolf whistled and I came to the sudden understanding that she appreciated the sticker as much as any of the straight guys did.

"Ajaya's known Astrid since you were what? Twelve?" Yoshida asked.

"Ten," I admitted.

"She know you got her on your bird?" Rift asked, eyebrow up.

"How could she? No one but me has ever seen Rikki till now," I said.

"Got a thing for the celebrity, huh?" Rift asked, a knowing grin on her face.

Jossom snorted. We all looked her way. "She goes out with movie stars and football players," she said, dismissing the idea.

"Big deal, Kayla. *He* saved her ass and most of her whole family. And they already know each other," Boyle said, Rift nodding in agreement to his words.

"Just friends," I said. "Our families don't exactly see eye to eye anymore," I said.

"They see things pretty damn quick when you're pounding AP rounds into the robots that are killing them," Rift said.

"Major, both men are still alive. At least one is concussed, likely the other as well. Also a bit dehydrated, but other than that, they should be fine," a voice said from speakers in our shoulders. Soldiers riding on the JTLV must have gotten inside.

"Thank you, Lieutenant. We should be setting you all down within approximately seven minutes. We'll disconnect from this end, so stay buttoned up till everything settles."

"Roger that, sir."

"Why?" I asked Yoshida.

He raised both eyebrows, unclear on my question.

"Why did Zone Defense send you all in? They've never rescued a team before. And why not go in and fight the drones in armor all the time?" I asked.

"Armor is new. This generation is the best so far but it has limitations," he said, waving an arm at the power cord that was plugged into his suit. We all had them, it being the first thing the special operators had all done as soon as we got settled. Rift had plugged mine in for me, like old-fashioned phone charger cords.

"Until our power constraints are solved, we must limit the duration of our engagements. These suits are also, as I believe you know, enormously expensive. I had to get Pentagon-level approval just to put you in that training suit. Producing enough suits to outfit even a company-sized element will rock a few budgets. We need other methods, cost-effective methods.

Like, say… partnered drones that fight alongside our operators," he said, glancing meaningfully at Rikki.

"So build them," I said. "We gotta have stuff more advanced than ten-year-old Russian designs."

"Oh, we do. By specs, they beat the pants off that thing, but in real-life action? Well, I've never seen anything like that reload maneuver that your Berkut did."

"That has more to do with his software."

"Please. We already have the original software developers in Russia reviewing the footage of the fight we were just in and they're baffled."

"Well of course," I said. "His software probably looks almost nothing like it started out. He rewrote it as he went. Plus I added different parameters a couple of times. Then I worked with him."

"Worked with it?" Rift asked, earning herself a raised eyebrow from Yoshida. "Sorry, Major."

"Yeah. I show Rikki what I want to accomplish and let him figure out ways to do some of it. I don't know shit about aeronautics, but he does. So that reload maneuver was something we developed through practice, but with him figuring out how to use his own systems and abilities to do it."

Yoshida frowned. "You're talking neural net type stuff. Nobody has that yet, certainly not ten-year-old drones."

I shrugged.

"We'll know more after we reverse engineer yours," he said, very matter-of-fact.

"What?" I asked, almost coming out of my seat. Thompson, Rift, and Estevez all tensed. The major did not. He just smiled. I didn't find it a comforting smile.

"Did you really expect that we would allow you to keep a functioning military drone?" he said. "Of course, we will pay you the bounty on it."

That motherfucker. That's exactly what I thought. Rikki was mine, by right of salvage.

"Salvage law only extends to non-military equipment," he said, reading my face.

"Non-military, or non-US military? *Zone War* uses all kinds of military stuff," I argued.

He just smiled a thin-lipped smile and shook his head.

"So let me get this straight. *You're* going to *take* Rikki Tikki Tavi and *destroy* him with no regard for his *self-preservation?*" I asked.

He frowned at my words, glancing quickly down at my drone. The Berkut still just sat there. Of course, the major couldn't feel the thrum of power as Rikki came online, not like I could—it was my legs touching the Berkut. Rikki wakes up when I say his full name. Then he listens for commands. His ability to filter out extraneous words is pretty good.

"Major, we are putting the JTLV down now," a voice, presumably the pilot's, said over our suit communicators.

At the rear of the Quad, the crew chief was opening the big hatch in preparation for something as the aircraft dropped lower. The major spun around to see the heavy steel ramp already opened to a half meter. "Close that hatch!" he yelled.

Too late. Rikki shot off the floor, straight across the compartment, and out the hatch before the chief could even turn to look at Yoshida.

Many sets of stunned eyes looked at me, then out the hatch, then at the major. *His* eyes, however, were locked on me and I felt like if I moved, he'd kill me.

"Get it back. Now!"

"He's operating on self-preservation mode. You've been identified as a threat. He will evade and escape. Nothing I can do will bring him back."

His eyes narrowed. "We'll see about that."

Chapter 16

Lots of talking, lots of threats. Lock me up, national security, blah blah blah. My attorney showed up about halfway through it. Nobody remembered that my personal AI was in my armor the whole time—recording. And calling.

Sarah Jarit was young, looked even younger. Small, petite even, with curly brown hair and light brown eyes. Most people thought she was a college intern. She was thirty-two and her pleasant, girl-next-door demeanor hid the sharp predatory mind of the human lawyer equivalent of a Berkut. Finished law school near the top of her class, two years younger than anyone else. Worked in a prestigious law firm for three years, then went out on her own. She was extremely good at the legal framework that surrounded the Zone.

"They thought they could keep me from seeing you," she said with a sharp little smile as she entered my plain, institutional interrogation room. "I sent them a clip of their own footage. Good idea having your personal AI on you, AJ."

"Which part?"

"Oh, part of the conversation with that major and some video of you and your robot killing almost as many drones as the rest of them combined. Explained that they had a PR nightmare on their hands."

"*My* AI got all that?"

"Copied everything the suit was recording. Probably good thing you didn't ask anyone if it was okay to bring it with you because there are all kinds of prohibitions against it. Seems the battle suit you were in had a more open network than the rest of them."

"It was a training suit. Probably less restricted or some shit like that. How much trouble am I in?"

"AJ, you released an active, deadly Zone drone into Brooklyn," she said. "That's a federal felony."

"Nope. Didn't do it. Yoshida told me to bring Rik- ah, to bring the Berkut. Then he was the one to talk about destroying it, which activated its self-preservation programming."

"That was one of the parts *I* played for him. He noted that it's quite apparent that you emphasized particular words, an activation phrase of sorts."

"Yes, I summarized his seizure of my property. Rikki took that as confirmation that he was in danger."

"Not sure about that whole property thing, AJ. It's a listed drone, with a very high bounty, by the way."

"Sarah, I'm no attorney, but I've read the Zone laws as much as anyone. There are absolutely no prohibitions on possessing anything inside the Zone. If I find a nuke in there, the Zone law says nothing about me not being able to possess it while I was in the Zone."

She frowned. "True, but you were no longer in the Zone."

"I was directed by the ranking Zone military commander on the scene to bring my captured Berkut out, intact and active. Until I turn it over to Zone Defense for the bounty, it's my property. Not my fault that the commander discussed taking apart an active drone in front of it. You could argue all day about if it was my paraphrasing or his words that alerted the drone, but there is no proof either way. The drones are artificially intelligent. The Berkut is near the top of the intelligence heap for those drones. Self-preservation is programmed into them, hence the reason they're still active five years past their expiration date. Rikki sensed eminent danger and fled."

"You named the thing?" she asked, uncomfortable.

"Yes. After the Kipling story," I said.

"They told me that. Implied that their case would make you look at best, unstable, and at worst, dangerously psychotic. You even call it a he." She looked at me carefully.

"Ah, anthropomorphism. Sarah, that unit was the one that killed my father. The only reason I didn't utterly destroy it was because both my parents told me to use it. Make something good out of something bad. So I made it my watchdog. Reprogrammed it to hunt drones, not humans. So what if I named the thing? Naming your dog doesn't mark you as crazy, does it? Rikki is smarter than any dog, has more personality than most people."

"But it's a killer drone from the Zone. No one is ever going to see it as anything but a crazed killing machine."

"Well, Yoshida saw it as the savior of Manhattan. That's why he wants it. To duplicate it so they can go in and hunt the drones."

"Then why not let him do that?"

"Because that drone is unique and Zone Defense will destroy that uniqueness trying to figure it out. And second, they used me to effectively *guide* their rescue operation with no discussion of remuneration, after freezing my license, then sought to destroy and replicate my property for only the bounty. Rikki is worth four times that bounty in software advances alone."

She looked at me thoughtfully, mind racing behind her deceptively soft brown eyes. "How dangerous is it to the public?"

"Not at all. He... it's programmed to protect humans, not hurt them."

"Where will it go?"

I looked at the mirrored wall meaningfully.

"If they are observing this privileged attorney-client meeting, they are in way more trouble than you," she said.

Like that would stop them. "Listen, I don't know where he is or where he'll go," I said. True enough. Had some strong hunches but didn't *know* anything for certain.

"How did you plan to get him back, then?"

"*I* didn't plan anything. Yoshida said they would reverse engineer him. I paraphrased it back to him. He didn't disagree. Rikki made the decision to leave at the first opportunity. Fight or flight. Rikki fled."

"AJ, if this thing hurts anyone, it'll come back on you. Probably on Zone Defense too, but you'll be the face of it."

"Not gonna happen. He won't hurt people," I said with every bit of sincerity I could. I wasn't one hundred percent certain, but I was pretty sure he wouldn't just harm someone. Hadn't shot me yet so, well, there ya go. "How long can they keep me?"

"I'll have you out in an hour. But AJ, they can still charge you," she said.

"Hell, they probably want me out so I can find Rikki for them. Then they swoop in, take the drone, and then charge me."

She looked at me, considering my theory. "A little paranoid— not entirely far-fetched though," she allowed.

"I think there's a lot of political pressure to win back Manhattan. They'll go to pretty far lengths to find a way to do it."

"Is that really so bad? Killing off the drones and reclaiming the island?" she asked.

"Not at all. I'm not opposed to helping, but they seem more interested in leveraging me, forcing me, than asking me. Never really gave me a choice on the rescue, but I would have done it anyway. Just don't like being bullied into stuff."

"You know there's a clause in your Zone license that lets them requisition your aid, right?"

"Ah, but it says *reasonable* aid. Not life-threatening aid. Big difference," I said. "What's reasonable?"

"Is that what it says? Exactly?" she asked, eyebrows up.

I couldn't stop the grin on my face. "Exactly."

Her eyes got real sharpish. The legal eagle preparing to dive on a kill.

"It'll be more like thirty minutes," she said, rising from her chair. "But AJ... you are extremely lucky you had your AI on you and recording."

"Yes, but Dad used to say luck was about being prepared to open the door when opportunity knocked," I said.

She tilted her head and thought about it. "Smart guy, your dad," she said, knocking on the door to be let out.

Chapter 17

"Ajaya Gurung, it's nice to meet you."

"Thank you, Cade Kallow. It's nice to meet you too. You've been in our living room almost every day for four years," I said.

"And yet I can't recall a single decorative detail," the host of *Zone War* said with a smile. Then he turned to the camera. "Here it is folks, as promised: an interview with the sniper who saved Team Johnson. As most of you know, I'm Cade Kallow, your host for a special edition of *Zone War*."

He turned back to me; his famous smile showing bright white, perfect teeth in a pleasant face that was not at all Hollywood perfect. Cade had been the narrator and host of *Zone War* right from the beginning, and it had made him an international star. A lean man of about a hundred and eighty centimeters, with ordinary brown hair, brown eyes, and a tanned, weathered face you might see anywhere. Till he smiled. His trademark grin was famous everywhere, along with his easy wit.

"So we have with us tonight Ajaya Gurung, solo recovery specialist, a Zone salvage expert with over eight years of experience. He's also the youngest salvager licensed for the Zone. At least that's what my notes say. Is that correct, Ajaya?"

"By a month and a half. Not really a significant amount of time to make a big distinction," I said.

A loud snort came from off camera. Cade whipped around to find the culprit. One of the six cameras aimed at us turned to take in the peanut gallery.

"Whoa, look at this audience of fine ladies," he said as if seeing them for the first time. Five faces smiled back at him. "Who all did you bring with you tonight, Ajaya?"

"On the right side is my mother, Barbara Gurung, next to her, my grandmother, Purnamaya Gurung. Next is my sister Gabrielle, my sister Monique, and finally, on the end, I believe you know the delicate snorter who is fascinated with counting days of seniority."

"Lovely ladies all. Are your sisters models, Ajaya? Or is it your mother and grandmother who work the cameras?"

"Now you've done it, Cade. They'll play that sound bite back till the speakers fail," I said.

"Deservedly so. They are all beautiful. But I do think I recognize the perky blonde on the end. She used to argue with me that she wasn't, in fact, the youngest salvage operator, and now I know why. Hello,
Astrid."

"Hi, Cade. See, I've been right all along," Astrid said. "Eventually you'll learn, as AJ did years ago, not to waste time debating me."

"AJ?" Cade asked, turning to me.

"My nickname."

"Bestowed on you by?"

"The twins. Astrid picked it up the first time we met."

"Over ten years ago, if my facts are straight."

"Yes. Our fathers were friends at the time. They met in Afghanistan."

"Your dad was Baburam Gurung, SAS sniper?"

"Yup. They ended up having two deployments where their units supported each other. They became friends and introduced their families to each other when they both returned home. Dad left the military and came to the US as a consultant so that we could grow up near my other grandparents and the rest of Mom's family. They mostly live in upstate New York."

He turned his head and looked at my mother. "Barbara, your met Baburam in the UK?"

"Yes, Cade. I happen to speak Nepali and was working with military families who had immigrated to the UK. My husband had brought Purnamaya with him from Nepal, as the rest of their family had passed. I worked with her to assimilate to her new surroundings while he was on deployment, and we were great friends by the time he returned," my mother said. Aama smiled at her and patted her hand. Those two did not have anything like the typical mother and daughter-in-law relationship. "We married in London, but I moved back here with Purnamaya when I was pregnant with Ajaya and my husband had another mission. I have a large family, and they made a big fuss over having us back. It was much easier with a baby, and then again when the twins came along."

"And somewhere along the way the Johnsons and the Gurungs met up?" Cade asked.

"Numerous times. I became very close with Karen, Astrid's mother. Ajaya and Astrid actually met a few times when they were little, but those were short visits and I don't think they remembered each other well when they came to visit here in New York," Mom said.

"That was ten years ago… Drone Night?"

"Yes," was all Mom said, her eyes glittering a little.

Cade gave her a sympathetic smile and turned back to me. "So you really met the Huntress on the actual night of the Attack?"

"Yes, Cade, but I think you mean the Driver, don't you? Not like she tracks them down with hounds and shoots arrows into them. I mean, she's more like a limo driver, right?" I said, carefully not looking to the women.

"Ouch, I think the gauntlet's been thrown down. What do you say to that, Astrid?"

I chanced a glance. She was casually looking at her fingernails. "Oh, he's much more the hunter type than I am, Cade. You know, the kind that dresses in silly looking green and brown clothes and spends an inordinate amount of time by himself, polishing his, ah, gun," Astrid said. "And I do drive a lot of very, very expensive vehicles. And yet I can still outshoot him."

It was my turn to snort. He spun back to me with raised eyebrows, clearly delighted with our rivalry. "Ajaya, I've heard from seriously qualified experts that your shooting from that tower was beyond fantastic, yet Astrid says she can outshoot you?"

"Cade, I think Astrid is locked in a memory from long ago when our families were vacationing in Vermont together and we did some range time. At *that* time, Astrid did score slightly higher on a long-range match, but that was the only time and I think she's perhaps dwelled too long on it. Peak of her career, so to speak."

"Grudge match," Gabby said suddenly, then looked embarrassed that she had spoken.

"I couldn't have said it better myself, Gabrielle," Cade said, nodding. "How about it? You two willing to shoot it out?"

"Anytime, Cade," Astrid said, giving me a mock deadly look. I knew her real death stare, and this wasn't it. She was clearly enjoying herself.

"Ajaya?"

"Sure, Cade. What are you thinking? A thousand meters?" I said. "Or is that too much for the, ah, lady?"

She crossed her arms over her chest and raised one eyebrow. "Anytime, Gurung."

Cade turned to the camera. "This is the absolute *best* interview I've ever had and we haven't even gotten to the good stuff yet," he said with a huge smile. "But speaking of which..."

"Nice segue," I said.

He nodded sagely. "That's why I'm the host. Skills, ya know. But let's get into it, shall we?"

I just nodded.

He looked at me for a moment, considering. "I dug around a bit. By which I mean my assistants dug around. You're the only solo operator in existence at the moment."

"That's what I'm told."

"And you've been doing it for almost half your life."

"Yeah, not so much when I was twelve, but pretty regular the last few years."

"What's it like? To enter the deadliest place on Earth, alone, on foot, no armor?"

"Mostly really quiet," I said. "You know, no loud engines, clanging tin cans."

His eyes widened just a bit, then he glanced where I carefully wasn't.

"As you can see, he has something of a death wish," Astrid said from the side, voice dry as a desert.

"Were you two like this in school together?" he asked me.

"Pretty much," I said, glancing at Astrid, who just nodded once. "Unless someone else picked on either one of us."

"You defended each other," he stated, as if things were suddenly clear.

"Let's be honest," Astrid said, smirking. "I had to defend him a lot more than he had to defend me."

Cade looked at me, waiting for a response. "Yeah, that's actually really accurate. She only had to face jealous girls while I was kind of a, well, wise ass."

"No?" he said, excessive disbelief on his face. "I find all that hard to believe. Girls jealous of Astrid? You having a smart mouth?"

"I know, right?" I agreed. "But that's the truth of it."

"Verbal abuse, or did it escalate?"

"Mostly verbal. Only a couple of physical bouts. Astrid could beat most of the boys in a fair fight and, well, I don't know if you know this, but she never fights fair. I did okay too. I wasn't very big, but, well, Ghurkas don't ever give up, and I'm pretty fast."

His expression had gone to amusement when I mentioned Astrid fighting, but it went dead serious at my last comment.

"Your dad was Ghurka," he said.

"Born and raised," I said.

"I'm told Ghurkas make some of the finest soldiers," he said.

"You were told some solid truth, Cade."

"And you were raised Ghurka?"

Aama snorted softly. I glanced at her with a mock frown. "Yes, Cade, although my training was a little cushy compared to my dad's."

Aama spoke to me suddenly, her tone brooking no argument. *"Timi ta Gookhaliko sartan hou. Sar zhukara hunnue pardaina. Teme Lai, taha cha kee timro sar jhukaunu pardaina."*

"What did she say?" he asked me. I didn't answer.

"She said *You are of true Ghurka blood. Don't let anyone get you down. You know what you are capable of,*" Monique translated.

Cade was silent for a moment. "Maybe we should hire more Ghurkas for the show?" he asked my grandmother.

She smiled and shook her head. "Only Ajaya. No one else would live," she said, looking my way and giving me a nod.

He turned back, looking surprised. "Wow, high praise indeed, AJ. Can I call you AJ?"

"Sure," I said with a shrug.

"So you go in on foot, wearing a stealth suit, carrying a heavy rifle and a pistol and a pack of gear. And you go *into* buildings and climb up them?"

"Yeah. That's where the best stuff is. Manhattan is a vertical city. Ground level is less than ten percent of the pickings."

"And you what? Just waltz past all the drones?"

"Sorta. I mostly avoid them."

"But how, AJ? They were designed to hide and ambush. How can *you* detect them when no one else can?"

"Ah, well, Cade, if I answer that, I'll be giving up my most important trade secrets. That's not smart."

His face went serious. "You would hide you techniques and let people die?"

I felt my own face get stern. "If I told everyone what I was doing, people would copy me. Well, *try* to copy me. Then lots of people would die."

"Fair enough as far as civilians go, but what about the military?"

"You know, I've been asked that question just recently. They let me roam around by myself for the last two years, as much as expecting me to die. Now they want to know why I didn't. "

"What about your dad? Did they ever ask him?"

"Yeah. He wouldn't teach them," I said.

"Ah, not exactly Ajaya," my mom said suddenly. "He taught one group. They all died. He refused after that."

"He what? When?" I asked, shocked.

"The second year after the breakup. He refused after that. Except for you."

"He was willing to risk his son?" Cade asked.

"That was my view. But Baburam had trained Ajaya from the cradle. He said our son had a gift that couldn't be taught. We argued enormously. Eventually I allowed a real short foray into the Zone. Ajaya did so well that, despite my better instincts, I let him go again, and then again," Mom said.

"That must have been insanely difficult," Cade said.

"Oh it was. But my husband always contended that he would die before Ajaya ever would. He contended that it was my son's natural element. Since his death, I have to say, Ajaya has proven him right beyond even his highest expectation."

"So pressing for details isn't going to get me anywhere?" Cade asked, already seemingly resigned.

"Right."

"All right then. Let's talk about the trap that almost got the Johnsons. Speaking of which, does anyone else find it odd that only one Johnson is in the house?"

My peanut gallery went still and the production crew all froze, waiting for a response.

"*Is* there any other Johnson? Really?" I asked, smiling. "I always thought there was just the one."

His eyes went wide. Not the reaction he'd been expecting. He glanced at Astrid. "You should marry this one," he said, his head snapping back to me before she could answer him. "So the feud is real?"

"There was a lot of bad blood. Nowadays, it's more that we've all agreed to disagree. Except for Astrid. She always stayed in contact. With Mom, with the twins, even with me."

"Even with you, huh?" he shook his head, smiling. Then he turned to Astrid, eyebrows raised.

"Mom and Barbara were close. Mom died before the breakup, the cancer too fast and aggressive to treat. I think her death had a lot to do with the whole mess. I doubt she would have allowed it if she'd been there. But Barbara was so supportive, even during and after the whole fallout. She never let it affect our relationship. Nether did the twins," Astrid said.

"What about AJ here?" Cade asked.

"I could get away with talking to the ladies, but Dad was volatile about Baburam and his shadow mini-me," she said, smiling a little.

"How did that make you feel?" Cade asked, turning to me.

"Oh, I knew exactly what was going on. I never blamed Astrid, but Brad? Different story there."

"Good thing you were driving that day, eh Astrid," Cade joked.

But Astrid didn't laugh, her face instead looking stricken. "I know. Believe me, I know."

Cade pulled back, maybe almost embarrassed. Then his face went smooth and he turned back to me. "Take us through it, step by step."

So I told him about that day, starting with my unimpeded trip to the building and climbing to the seventeenth floor. About recovering the notebook computer and then hearing the sounds of combat. About looking out the window and seeing swarms of drones.

"When did you know it was the Johnson LAV?" he asked.

"Immediately. No one else uses orange and white."

"Could you see into the rig?"

"I could see Astrid driving."

"What was your first thought when you saw her?" he asked.

I was kind of back in the moment when he asked and my mouth just opened and spoke without my brain putting a brake on it. "No. I thought no. Not today. Not ever, if I'm around."

"No what, AJ?"

"No, she's not gonna die in the Zone," I said, locking my eyes on his so that I couldn't look her way.

"You thought you could help? That you could prevent her death?"

"No. I *knew* I could. It wasn't gonna happen, Cade. Not on my watch."

His eyes gleamed like he had just been handed a baseball-sized lump of gold.

"What did you do next? How did you put your plan together?"

I shook my head. "I didn't *put* it together… I didn't sit down and draw it out. There wasn't time for that. It just popped into my head. Steps I needed to take."

"Steps? What steps?"

"Range the shots. Get a shooting position. Prepare an egress. Take out the Spider, destroy the machine-gun sight, kill the missiles, and break the cable. Then get out of there while setting off the bomb."

"All of that just *popped* into your head? With details?"

I shrugged. "How do you know what questions to ask me? You aren't looking at notes, and my answers aren't always what you expect. How?"

A light of understanding appeared in his eyes. "Experience. I've done this for years and years." He paused and looked at me. "And so have you. I keep forgetting that you've been at this almost half your life."

His hand came up to his earpiece and he listened for a second, his eyes going wide. "Although *I* apparently need a nudge now and then. Spider? You said a Spider? As in a Spider CThree?"

"Hunter-Killer units are super rare; only few came off that ship. Nowadays they've mostly used up their ammo, so those two must have been held in reserve. Plus, they don't set complex traps like that on their own. So I knew there had to be a Spider running it. It was on top of the Customs House. My first shot took out its vision sensor. The shot was suppressed and subsonic. Then I shot the other four rounds that you know about."

"So you shot at the Spider with an underpowered round to keep the element of surprise for a second?"

"Yup. Drive the boss away. Take out the dangers, free the LAV, then get my ass into the elevator shaft."

"That's how you survived the blast. In the elevator... *shaft?"*

"I propped open the doors, attached cable descenders, and set out the bomb. After my last shot, I rolled off my platform and ran for the shaft. Set off the bomb as I started to descend... as the first wave of UAV's came through the window."

"A controlled fall down an elevator shaft?" he asked, face incredulous.

"More or less. Kind of jammed up my leg on the car. Crawled out of the basement through a utility tunnel, then got to the street as quick as I could."

"As quick as you could? Why not stay down in the tunnel?"

"Rats, Cade. The tunnels are full of rats."

"And you're more afraid of rats than drones?"

"Millions of hungry rats that grew big eating human remains? I can fight drones. I can't fight a thousand rats all at once."

He shuddered. "Okay, *that* visual's gonna stick with me for, like, ever. So you're back on the street. What next?"

"There were quite a few extra drones about, but I avoided them. Almost got busted by a Kite and its Tiger unit, but they both got distracted."

"A Tiger? And it got distracted?"

"Falling debris, I think. Probably loose stuff from my bomb. Anyway, I got past them and made it to my safe house. Spent the night and then came out in the early morning."

"Wow, there's so much to unpack in those sentences. Safe house?"

"Yeah, I have little havens set up all over the island, for exactly those kinds of situations."

"Oh, like situations where you take on a Spider, two Hunter-Killers, a buttload of Wolves, and about a bazillion UAVs, then fall down an elevator shaft, crawl out of rat-infested tunnels, and play hide and seek with a frigging Tiger unit?"

"Ah, yeah."

"Ya know, some people are gonna say you're making some of this stuff up," he said.

I shrugged. "I don't give a shit what they think. Never have. I'm not part of this show, Cade. I do my job and support my family and that's it. I work in the shadows, not the spotlight. *You* guys asked *me* to be on this interview, remember? If you don't believe it, I don't care." I realized as I finished that I was leaning forward, maybe a bit aggressively.

Cade had pulled back. His hands came up. "I said *some* people. Not me. What about you, Astrid?"

"Every word. Although, knowing AJ, my suspicion is that he's actually underplaying much of what happened. Some people, you have to believe half or a quarter of what they say. With AJ, you gotta add that much back in," she said, giving me a head tilt and a smirk when I looked her way. I automatically gave her my innocent face. We were falling back into routines from school years like no time had passed at all.

"So a Spider. They're still there, or at least one of them?" he asked.

"At least two. I've seen two at once. I would guess all three are operational."

"And they're setting traps, like the one that got the Destroyers."

"Yes."

"You heard the military actually extracted them, alive and okay?"

I just nodded. He watched me for a second, looking for something. Then he flashed his trademark smile at the camera. "And we'll be interviewing both of them tomorrow. Zone Defense has declined to comment on either the rescue or why one was mounted. We'll keep working to get to the bottom of that story and, as always, will keep you posted.

"So, AJ... when are you headed back in?"

"Not sure, Cade. My ankle is still a bit tender so I'll let it heal before anything else."

"I heard a rumor that Zone Defense suspended your license? Why would they do that?"

"You'd have to ask them. They haven't been very clear with me on that topic."

"You don't seem worried."

I laughed. "Let's see. The powers that be tell me I can't go risk my life in the most dangerous place on Earth. I just got paid on my last trip, I've still got items for sale on my Zoneite site, and I think you all are adding a little something to our family fund. I'll find something."

"I, for one, would rather see you do almost anything else," Mom said suddenly.

Cade gave her a sympathetic look. "Hey, who knows, maybe you could be a consultant on *Zone War*? Where's Trinity?" he looked off-camera, moving his head till he spotted her. "What do you think, Trinity?"

She smiled. "Oh, we could probably work something out."

"Maybe we can," I answered.

Chapter 18

It was a late-afternoon interview for the show and when we got done, Trinity wanted to take us all to dinner. We ended up at a Spanish place, feasting on tapas. The twins were beside themselves with excitement at being included on the show. They alternated with hanging on Trinity's every word and wanting to get home to start responding to the messages they were getting from their friends at school. Mom's rule of no AIs at the dinner table was wearing on them, but the extra hang time with the producer of *Zone War* went a long way toward salving that injury.

Somehow, Astrid and I ended up sitting next to each other. Myself, I suspect the plotting of teenage girls.

"You don't honestly think you can beat me, do you?" she asked me.

"Vermont was a long time ago, Trid. I shoot long-range shots all the time."

"But how far? Two, maybe three hundred meters? The Zone is too cluttered with buildings to get long shots. *I* have access to a thousand meter range."

"You do know that if you climb to the top of a building, you can see for kilometers, right? Oh yeah, you guys are strictly ground floor. I regularly shoot UAVs out to fifteen hundred meters."

"Right out in the open? Exposed to other drones?"

"Well, I make sure my area of operations is clear of anything first, then take the shot on a decent unit like an Indian Falcon or Chinese Air Raptor. Then I clear out. Get the drone I shot next time I'm in the Zone."

"How do you do it? How do you *know* an area is clear?" she asked, blue eyes earnest.

I hesitated. Her eyes started to narrow and I spoke before she could. "I have technology that detects the drones."

Annoyance changed to interest and then to confusion. "How? Anything electronic would emit EM signals."

"That's fine if the signals are part of the drone communication net," I said.

Her eyes widened, getting bluer, if that was even possible. She sucked in a quick breath. "You reprogrammed a drone," she guessed.

I gave her a little nod, taking a bite of food. Her eyes searched my face while I chewed, impatience building. I gave her a grin, chewing slowly to drag it out. She smacked my arm.

I swallowed even as I laughed, then almost choked on the tapas.

"A Berkut," I said.

Her eyes got big. "Wasn't your dad..."

"Killed by a Berkut? Yes. The same one."

"And you reprogrammed it after it did *that?*"

"Yeah. I know. We didn't know Dad was bleeding out. He was the one who shot it. He got all excited about the chances of using it. Then he fell asleep and never woke up. Mom wanted to know exactly how he died. I told her everything. She was the one who insisted I use the Berkut. She told me that based on what he'd said to me inside the Zone, that it was his dying wish.

She reminded me that he strongly believed in getting good out of bad."

"Wow. Okay," she said, glancing at my mom, who was chatting with Trinity at the other end of the table. Astrid got a thoughtful look on her face, then suddenly turned to me. "That's why you lost your Zone license, right?"

"Yeah, I think. See, they cancelled it and wouldn't really give a reason, then they begged me to go on the rescue. Rikki helped me during the rescue, and then they wanted to tear him apart and copy him."

"Rikki? You named it after the mongoose? Of course you did," she said, laughing softly. "Wait... *you* were on the rescue?"

"Yeah," I said, not adding any detail. She looked at me with that cute frustrated look she always got in school when I yanked her chain. I could just about see the moment when she decided to forge ahead.

"What happened to it when they took it apart?"

"They didn't. If you talk about destroying an autonomous drone in front of it, you might expect that it'll opt for a resounding no. He took off and is at large somewhere in Brooklyn, I'd guess."

"AJ, you let a Berkut loose in Brooklyn?"

"No, dammit. Everyone keeps saying I did it, but it was the major in charge who told Rikki he was going to destroy it. It winged out of the Quad before they could stop it."

"Then it could be anywhere... hunting people," she said, worried.

I raised a single eyebrow and gave her my most put upon look.

"You know where it is?" she asked.

I shook my head, smiling a little. "Rikki won't hurt humans."

"But you're okay with it just lurking any-old-where?" She didn't believe that I didn't know where it was. She knows me really well. Of course, I didn't know exactly but I had my guesses. Not gonna help the G-men out though.

I shook my head and pointed at my ear. She frowned, confused. It was a pretty friggin' cute look on her, if you ask me. Then understanding blossomed across her face. She tucked a strand of blonde hair behind her right ear and then casually looked around before looking back at me with a raised eyebrow. I nodded. She thought about that, then changed the subject.

"So, back to the rescue? You were really there?"

"Yeah. In a suit. Armor," I said.

Her response was instant—a sharp shove on my left shoulder. "Get the f... get out!" she said, glancing at the others, who were now looking at us.

We had talked a lot about powered armor back in our early high school years.

"What was it like?"

"Really frigging cool. I was dialed way down because I didn't have any training, but it was still amazing. And the operators at full power were jumping around like fleas. Punching holes in solid walls, stuff like that. It burns power fast, though. Makes it only for limited engagements."

"Did you use an M-45?" she asked.

I shook my head. "Not checked out on one. Used a SCAR-M," I said.

She smirked at me.

"What? Oh let me guess... you've used an M-45?"

She nodded, still grinning like a maniac.

"I pretty much hate you," I said.

"Please, says the punk who got time in powered armor," she waved me off. After a second, we grinned at each other. Then her right eye turned red. Incoming message on her contact.

She looked off to the right, a pleased little smile on her face. My good mood evaporated.

"Music man?" I guessed.

She frowned. "Like you've never heard his name before?"

Of course I had. Everyone had heard of Xavier, one of the current *it* performers. Their recent spate of dates had been grossly overpublicized, in my opinion.

She frowned again, this time at something she was seeing on the inside of her contact. Her fingers came up and flickered as she responded.

I turned away, taking another bite of food before accessing my own AI. For a few hours, it had seemed like the old times were back. Wrong.

>Status of Ghost query?< I typed.

>Pasha Gachev agrees to meet tomorrow. 10AM, his house. Address loaded for travel.< appeared in my own iContact.

Well, there was that. Maybe he could tell me enough details to shed some light on the girl in the Zone or send me in a new direction.

When my own contact had cleared, Aama caught my eye and nodded at Astrid. I turned and found her frowning at her plate.

"Everything okay, Trid?" I asked.

She snapped around, glaring, but then it faded. She shrugged and turned back to her plate, poking a tomato with her fork.

"Brad giving you shit for hanging with the Gurungs?" I asked.

"No. He's staying quiet. Makes me a little suspicious but then again, we did almost get killed in the Zone, and he knows it."

"X-man giving you shit?" I asked.

Her frown deepened and her fork poking took on a stabbing sort of energy. "Shacking publicity hound," she said, almost a whisper. "So, what's your plan? You know... for the, ah, well, you know?"

"I don't have one."

"What?"

"That's kind of the whole point of it. It plans for itself," I said, spearing her worn and beaten-down slice of tomato along with the piece of cheese next to it. Popping both in my mouth, I gave her my own smirk.

"You're just going to let it do its thing? Really?"

"Yup. Because I programmed its thing."

"But they're self-programming. It will do its own thing."

"Sorta. I give it a thing, it then works out how to do that thing in the best way possible. So right now, I'm confident it's doing its thing."

She glanced at the sky out the restaurant window. "Have you seen something?"

"Hints of something. Tiny little flickers of something." She looked at me with those eyes, then back out the window, frowning in maybe the cutest way possible. I wanted to tell her she was looking too high. Way, way too high. But I was pretty sure other ears would hear it as well. Zone Defense had access to too many really good micro drones for me to feel secure. "More importantly, I know the capabilities in question."

"Awfully confident, aren't you?"

"I guess I am. Do you think that's stupid?"

"No," she said, studying me for a moment. "You've changed since school, AJ. It looks good on you," she said, then turned to talk to Monique, who immediately asked her about Xavier.

Whiplash. Pretty sure girls go out of their way to give you whiplash. Are there secret classes for that?

Chapter 19

Pasha lived in the Bronx, one of the more gentrified sections, another outgrowth of the Manhattan exodus.

He had the whole top floor loft of a converted factory building, which seemed to indicate his time on the show and his forays into the Zone had paid pretty good dividends.

"Come in, come in," he said with only the very slightest accent. I had spent my evening, after the dinner out, watching the seven episodes that the City Slammers had been in before they had quit the Zone and the show. Pasha had immigrated to the US when he was a preteen; now he was in his early forties. His loft was decorated in a combination of US industrial design and Euro design, like upscale IKEA meets old manufacturing.

Lots of sleek wood, light colors mixed with heavy, dark iron, brass, and bronze. Open floor plan with a few walls that didn't quite reach to the three-meter-high ceilings. Iron beams, brick and black ductwork. He led me past the living room furniture and parked me at the concrete kitchen island. A glass of ice water waited for me, a slice of lemon floating inside. He, himself, moved around to the working side of the island, where a whole mix of greens appeared to be involved in becoming some kind of juice or smoothie.

"I like to cook now. It was always a bit of a stress reliever after Zone runs, and now I find myself fully involved in the foodie lifestyle," he said, sounding just a tiny bit embarrassed.

"Hey, eating is one of my favorite ways to deal with the stress. I just don't know how to make much," I admitted.

"I saw your interview yesterday. I think I remember seeing you around one of the Zone entrances a time or two, but I never realized you went in on foot. You have to be one of the craziest badasses I've ever met. Every trip was a panic attack for me and *I* had no less than two inches of hardened steel armor between me and those things."

"It's all what you know. I've never been in an armored vehicle. Probably get claustrophobic. Anyway, thanks for seeing me. I saw something my last trip in and thought I must be crazy but I found a quote where you saw almost exactly the same thing," I said.

He paused in the act of putting spinach (at least I think it was spinach) into his auto-juicer. He turned to look at me, his whole demeanor different. He didn't, however, say a single word. Just looked at me, his expression mostly unreadable. Mostly. I could see in the confusion that was his face that fear looked back at me from deep inside the emotional mix.

"I saw a girl. Young, maybe my age. Black hair, dark eyes, something silver on her cheek," I said.

His eyes shifted to the door, then the living room windows. I waited. He put down the spinach, expression undecided, then it shifted—to decided. He left the kitchen, beckoning me to follow.

We moved deeper into the loft, headed toward the center of the building and the heavily constructed central column that held the old freight elevator. We actually went into the elevator and then out the other side, closing both sets of mesh steel gates behind us, and then into a smaller room with a regular eight-foot ceiling and solid brick walls. He closed the old metal door and turned to face me.

"I should never have given that interview," he said, pushing one hand through his short, bristled salt-and-pepper hair.

"There was trouble?" I asked.

"You have no idea. A pair of dark suits showed up the same day the article came out. Government ID's."

"They questioned you? Threatened you?"

"No to the first, yes to the second. They basically told me I was crazy, had seen a hallucination, was spreading false information about the Zone, and could be charged with major federal crimes. Threatened me under the Terrorist Acts. Complete seizure of property, prison, or worse."

"Or worse?"

"Under the terrorists laws, they can hold you indefinitely without due process. You just disappear. Like that guard did."

"The Zone Defense guard disappeared? The one quoted in the article?"

"Gone. I don't think he had any family and he just vanished. Maybe he took off on his own, but I always felt like the feds were involved."

"What did the feds look like?"

"Basic government drones. One white, one black. Nothing distinctive about either one," he said.

"Shit. I think I've met them," I said. "They took away my Zone access."

He stared at me, really frightened. "You've already met them?"

"Well, they weren't as threatening as you described, but then I think it's 'cause they want something from me."

He stared at me, then suddenly nodded. "Your secret, the secret to how you move around the Zone. They're all about the Zone. Did... did you mention the girl?"

"Not to anyone. You're the first person I've said anything to."

"Keep it that way. Listen, it was nice to meet you, but I can't add anything else, and I wouldn't even if I could. I've got a good life and it's pretty clear they can wreck it on a whim."

"Just one last thing... where were you when you saw the girl?"

He was silent. "Okay, but this is it. We were in lower Manhattan, near Wall Street. That's all I'm going to say. You have to leave."

I left.

My AI came to life as I exited the freight elevator, confirming to me that the old structure with all of its steel and brick was pretty good at blocking electromagnetic signals. It was the same kind of structure I preferred to use for my hideouts inside the Zone.

"Ajaya, you have voicemail messages from your mother and from Trinity Flottercot, and eleven thousand, four hundred and sixteen new email messages."

"Play Mom's message first."

"Ajaya, it's your mother. Trinity called the apartment looking for you. She told me that she wants to offer you an episode with the Johnsons... going back into the Zone. I want you to promise me that you will discuss this with me before agreeing to anything! I'm serious, Ajaya."

"Play Trinity's message."

"AJ, Trinity here. Listen, yesterday's episode was a runaway hit. Almost as many real-time viewers as the Wall Street trap episode and actually more secondary viewers chose to watch the recorded version last night than any other we've ever produced! I want to capitalize on this and follow up with a new one... one where you accompany the Johnsons back into the Zone. What do you think? It's just like you suggested, right? Call me back, soonest."

A shadow flickered on the ground in front of me, cast from overhead. I looked up. Saw the quickest image of a drone. It was just a glimmer. It was enough. Idiots.

Drone Hunter units were deployed for several years all along the Zone wall. Advanced autonomous net shooting units to capture the terrorist drones intact for military study. They caught like ten, maybe eleven Zone drones. By then, the drone network inside the Zone had adapted. A little UAV like a Kite would tease the DH units and when they came after it, a more lethal unit would ambush the Hunter, burning off its power supply with a laser or blasting a spray of flechettes into its rotors. Zone Defense lost like forty of the expensive Hunters before scrapping the idea and just leaving the skies to the big armed and armored Render drones. Now they had one tailing me like it was gonna spring the net on a freaking Berkut.

"Ajaya, you have three email messages from the same source. A freelance reporter named Mitchell Lee. That's the same reporter who authored the article in the Ghost file with Pasha Gachev's interview and the Zone guard. He is requesting an interview about your interview."

"Write him back and ask if he can meet in a half hour. If yes, let's set it for the Honest Bean coffee shop."

I walked for a while, feeling out my ankle and attempting to loosen it up. I avoided looking up, but occasionally there were shadows that seemed much too large to be birds.

"Ajaya, Mitchell Lee agrees to meet you at the Honest Bean thirty minutes from now. I have ordered an Ublyft car to ensure your punctuality."

"Thank you." Me and my AI politeness.

Chapter 20

Mitchell Lee was taller than me and really thin, almost skeletal. He had really, really curly dark hair and a tightly trimmed mustache. Wearing khakis and a checkered button-up, he reminded me, at first sight, of a modern Ichabod Crane.

I waved an arm from my booth in the corner of the coffee shop, probably unnecessarily, as so many people were glancing my way, he probably could have figured it out on his own. Plus my waitress never seemed to be more than twenty feet away. How did Astrid deal with all this attention? Truth told, she had been dealing with male attention from about fourteen on, so maybe the extra amount supplied by celebrity status wasn't a big stretch for her. Bothered me, though. Snipers like to hide.

"Ajaya Gurung, so nice to meet you," Mitchell said, shaking my hand.

"Really? You think?"

"Well, yes, of course. The man who rescued Team Johnson? Who wouldn't want to meet you?"

"Probably Teams Uptown Girls and Bone Shakers. They'd have a shot at number one, wouldn't they?"

He pulled back, his grin fading. "That's pretty... cold."

I laughed. "I'm kidding. This newfound attention is disturbing. Nobody cared a few days ago; now I'm somehow interesting to everybody. I don't trust it," I said, waving a hand at the faces turned our way.

His disturbed expression cleared and he nodded. "Oh, yeah, I can see how you might feel that…" he said, but then the waitress was right there.

"What can I getcha?" she asked, directing her comment at me instead of him as she topped up my already full cup.

"Ah, mocha latte, please," Mitchell said.

"Sure thing," she said, smiling at me. Not sure if she even glanced his way.

"See what I mean?" I asked as she reluctantly left the booth. "A week ago, I couldn't get her attention for, like, ten minutes."

"Yeah," he said, frowning a little. Then his expression cleared and he became excited again. "I'm so glad you accepted my email. You must have dozens of interview requests."

"Yeah, like fifty-three at last count, but none of them had what you have," I said.

"What *I* have?" he asked, confused looking.

"Yeah, this will be a quid-pro-quo-type deal. I'll answer your questions if you answer mine."

"What, ah, what questions do you have for me?" he asked, much less sure.
"You wrote an article a while back, about ghosts in the Zone. I have questions," I said, watching his response. If it was I, and I had written an article about sightings of people in the Zone, I would have been instantly curious about that question. Instead, his eyes got wide and he looked suddenly uncomfortable, maybe even worried.

The sound of fast-moving feet hit my ears and I spun around, my brain realizing just in time that the feet were very, very small. A small blonde pixie came to a crashing halt in front of me, her mother approaching with an embarrassed expression.

"Momma said you saved Ashhtrid," she said, possibly six or seven years old. Both of her middle two upper front teeth were missing in action.

"I, ah, helped her. She's my friend, so we have to help friends, right?" I asked. Behind her, the woman froze, a tentative smile on her face.

The little girl nodded, then dove forward to hug me. At least six people were touching the sides of their right eyes. I hugged her lightly, giving her mom a smile back.

"Come on, Joelle. Let's leave Mr. Gurung to his coffee, okay?" the mom said, gently peeling the little person off me. Secure in her mom's arms, Joelle waved at me as her mother took her back to their table.

Mitchell still looked uncertain but his eyes held a gleam much like the one Cade Kallow had when we were doing the big interview. He nodded. "How about question for question?" he asked.

I nodded. "Lead the way."

"What's it like when you come across human remains... in the Zone? Or do you not even notice them anymore?" he asked.

"I come across them every single trip inside. They're everywhere and no, you never get used to them. Most of the time, I try to figure out what happened to them, how did they die. I'm always careful not to disturb them. I think that would be very disrespectful. In there, it's human against machine, so I feel for every human I find."

He opened his mouth to ask another one, then closed it at my raised eyebrow. Then he nodded. My turn.

"Did you find any other credible accounts of people living inside the Zone?" I asked.

He scratched his head, sighed, and finally spoke. "Yes. A couple of others, all Zone Defense. But between responding to my ad for sightings and me contacting them, they all changed their minds and refused to talk to me.

"You've refused to go on *Zone War* for three years. Why now?" he asked.

"They always wanted to put cameras on me before. That would be a real quick way to get dead. This was an on-air interview, not putting me at risk inside the Zone," I said. "Where, in the Zone, did those other good sightings happen?"

"Only one responded with that much detail when they emailed me back. Said it happened on the lower west side of the island, about level with SoHo. What drives you to keep going back into the Zone?"

"I have a family to take care of," I said. He raised both eyebrows, the message being that there were other ways to earn a living. I explained. "New York is expensive, nowadays even more so than London or Tokyo. There are five of us. The only skill I have that lets me meet those financial obligations is Zone salvage. Did you get into trouble for that article?"

He looked troubled, glancing around to see if anyone could hear us. "I was warned by my editors that it was extremely irresponsible to suggest people could live in the Zone. It was suggested that I should post a follow-up that basically admitted that my first article wasn't even close to being true, just spooky ghost stories of the dead. What do you think about the Zone Reclamation Bill?"

"I don't know any of its details. Saw something on the news that said it would require the military to go in with boots on the ground. As much as I would love to see Manhattan drone free, that would be a bloodbath."

He jumped in before I could ask my question. "But then you'd lose your way of living? That flies in the face of your previous statement about supporting your family. You don't really want to lose the Zone at all, do you?"

"It's my turn. Were you ever visited by government agents regarding your story?"

"I'm not answering that. You're not being straight with me. I think I have enough," he said, reaching up to touch his right temple.

"Well, Mitchell, so do I," I said, touching a button on my shirt. People get so used to iContacts that they forget about more mundane recording systems. "Be very careful what you write. You bailed early. My answer to your last question is kind of a doozy. But now you won't have it. Maybe another reporter would like the story. Maybe Agents Black and White would like to see how *you* responded to *my* questions?"

He grimaced and started to say something but then glanced around quickly, seeing all the faces still turned in our direction. Then he picked up his latte and left. The door closed behind him as I realized he'd just stuck me with the bill.

Chapter 21

Back home, I found Aama cooking in the kitchen. After giving her a peck on the cheek, I went into my lair. My window was open, maybe halfway. Aama sometimes did that to air out my room when my stuff got stinky. A pile of dirty clothes including my stealth suit was on the floor, so that seemed pretty likely. Mom wasn't home yet, but I had called her back on the ride from the coffee shop. We'd ironed out an agreement on the Trinity thing.

"Map of the Zone please."

Manhattan appeared on my wall. "Plot approximate position of sightings, including my own."

Four dots appeared, two near Wall Street, two spaced out on the West Side, moving up toward SoHo.

If the dots were connected, they'd form a kind of sideways curve, like a left-hand parentheses that had slipped down.

"Highlight the area inside the curve."

The inside of the parentheses became a sunny yellow. It covered Wall Street, Broadway, part of Trinity Place, West Street, and too many others to list.

"Zoom in on the yellow area. Plot the center of the area please."

The highlighted part expanded, as did the detail, and a red dot appeared near the beginning of Hudson Street.

Hudson Street. Something about that street... some tidbit I had tucked away a long time ago.

"Any buildings of note near the dot and particularly on Hudson Street?"

"Ajaya, 60 Hudson Street is the site of the old Western Union building. After Western Union moved its headquarters to New Jersey, the building became a massive Internet interconnection hub via fiber optic cables. The hub is still active to this day, as the connections were made entirely maintenance-free just prior to the Manhattan Attack."

Bing, bing, bing, bing... we have a winner. Now to get back in. I leaned back in my chair and turned to look at the big road map of Manhattan I'd thumbtacked up (don't like those sticky alternatives; they always fall down on me) when we'd first moved in.

Zone Defense was a lot of things—arrogant, autocratic, and remarkably unhelpful to the salvage operator—but they were competent. Getting into or out of the Zone without them knowing was... hard. Back in the day, Dad and I played a what-if game. What if we discovered something so valuable that we had to sneak it out? How would we do it? Or what if we left something valuable inside the Zone and they wouldn't let us back in to get it? We constructed elaborate scenarios for fun but then systematically destroyed those plans, step by step, cutting away the crazy and complex, replacing them (where we could) with simple, more effective ideas. In the end, we weren't left with much. But a few of our schemes might actually work. However, it wasn't time for those.

"Call Trinity."

"*Calling Trinity Flottercot...*"

"Hello, Ajaya. Thank you for calling me back."

"Hi, Trinity. Whatcha got cooking?"

"Well, I'd like to follow up on that team approach thing you suggested. Have you go in with Team Johnson, then go off to provide over watch. Brad's not excited, mind you, but he's willing to listen. The problem is, I'm not sure of what target would be valuable enough to risk it?"

My wall map has old-fashioned colored pins to go with the thumbtacks. Red, green, black, and gold.

The red represents what it always does—danger. Places to avoid for various reasons: structurally unsound buildings, rat nests, dog packs, and clusters of drones.

The green ones are mostly my safe havens, although a few represent some untapped resources like the FBI satellite offices that probably have excellent weapons armories.

The black ones are reminders of places I've almost died. They're like little reality checks to keep my ego beat down around my ankles. I got up and put in a new one near the green pin that represented my beer cooler safe house.

There are only two gold ones, one at the top and the other near the bottom of the island. Gold is the universal symbol of bling. Wealth, money, assets. I used to have more gold pins. They used to represent untapped money sources that I had identified, but I emptied all those long ago. But, along the way, I created some other potential sources of income. Those two dots were the reason I wouldn't lose a second's sleep if the drones all died and Manhattan was reopened to the masses. That reporter shouldn't have bailed.

I often avoid drones altogether when I go into the Zone. Ghost around the little bastards, which, with Rikki's help, isn't all that difficult. But don't think for a second I don't hate the things, even as much as they fascinate me. I've spent days on days doing nothing but trapping or shooting drone after drone. Especially the last two years. I wasn't kidding when I told Astrid about long-range sniping UAVs. If anything, I just didn't convey to her how often I did that. The problem is that while hundreds of drones have fallen prey to my traps and bullets, I've only been able to bring out a small percentage. But my dad trained me to be neat and tidy, to organize, observe, and keep what I kill.

The gold dots represent drone depots, caches of dead drones I've been adding to almost every trip into the Zone.

"I've got a pretty good idea of something he might be interested in," I said. "How about a storage container with a whole pile of dead drones in it?"

The sound of her sucking in a tiny breath was all I heard for a few seconds. "How many and what kinds? And for Christ's sake... how?"

"I'm a hunter, Trinity. I hunt drones. The container I'm thinking of has between a hundred and two hundred drones in it. A whole slew of UAVs but also a few Leopards, probably twenty or more Wolves, and at least three Tigers."

"You've been stockpiling," she said.

"Got no way to get them out. You'd need something like an eight-wheeled armored vehicle to get them all. Know anyone with such a thing?"

179

"You'd split the proceeds?"

"I'd go one third to the Johnsons and two thirds to the Gurung family. I already killed them and stacked them. We just gotta drive in, empty the container, and drive out."

"Where?"

"Nope. I'm keeping that close to the vest."

"You don't trust me?" she actually sounded hurt.

"I'm more interested in operational security. The Spiders set traps ahead of both your last missions... how did they know? But also, I don't trust Brad."

"You think we told them?" she was getting upset.

"Indirectly. They listen, you know. They put sensitive units as near the walls as they can get and they monitor the soldiers monitoring them. One of the major reasons I've kept turning you down. Listen, why don't you talk to Brad. If it's a go, if he's interested, I'll give you the general area, but only in a secure setting. I'm not telling Brad the exact location till we're almost there. I learned from the lesson he taught my dad."

She was silent for a few moments. "Alright. I'll talk to him. What's your guess on the bounty value?"

"Between seven hundred and fifty thousand and a million—give or take."

"Holy shit, Ajaya. You've been sitting on this for how long?"

"A while. It's not as exciting as you think. Zone Defense would likely try to lowball that many drones at once. They get a little stingy when you hit them with a bunch. Partly why I created this rainy day stockpile. Always figured I'd bring the drones out in small numbers. That, and the whole lack of a vehicle thing. Realistically, I think we would end up with as much as nine hundred thousand or a little more. Brad could pull in three hundred thousand for an hour's work."

"And you'd get six hundred thousand?"

"I already took all the risk in killing the damned things. Not to mention dragging them and stockpiling them. And I'll want that two-thirds guaranteed to my family, whether I'm alive or dead."

"Ajaya, this is... fantastic. Let me talk to Brad and I'll get back to you."

"Roger that, Trinity. Talk to you later."

I didn't tell her about the other, bigger depot.

"Are you interested in beginning planning, Ajaya?" my AI asked.

"Yes, although I would feel better if I knew where Rikki was before going into this," I said, picking my stealth suit up off the pile. It was going to need cleaning and some minor maintenance before taking it into the Zone.

"The equipment in question is currently located two point seven meters from you. Northeast."

Morning sun came in my window so northeast was... my closet. "You're kidding me?"

"You specifically curtailed my humor settings. You should find what you requested inside your clothing storage closet."

I didn't move. "Likelihood of active monitoring of this apartment by outside agencies?"

"Monitoring devices exist in four rooms of this living unit, including this room. However, the active listening capability of this equipment is being actively blocked by the device you requested, which is, again, currently in your closet."

I moved forward and slid open the closet door. Sitting on top of my stack of clean jeans was Rikki Tikki Tavi, LEDs lit green although his fan blades were not moving.

"Any sign of official or suspicious vehicles approaching the neighborhood?" I asked my AI.

Rikki answered. *"No abnormal traffic within a three-block radius, Ajaya. Currently projecting interference, which is utilizing active replay of media programming considered nominal for this location."*

Rikki has never been one to initiate anything like this before. Although, he's also never been outside the Zone before, but still, this seemed advanced.

"You are actively replaying footage from when?"

"This unit has copied and pasted emissions from currently broadcasting editions of Zone War *program onto the CPU of the listening devices in this room and the bedroom next to this one. Software or individuals monitoring currently will hear real-time programming instead of this discussion."*

Holy shit. Holy, holy shit. Rikki was deploying active masking measures by linking what was playing on the net directly into the listening devices. Not only was I unaware you could even do that, I was mildly terrified that the Berkut was autonomously capable of such sophisticated electronic deceit.

"Describe logic chain leading to current masking strategy."

"The active listening sensors in this room are similar to those deployed by drone units inside the active Zone. Deception through data overlay is standard procedure by Rikki unit during movement of Ajaya Gurung throughout the Zone. Technique usage in current situation deemed even higher in success probability than in previous situations. You request masking of such sensors one hundred percent of the time inside the Zone. Probability you would authorize similar actions in this instance deemed in excess of ninety percent."

So Rikki copied the same technique we used inside the Zone. That made me feel a bit better, but damn. It was still surprising though. My modified drone was doing things I never imagined it could. Hiding from searchers in such an electromagnetically active area as Brooklyn was one thing, probably relatively easy for an AI that hides in the electronic desert that was Manhattan. But Rikki had taken the initiative to mask the bugs that someone, likely Agents Black and White, had seeded throughout my home. That was advanced. Really advanced. Like nothing I had ever heard of advanced.

"Current condition of Rikki CPU and core programming?"

"Within ninety-four percent of nominal processing."

Rikki usually reported a higher percentage than that, like ninety-eight.

"Was any damage sustained during last mission?"

"Number four prop bent. Replaced by Ajaya. RAM chip sustained minor code damage due to power loss during stasis. Missing code has been replaced."

"Who rewrote the code?"

"This unit, designated Rikki Tikki Tavi, rewrote code using adaptation of other sub programs."

Rikki rewrote his own codes. Not surprising, as the original Berkut programming was one of the more sophisticated code packages among the original drones. Not like the spiders, but really pretty good. My upgrades and rewrites were, not to toot my own horn, pretty darned good too.

"What code was damaged?"

"Mission completion processes."

"What about core mission code?"

"Intact."

Whew. The biggest change I made to Rikki was completely rewriting his core mission. I changed it from Kill All Humans to Protect Humans, with special emphasis on Gurung family members and Astrid. If that had gotten damaged, he might have reverted to the kill orders or something less dangerous but useless. Like Protect the Tomatoes.

"How did you evade capture by Zone Defense?"

"Extreme low altitude tactics. Zone Defense capture resources utilize search techniques above three meters in altitude. Access to hostile force command and communications network provides real-time data on deployment of assets arrayed against this unit. Noncombatants evaded in similar manner. Detection by domesticated mammals and free-ranging avian species unavoidable."

"So you stayed low and listened to their comm chatter? And dogs, cats, and birds saw you."

"Affirmative."

"How did you find this location?"

"Access to information network designated internet far more pervasive than inside the Zone. Internet sources assimilated to provide most likely rendezvous location for Ajaya."

"Explain Internet access being more pervasive than inside the Zone?"

"Access to Internet is broadcast in these locations. Inside Zone, access is limited to active optic network locations."

"You've accessed the internet by tapping fiber optic lines? At what locations?"

"Affirmative. Primary access node is Hudson Street interconnection hub."

Hmmm. Same place that popped up in my ghost in the Zone research.

"How do you get the information? You don't have a dedicated optical receiver."

"Implanted Mole units provide interconnection for authorized drones."

"Who, or should I say, what authorizes a drone to use the Moles?"

"CThree units authorize all access and coordinate information processing."

"The Spiders are actively accessing the internet? For what purpose?"

"Intelligence gathering to best accomplish primary mission."

"The primary mission was to kill humans. There aren't any more humans in the Zone."

"Affirmative. Primary mission to kill all humans. Mission in Zone has reached ninety-nine point nine-nine-nine elimination rate. CThree units seek additional targets."

Whoa... there was a lot to unpack in all that.

"Why is completion rate not one hundred percent?"

"Drone network units consistently report readings of human activity. False positive sensor alerts also too prevalent to disregard. Information gathered is consistent with Ajaya AI project designated Ghost."

"Are you saying the drones themselves are aware of the girl in the Zone? And you hacked my AI?"

"Affirmative to both queries."

"AI, how did Rikki compromise your security?"

"Ajaya, Rikki unit had authorization from previous connection during code rewrite."

Okay, that made sense. I had used this very AI, minus about twenty upgrades, to program, test, and reconstruct Rikki. That an embedded authorization still existed wasn't surprising.

"Ajaya," my AI interrupted. *"Call from Trinity Flottercot."*

"Put it through. Hi, Trinity," I said when I heard an open line.

"Ajaya, Brad wants to have a meeting. He's interested in your proposal, although he wants forty percent of the total value."

"I'll meet him and I'll go as high as thirty-five percent of the total *net* proceeds. None of that total value crap. I'm not giving him a designated percentage of a gross value. Only a part of what we have left over after Zone D gets done tearing that number down."

"Okay, I'll pass that along. Can you come down to the studios in, say, two hours?"

"Sure. See you there."

Chapter 22

It wasn't till I was in a self-driver, headed to the studio, that it occurred to me to wonder how Rikki got the window open. That thought fled as I arrived at the studios.

The studio gates were both automated and manned. Why? Jobs are important in today's world, even if perhaps redundant. I had heard that the Flottercots insisted on keeping the human staff, even the old guy that manned the main entrance. He stepped gingerly out of his booth and peered at me through the window that the car helpfully lowered for him. The barrier had already opened, the security AI having already identified me and checked off my name against expected visitors.

"Ah, the new recruit. Good to see you back. That show desperately needs fresh blood," the old-timer said.

"Well, that's not fully decided yet, but who knows, right?"

"Oh, I do hope you come aboard. That was some exciting stuff you did. I'm sure the Johnsons are very thankful."

I just nodded at him, not willing to explain that not all the Johnsons were fans of mine, no matter what I did.

My musings were pretty much confirmed as soon as I was ushered into the conference room by a male receptionist whose excessive good looks probably indicated a hungry actor hoping to break into the business from the inside.

Only two of the multitude of faces smiled at me, although most of them were just blank and only two looked potentially hostile.

Trinity hopped up from her seat at the head of the table. Astrid was seated on one side of the young producer and JJ on the other. At the far end of the table, Brad took the other dominant spot, Martin at his right hand. The other four people seemed to be production crew and staff members. Trinity grabbed my hand in a tight handshake, guiding me toward the empty seat next to Astrid. "Ajaya, great you could make it on short notice," she said, patting my shoulder as I sat down. Across the table, JJ gave me a solid nod, while at the other end of the table, Martin sneered and Brad looked cold and unimpressed.

"So, Ajaya, we were just discussing the new episode—" Trinity said, but Brad interrupted her.

"*Proposed* episode. Not sure I even believe this drone stash you're bragging about," he growled.

When I was little, I was immensely impressed with Brad Johnson. He frowned a lot, looked super serious all the time, and talked in a deep, manly voice. He was rugged and muscular, every inch the modern warrior soldier. Now, grown up, I saw him a lot clearer.

"Really? Look, everyone. Here's my surprised face—Brad Johnson doesn't believe me. Oh dear," I said, keeping my tone flat and low. Reaching into my daypack, I pulled out a little leather binder, a piece of salvage from a bookstore on Madison Avenue. I paged through it, making a show of it, letting it sit open so that everyone could see the pictures glued to the pages but not get a real good look.

I arrived at a picture of the inside of a room stacked with dead drones. Then I turned the page, finding a second picture of a different stack of metal and carbon fiber carcasses. "Here's the one." I pulled the picture and tossed it down the table at Brad.

"Are those Polaroids?" the woman on my left side asked.

189

"Yeah, digital is a bad idea inside. But Polaroid cameras and film are still around. Film's getting old, so you sometimes have to use a whole roll to get one good picture," I said.

Brad was looking at the photo, Martin leaning around his shoulder to see it too. Brad's eyes flicked to my book, really fast, then up to me. "This just shows stacks of drones. Doesn't prove they're still there."

"Nope. It doesn't."

He waited. I waited too.

"You want us to go after drones that might not even be there," he finally said.

"And just where would they have gone? You think I backpacked out three Tigers? It's why they're there in the first place."

"It's your insurance for the eventual end of the Zone," JJ said suddenly.

I nodded. "I tagged them all and filed the tags with Zone Defense. Can't get paid till I present proof, but will still get paid if the Zone suddenly gets cleared and I can U-Haul them outta there."

"You really have been shooting drones down, haven't you?" Astrid asked.

"Yes. That's the smaller of the two," I said.

"Two what?" Trinity asked. "Wait... two containers of dead drones?"

"Yes. The smallest. Also the closest."

"None of it is any good if we can't depend on you," Brad said. "You *are* your father's son."

I nodded. "And both of us have saved your ass."

He leaned forward aggressively. "You didn't save *my* ass, you saved *hers!*" he spat, finger pointing at his daughter.

"Too true, Brad. Too true," I said. "Most fathers would appreciate that sort of thing, but you aren't most or even much of a father, are you?"

"Shut the fuck up, you little bastard. *My* father is ten times the man yours was!" Martin suddenly interjected.

"Ah, there he is. Been waiting for your contribution, but then so has everyone else… for most of your life," I said.

"Enough!" Trinity said, standing up abruptly. "So there's bad blood and hard feelings. We knew this. Get over it. Be the professionals you say you are."

"It's about trust, Trinity," I said.

She nodded, thinking about her next words. Another voice beat her to them.

"I *trust* you Ajaya," JJ said. "I trust that you've got boatloads of dead drones because you hate them and I *know* how you shoot and how you were raised. I *trust* that you would do everything in your power to protect my sister. Thank you for that, by the way. So I have no issue riding into the Zone to a big old box of dead drones with you on overwatch, loading them in and hauling ass out. Be the easiest salvage ever… for us. You're the one whose gonna have his ass hanging in the wind when the big guns show up, with just your .338 for company."

"Thank you JJ. I appreciate that. But when did I ever say I was gonna just have a .338?" I asked with a smile. "You wouldn't believe some of the stuff I've found. All those military and federal facilities all over the place. National Guard, Homeland Security, Counter Terrorism. This book only has two drone caches in it. The rest of the pages are stockpiles of weapons, explosives, safe houses, and more. Oh, and it's all in code, Brad."

His eyes snapped up from the book, the greedy little gleam changing to instant anger. His eyes flicked to Astrid, then back to me. Either he was remembering to act civil in front of her or he was wondering if *she* knew me well enough to decipher my code. Or both.

"JJ brings up good points," he finally said. "Ajaya's been in love with my daughter since he fumbled his first meeting with her on Drone Night. He may be hopelessly pathetic, but he's at least consistent."

"Dad!" Astrid said. He ignored her, looking at Trinity. "We'll do it."

"Ajaya?" Trinity asked, body tense as she waited for my answer.

"As long as my family is guaranteed payment if I don't make it," I said.

"I'll sign a contract that says they can have my share if you don't make it out," JJ said.

"Me too!" Astrid said, flicking a glare at her father.

"I have no issue with that covenant," Brad said.

"Okay. We have a mission and an episode to plan. Let's get to it," Trinity said, eyes gleaming with unfettered excitement.

Chapter 23

The container of drones was, surprise, on the south end of the island.

Both caches were located on the outside edges of Manhattan, right up close to the docks. Each was also fairly close to a major entrance to the Zone. Shorter retrieval distance, potential use of a boat, some protection by wall defenses.

I chose the southern one for obvious reasons... I wanted to be near as possible to Hudson Street. Once I had access to the Zone, I needed to use it for all it was worth.

"Wait. I thought we were going to pick you up on the way out, like Dad and JJ used to with your father?" Astrid asked during the planning.

"That might have worked back then, but nowadays, you all have got to go pedal to the metal and haul out of there. I'll exfiltrate on foot, like I always do. Believe me, it's safer," I said, giving her a meaningful glance. I saw the exact moment she realized what I was really saying.

"Oh, so you've got that whole exfil technique you were telling me about?"

"Yup. Ajaya's secret sneaking techniques," I said with a nod.

The others were looking at us funny. Well, Brad and Trinity were. JJ was studying the map and Martin was cleaning his Sig Sauer 10mm Caseless like a broody psycho.

"The cache is booby trapped, but easy for a human to disarm. I'll go over that with all of you next. Astrid, you'll be able to drive all the way around the container and park facing back toward the egress. It's located on the Lower East Side, between the Battery Park entrance and the Brooklyn Bridge, which gives you two possible exits almost equal distance apart."

"That's pretty near the ship that originally brought the drones in," Martin said, lifting his head from his disassembled gun.

"Real close. I was originally gonna use the ship itself, but it got a lot of flooding from when the military bombed it."

"You've been in it?" JJ asked, fascinated.

"Yeah, all through it. Mostly a wreck. Some interesting stuff though."

"Like what?" Trinity asked. Everyone in the room was staring at me now, hanging on my words.

"A couple of bodies, some booklets of programming notes, some spare parts, a few drones that never made it off the ship."

"Bodies?" one of production staff asked.

"Yeah, three. I think it was two sailors and one of the drone techs."
"How'd they die?" Trinity asked. Everyone was still listening.

"Spider sting," I said.

"Sting?" Trinity asked.

"Spider CThree units use their seventh limb as a weapon. It can extend out further than their regular legs, and the end is a sharp claw. Leaves a distinctive hole in the victim," Brad Johnson said.

"Distinctive?" another staffer asked hesitantly.

"Big round hole like the diameter of a baseball," Martin answered, smiling a little.

"It killed the person who let it loose?" Trinity's assistant asked.

"I think a lot of the shipboard personnel died that night. Whoever set the whole thing in motion had placed really deep, extremely dominant mission parameters. Basically: Kill All Humans," I said. "Much of the ship sank and flooded when the Air Force bombed the hell out of it. These three were in the front drone hold, the only internal part of the ship still above water."

"That would make amazing footage," Trinity suggested, staring right at me.

"Amazing and really, really short. You'd get about five minutes of footage before the camera operator was swarmed by drones."

"Programming notes?" JJ asked.

I smiled. "Yeah. Interesting stuff."

"Those would be worth a small fortune," he said, giving me a raised eyebrow.

"I'm sure they are," was my only response.

"Just how much stuff do you have squirreled away?" Brad asked.

"We spent the better part of six years sorting through stuff, pulling some out, stocking hideouts, storing some things away."

"Spent your whole life sneaking around, stealing other people's stuff," Martin said.

"As opposed to *driving* around and stealing their stuff?" I asked.

"We killed drones by the dozens," he said.

I waved a hand at the photo. "As I said, that's one of two—and I shot all of the drones in those storage sites in the last two years. Between us, Dad and I have filed more drone kill tags than all five of the current *Zone War* teams combined. You can check that factoid with Zone Defense."

Martin opened his mouth to reply but his father held up a hand. "The proof, Martin, will be in the storage container Ajaya's taking us to. All the rest of this is just dick measuring," Brad said. "Sorry honey," he said to Astrid.

She waved a hand, brushing the comment away. "None of this matters. How do we avoid being trapped and killed again?" she asked, looking at all of us but ending with her eyes on me.

"First of all, nothing said in this room gets written on any electronic instrument, email, AI, or spoken about on a phone call. That's why I asked for an electronics-free meeting," I said.

"You think the drones can somehow monitor what happens out here?" Martin asked, incredulous, turning to his brother and father like I was crazy.

"Yup. Op Sec is paramount. I've found indications that the Spiders have access to the Internet via fiber cables that pass through the Zone. Hence why you all changed your mission and *still* got hosed. Also why the Destroyer boys got whacked so easily."

"You have evidence of internet access?" Brad asked. "And you didn't share it?"

"Not what I said. I have *indications*, not evidence. Nothing I can bring to General Davis and prove. Just some intel I've been putting together, but it's borne out by what happened to you and the Destroyers. I'm hoping to get some concrete stuff soon."

"So every time we file a mission, the drones know about it?" Brad asked.

"I think that's a recent development, which might mean they've only just hacked some server or processor somewhere in the information chain. Or else they'd have killed all the teams by now. The amount of prior preparation used in the attack on Destin and Troyer would indicate a long lead time," I said.

Martin looked back and forth between his father and brother, but their troubled expressions showed that they likely believed my story.

"I've read everything written," JJ said, then glanced at me, "at least publicly available, about the prior programming of the drones. Nothing like this was a part of it."

"The upper-level drones, particularly the Spiders, all had advanced AI-specific computing chips installed. The Chinese were actually a bit ahead of everyone else at the time of the Attack. The Spiders were their very best design, with maybe the most adaptable machine learning systems of their day. They've spent the last ten years learning under combat conditions. I don't think anyone on Earth knows what they're capable of."

"But preparing ambush and trap sites that elaborately?" JJ asked. "Where did they learn that?"

I kept my mouth shut. No real reason to point out that I'd been trapping and ambushing drones successfully at a really high level for the last two years.

197

"So operational security is paramount. Trinity, you have to ensure this information is locked down," Brad said, looking at all the staffers.

They in turn looked to their boss, each giving her a nod. "You have my word," Trinity said.

Brad frowned. "No offense, but this is our lives here. I think this mission has to go first thing in the morning and we file a broad plan with Zone Defense five minutes before we kick it off," he said, looking at JJ, Astrid, Martin, and finally, reluctantly, me.

"Let's do it," JJ said.

Chapter 24

"Where are your weapons?" Trinity asked as I walked up to the Johnson LAV. She looked at my small pack but I shook my head.

"No Zone license, so I can't retrieve anything from the police station," I said. "All I have, for the moment, is this," I said, pulling my kukri from behind my back.

She looked horrified. I smiled. "I'm not using any of those weapons anyway. Everything I need is inside the Zone. The Johnsons will drop me off right on top of one of my weapons caches."

She looked uncertain, but my calm smile must have convinced her. A Zone soldier came up and held out his hand for my pack. Two other soldiers flanked him, their G45s unslung and pointed at the ground between us. Idiots. Did they think I'd bring Rikki inside in my backpack?

I gave him the pack, he dropped it to the ground, and his fellows poked it with their rifle barrels. Yup... that's exactly what they had thought.

Astrid poked her head out the rear of the LAV. "Hey, get in here already. I need details," she said. I nodded to Trinity, was ignored by the soldier now tearing open my pack, and headed into the rear of the LAV.

I tried to pay absolute attention to the vehicle's details as I followed her, but Astrid's one-piece battle coverall must have been custom tailored because it fit her like a surgical glove. Focus, Ajaya. Focus.

The Johnsons' vehicle was a secondhand retired Canadian LAV 6, refitted with a hybrid electric drive/diesel drive unit and customized at great expense. Theirs had the remotely controlled GAU-17 minigun mounted above the front of the vehicle, which left the top hatches clear to open for salvage. An interior crane let them hoist heavy objects into the LAV, and the whole back of the vehicle was open and roomy as opposed to most armored vehicles' claustrophobic interiors.

Astrid drove from the left-hand seat while her brother, Martin, usually occupied the rear-facing gunner's position. With practiced grace, Astrid slid into her seat and pulled up a map on the LCD screen. I had a feeling that even the current military vehicles didn't have as many bells and whistles as this one did.

Which made sense. Military units needed to survive active warfare. The Johnsons needed navigation, cargo room, drone-specific weapons, and urban maneuverability. Before they faced off with the TKs, they had never faced such heavy fire. I had seen new armor patches welded to the exterior where the heavy machine-gun had torn up the original metal hide of the rig. I hoped it was just as tough as the original armor.

"Here's the site," I said, leaning forward to type the address into her nav unit. She smelled like strawberries, her head pushed close to mine to study the route.

"Out of the way, dweeb," Martin said from behind me. "You're blocking my spot and this baby doesn't go anywhere without its weapons pod live."

I squirmed backward, letting him squeeze past me. He too wore a dark green coverall, his Sig holstered in a cross-chest kydex rig. Astrid didn't carry a handgun. She had a compact Israeli Tavor rifle mounted in a locked rig on the left side of her compartment.

Brad was already in the commander's chair, so I moved back to the main troop compartment, finding JJ coming into the vehicle, my pack in his hand. "Zone Defense says your pack is clear, Ajaya. Any reason why they were so aggressive in searching it?"

"My grandmother's cookies are pretty sought after," I said.

"Your Aama bakes regular cookies?" he asked.

"One of the first things she learned to do when she moved here. My other grandmother taught her. Killer chocolate chips."

He laughed as he went about securing his gear. He was wearing armored chaps over his battledress, but his armored jacket was hanging from a hook by the door. JJ wore a cut-down semi-auto shotgun in a thigh holster. I think it only held like three shots of 12 gauge but really, how many shots are you going to get when facing a drone? I'd noticed Brad had a well-used HK UMP .45 in his own chest holster.

"You got stuff waiting for you inside, I hope," JJ said, waving a hand up and down my un-gunned body.

"Yeah, I'm gonna have Astrid drop me just about right on top of some things I've been saving for a day just like today."

He scratched one side of his big, blond head, his eyes flicking toward my pack. "You're packing light because you've got some heavy stuff inside," he guessed. His hand hit a button on the ceiling of the LAV and the back hatch drawbridged up.

"Yup. Gonna weigh like a bitch but it'll ruin anything in the Zone's day."

"You're not going to shoot some military anti-tank missiles, are you?" Martin asked. I felt the LAV move but Astrid must have been using the electric drive because I didn't hear a thing.

"He's not an idiot, Martin," JJ said, then leaned down close to my ear. "You're not, right?"

"Not to worry, boys. No missiles, although you'd be amazed at what the military left lying around."

An inside monitor came to life on the left-hand wall, the view showing the outside of the troop carrier.

We were just leaving the Battery Park tunnel, the massive steel flood door still swinging away from us.

I reached inside my stealth suit and pulled out a folded paper. "This is a diagram of the booby trap on the outside door of the container. It's real simple and there aren't any extra surprises. Just a pair of flash bangs tucked inside a tube of ball bearings. The trip wire secures to a pin on the left side of the door. Slide the pin out of its brackets and you're good to go."

He looked at the rather elaborate drawing, then back at me. "As much as I appreciate the preparation, now it looks like you're wondering if *I'm* the idiot."

"Just being careful," I said. I felt a turn to the left and the monitor showed us swinging around onto FDR Drive, headed south to Battery Place. We had agreed this approach would keep us more in the open, let us travel along to State Street, then South Street, the route staying near the water and Zone barriers as we moved up the east side of the Island.

It was early in the day, the sun still coming up, and there was no sign of any drones. "JJ, would you give AJ the sling pack that's in my gear locker?" Astrid said from up front. "AJ, we're getting close to your drop-off."

With a bemused smile, JJ opened a small locker door and pulled out a sports bag that seemed like it held a small, ball-shaped object.

He handed it to me as his father and brother looked on, all three intensely curious. Up front, I could see Astrid glancing at me in the little mirror over her position.

Why try to sneak forbidden stuff past the government when you can have a beautiful blonde girl do it for you? Nobody had searched her stuff in years.

I opened the bag and Rikki spun up his hover fans, lifting smoothly out into the open.

"Holy shit!" Martin yelled while Brad and JJ just froze at the sight of the Berkut.

"Relax. This is Rikki Tikki Tavi. He's my ace in the hole."

"Ace up your sleeve or in this case, in the bag," Rikki said. Shit... that wasn't... couldn't be... a joke?

"Did it just make a joke?" JJ asked.

"Rikki's quite a bit more advanced than your typical Berkut," I said, like he did it all the time.

I reached up and hit the back hatch button as Astrid pulled to a stop. It powered open and Rikki shot out as soon as there was space.

"Immediate area clear," my constantly surprising drone reported, hovering outside the LAV.

"Let's go with high altitude coverage today, don't you think?" I asked him.

"Concur," Rikki said, segments sliding open into Delta mode. A second later, he shot up into the sky.

"That's how you've been doing it?" Brad asked. Then he turned to Astrid. "And you knew?"

"She didn't know till just recently. Long story. Gotta run now. We'll have you under overwatch in like ten minutes," I said, then I bolted out the back of the vehicle and ran across the street to the building on the heliport pier that shoved out into the East River.

Maps of the city still called it the Downtown Heliport and in its day, it saw many of the world's richest people ferry into and out of Wall Street. The burnt-out husk of a Bell helicopter was a bitter reminder of the end of New York City as the financial center of the country. Drone night killed hundreds of thousands, but the day after had killed billions of dollars of wealth and corporate capital. Beyond the Great Recession, worse than the Great Depression, the interconnected economies of the entire planet had fallen deeper and further than at any point in history. Only a few people had been lucky enough to have shorted the markets on that day. In twenty-four hours, they had jumped to the top of the list of richest people, the previous titans laid low by terrorists and drones.

The reinforced steel mesh barrier that surrounded the Zone rose out around the pier, glittering steel mesh that could be electrified in a second. Lights, sensors, and a few widely dispersed laser units bristled across the top of the Zone barrier. Beyond the fence, automated aquatic and aerial units patrolled, ready to instantly destroy any breakouts.

A squat two-story building anchored the land end of the short pier, a facility that had housed flight operations, VIP and pilots lounges, a passenger area, and administrative offices. It also, in the back of the lowest level, behind the terminal operations office, held a pretty heavy-duty set of lockers. I had replaced the lock in the heavy metal door with a push button combination model, and that let me into what might have been a secure room for special cargo or ultra valuable material. One whole wall was heavy gauge steel lockers, and I had taken occupancy of four. The handy thing about the Zone was that you could find the absolute best of the best of virtually anything and none of it cost a dime. Four ultra-heavy-duty Abus padlocks, all with the same combination, guarded my cache.

I unlocked all four, first pulling a HK MP-5 submachine gun from its hooks, racking the bolt and slinging it over my shoulder. Next, a bag of thirty-round mags for the HK. Then in the next locker, a NYPD Barrett M-82A1 .50 caliber rifle, a so-called anti-material rifle. Anti-everything rifle, if you ask me. An ammo can of assorted .50 caliber flavors came out with it. The third locker held a shorty, NYPD Mossberg 590 shotgun with a fourteen-inch barrel, and a rather special AR-15. I loaded the shotgun with six rounds of buckshot and slung a bandoleer of shells over the barrel. The AR already had a mag in place so I just pulled the charging handle and chambered a round. Finally, in the fourth locker, laid a little surprise I had found while ransacking a US Army depot, something I had only read about until I found it. I had played with it a bit, but now was its time to shine. It too had an ammo box of goodies with it and I grabbed the two heavy weapons and hauled them up to the second story and out onto the roof. Then I raced back down and grabbed the ammo cans and mag bag. The shotgun and AR stayed at the bottom of the stairs.

Outside, the roof rose up to a long, angled ridge, a fairly gentle incline that let me set up on the south side with my weapons pointed to the north, with a great view of the next pier up. My drone container was right at the beginning of Pier 11, as near to the street as possible. The Johnson LAV was already backed up to it as I set up shop.

Bipod opened, ten-round mag of armor-piercing ammo in place, lens caps off the Leupold scope, and the Barrett was good to go. Then I set up my other surprise.

The XM-25 was an experimental weapon for shoulder firing 25mm airbursting ammunition. Equipped with a sophisticated fire control laser range finding computerized sight, it held five rounds of 25x40mm grenade ammo. After racking a round into the chamber, you simply put the laser dot on the structure nearest the target—in this case, the corner of the building just across the road from Pier 11—pressed the ranging button, and a firing solution was fed into the chambered round's warhead. Then you just waited for the right moment. A swept-winged shadow fell over me as Rikki took up a security position overhead.

JJ had the metal container doors open and he, Brad, and Martin were hauling dead drones into the back of the LAV as fast as they could drag them. They rushed around like they were late to a party.

"Incoming UAVs, four, right up Gouverneur Lane," Rikki said softly over my shoulder. That was right near the building I had laser ranged. *"Fire in 3, 2, 1, Mark."*

The XM-25 fired right on his mark and the heavy gun kicked my shoulder as the round shot across the open area. Four hovering combat drones appeared around the corner of the building just as my grenade went off. Three of them instantly fell, rotors torn to shreds by the shrapnel spraying in every direction.

On the pier, all three Johnson men instinctively ducked at the sound of my gun firing, then jumped again when the 25mm warhead detonated. From the corner of my eye, I could see them looking around widely, even as I fired a second round at the remaining drone. Round two exploded behind the survivor, but the beauty of air bursting munitions is just like the old line about horseshoes and hand grenades... you only have to be close enough.

The blast itself knocked the Kite sideways before gravity pulled it down to the hard streets. I dropped the gun sight down to road level just as its Tiger came bounding out from between the buildings. Lase, fire, lase, fire. Both rounds exploded just behind the lethal ground robot, but Tigers have thick armor and the blasts only rocked it around a bit.

I dropped the XM-25 and rolled sideways, pulling the Barrett's stock into the pocket of my shoulder. My eye found the scope just as the deadly bot landed on top of the LAV. I fired as it gathered itself, the huge round striking low, bouncing off the armored vehicle and just clipping one of the Tiger's hind feet.

Just a glancing blow, but the beauty of John Browning's heavy machine-gun round is its breathtaking power. Multiple tons of kinetic energy, even at three hundred meters, so it was like a car had clipped the robot's foot.

The metal monster spun sideways, only the claws of one front foot keeping it on the LAV at all, leaving it to scramble it's other three feet back under it. Plenty of time to send another super heavy round downrange, this one blasting the close combat bot right off the top of the personnel carrier, flipping it up into the air to land on its back, legs and head twitching.

JJ shot the Tiger twice with his shotgun, reloaded, and then gave me a wave. The Tiger was winding down its repetitive twitches as JJ picked up the two Wolves he'd dropped when the Tiger appeared, marching them into the back of the LAV.

"HK unit converging on this position. Additional UAVs approaching from multiple angles. Attention has been diverted from Johnson vehicle."

"You saying I'm the new target?" I asked, putting a new magazine into the XM-25. I lasered a spot on FDR Drive to at least put an intermediate range on the chambered grenade's fuse. Then I laid out a second magazine and reloaded the Barrett.

"CThree unit approaching from the west has designated you as highest priority. Drone network is calling all units within a one-mile radius."

I had known that unsuppressed gunfire, particularly the heavy blasts from a Barrett light fifty, would bring everything running. Hadn't counted on a Spider coming too.

The sound of Rikki's gun startled me and I looked up from my flinch to see him blast a second shot into a Raptor drone swooping in from behind us.

"Roll left now," his voice said, and I instantly did as he said, rolling over twice. A massive thunk sounded where I had been. A black delta shape was stuck nose down, titanium and carbide beak speared right into the metal roof of the terminal. At first, I somehow thought it was Rikki, but then *my* drone hovered down and shot the other Berkut twice, killing it stone dead.

"Aerial units at our eight and ten o'clock positions."

I turned and fired the XM-25 twice without lasing the shot. The mini-grenades exploded over the street, just in front of the cloud of UAVs that were accelerating our way. A couple fell but the bulk of them kept coming. Time to go old-school.

The XM-25 clattered to the rooftop as I pulled the MP-5 from its slung point around my back. A very familiar gun for me, as I had a ton of trigger time behind the sights of Heckler and Koch's famous contribution to the submachine guns of the world.

Perhaps the most widely used sub gun on the planet, the compact weapon was still in use pretty much everywhere. Dad and I had found them in police stations, federal offices, and even in some likely criminal establishments.

The gun I held had a four-position selector switch. Safe, semi-auto, three-round burst, and full auto. I had it on the three-round burst mode and started to feather the trigger as my sight picture filled with hovering drones. Five UAVs had survived the 25mm grenades and my first three bursts killed two of them. Rikki shot the third and then we both shot the last two.

Reaching into my daypack, I tossed him a new ammo block. He cleverly ejected the partial one in such a way that it slid down from the peak of the roof to stop at my feet, twisting himself to catch the full one.

"HK unit arriving in ten seconds."

My over watch was working better than expected... too well. We'd planned for me to get a lot of attention, but this sounded like I was gonna get *all* of the Zone's love and affection.

I put the partial ammo block in my pack and pulled out a flash bang grenade. Love these things. The SWAT team favorite for entries and hostage rescues, they didn't fling any shrapnel but the sheer blast effect was really hard on UAVs.

"Rikki, prepare to execute Red Baron."

"Jawohl," he said.

Wait... was that German? What the F had happened when he rewrote his own code?

He floated down and the underside of his fuselage opened in two places, short perching talons extending from his body.

Ignoring his odd comment, I placed the flashbang in his feet, careful to get the trigger spoon inside his grip, then pulled the pin. Immediately he shot upward, all fans on maximum thrust. Within seconds, he was gone from view, his light underside fading into the sky.

Alone, I had time to replace the partial mag in my MP-5 with a full one, then got my body prone and the Barrett snugged to my shoulder as the clank of treads announced the arrival of the Tank Killer. It came out Old Slip Street and I fired two rounds at the first sight of its armored front end. Both rounds impacted the front right drive sprocket and the tread running around it. The little tank lurched, the drive mechanism fouling up, but it still had enough power to spin itself toward me and bring the laser to bear. I ducked as soon as I saw it and still almost lost my face as a superheated wave of air announced the passage of the otherwise invisible infrared laser beam. I rolled sideways four times, leaving myself dizzy but eight or nine feet from where I had been, the big Barrett rifle banging against me as I held it tight.

Over the lip of the roof, I could hear the metal buckle as it was heated instantly to the point where the colored coating melted and the aluminum started to actually burn. Then came the fantastic sound of the LAV's M-134 minigun ripping off the better part of five hundred rounds of 7.62mm armor-piercing ammo.

The burning sound cut off and I instantly pulled my hand into my sleeve, then pushed the polished mirror metal part of my stealth suit over the roofline to check the tank. I caught a tiny image of the tank with its gun still pointed my way and yanked my arm down as the cuff melted right off my suit. Tricky bastard with machine reflexes.

The Johnsons' mini gun sounded again, a deadly burring thrum of power, and the laser cut off in a crunch of sound. This time, I came up over the roof peak with the Barrett's barrel leading the way. The TK's gun was smoking and sparking in ways the manufacturer never intended. I sent four more armor-crunching rounds at the robot, concentrating on the laser gun and the juncture where the turret met the body of the beast. The minigun's burr came again and again, tracers making a solid beam of light like a sci-fi ray gun blast, followed by the dull whump of an explosion as the front of the robot tank burst open with a billow of black smoke

The air behind me filled with whirring sounds and I dropped the big rifle, rolling to my back, scrambling to get the MP-5 out and up. A dozen various flying drones announced my demise, the flock coming toward me from the southern Battery Park side. My gun snagged on all the buckles and crap adorning my body and a sudden dump of imminent-death adrenaline made my hands jerky and clumsy.

A black speck fell into the midst of the drone flock, exploding in the densest part of the bunch. Rikki dove down behind his bomb, gun firing at stunned survivors. My sub gun came free, death took a step back, and I was quickly adding my own fire to my Berkut's.

The twang and crunch of metal brought me around to see a Wolf standing on the roof, the claws of a second one embedded in the edge as it struggled to join its partner. My thumb pushed the selector to full auto and I fired off the rest of the mag, then dove for the Barrett.

The 9mm rounds from the MP-5 knocked the standing Wolf backward, but its frontal armor was too thick for the bullets to penetrate and the rearward momentum stopped suddenly as powerful motors kicked in. Rocked back onto its hind legs, the Wolf tried to bring its head-mounted flechette gun down far enough to shoot me. Servos whined and its body began to drop toward me while its partner started to pull itself up.

I shoved the big Barrett forward on the metal roof, hand on the pistol grip but shoulder nowhere near the stock. No time. Twisting my arm to swing it around, I pulled the trigger as soon as the muzzle seemed on target.

The standing Wolf disappeared and something punched my right bicep hard enough to knock me sideways on the roof. Stunned by the recoil of the loosely held fifty caliber, all I could do was stare. My right arm was completely numb.

The climbing Wolf had just two claws still in the metal sheathing, almost knocked completely off by the violent demise of its partner. It twisted and scrabbled in an odd, bizarre, non-living way. Then it stopped and, after a pause, started to swing its hindquarters.

The onboard computer had analyzed the problem and applied physics. Soon it would pendulum high enough to get its other paw in the roof.

With my left hand, I dragged the Barrett down the roof toward the access. The robot Wolf swung farther. My right arm gave up being numb and started to throb. I stood up and stumbled closer to the exit. The XM-25 lay in front of me. I kicked it through the access port, dumped the Barrett down the hatch and then, one-handed, twisted the MP-5 off its sling and threw it through. The Wolf got its second paw on the roof, metal crunching under its claws. My feet went on the ladder and I hooked my flopping right arm through a rung, grabbed the metal hatch with my left, and swung it shut just as the Wolf thrust its body up and onto the top of the building. Metal tinged as flechettes whined off the steel hatch.

I dropped down the ladder, which thankfully was only about six and a half feet long. Grabbing the guns, I dragged them and myself downstairs and to the lockers. All three went into one locker and I snapped the big padlock shut. No heavy caliber weapons in drone hands today... or claws?

My right armed throbbed really painfully, but I had some use of it so I set the pain aside and picked up the special little AR-15. When I had found the AR six months ago in a police station gun room, an NYPD armored vest with mag pouches was sitting next to it. The name tag read *A. Goldman* on the vest and I wondered if Officer Goldman had lived or died on Drone Night. Maybe I'd have my AI do a search when I got out. If I got out.

The vest was the kind called a plate carrier. It wasn't ballistic armor itself, but it held big armor plates on the front and back, the sort that can stop rifle bullets. Magazine pouches held six standard mags; but these could only hold ten of the special rounds rather than the normal thirty. That's because each was twice as big as a 5.56 mm round, being as they were .458 SOCOM rounds.

I researched the caliber after I found it. The idea was to pack as much power into a cartridge that could fit and run through a standard AR with a new barrel, chamber, and bolt assembly. This round was probably close to that. Basically the same as an old Wild West .45-70 buffalo round, moderned up for the twenty-first century. Over a metric ton of energy at the muzzle. Big heavy bullets that could bulldoze through armor and solid cover with ease. Sounds like drone medicine to me.

I struggled into the vest, ignoring the sounds of the access hatch getting yanked and tugged on. Then I slung the shotgun bandoleer over my shoulder. The shotgun itself went over the left shoulder while the AR was kept in my arms.

Gunshots sounded up on the roof, then the whine of flechettes. Rikki was engaging the Wolf. I went back upstairs, pointed the muzzle of the rifle at the hatch, and yelled, "Back off, Rikki. Fire in the hole."

The gunfire stopped and after a moment, so did the flechettes. The Wolf, who didn't know what my words meant, went back to worrying the hatch. Right up until I fired a round through the metal hatch and through the drone's metal head. A loud metallic thump followed the echoing boom of the shot. Wolf down. Time to go.

Chapter 25

It looked like a freakin' drone reunion outside. Peeking out a window in the Zone is a great way to get a laser through the skull, as almost every drone is programmed to look for exactly that kind of behavior from humans.

Instead, I used a makeup compact I found in the receptionist's desk. Don't know what happened to its owner, but the building was remarkably free of skeletons, so I had hopes she'd made it out okay.

Keeping to the shadows prevented flashes of light that would bring the same deadly response as poking my face up against the glass, but it was frustrating trying to get a full picture of what was happening. I'd already mirrored Pier 11 and my storage container, but the Johnson LAV was long gone. That's what we'd agreed upon. If and when things got dicey, they'd go their way and I'd go mine.

Except, mine looked full of drones and theirs looked pretty empty. Scoping around with the mirror eventually found the reason why. Clinging to the side of a building across the street was a seven-legged horror with a cracked ocular lens. A Spider... apparently *my* Spider. Like it wanted payback or something.

At least that's how my primitive, superstitious side wanted to look at it. Logic told me that the Spider had simply identified me as a bigger problem that might be easier to kill than an armored LAV. So easy, in fact, that I wondered why the assembled drones hadn't simply stormed the building already. A fast-moving, swooping shadow gave me the most likely answer.

Rikki was distracting them. But probably not for long. Time to get to work. Staying back in the shadows, I built a little shooter's hide. The reception counter gave me a structure. Desks and shelves shoved in front of it gave me thicker cover. A stool behind gave me a seat and I laid the .458 on top of the counter, looking through the Trijicon optic. Using a combination of fiber optics and tritium illumination, the Advanced Combat Optical Gunsight didn't generate any electromagnetic signature for dronedom to pick up on.

I put the reticle on my greatest immediate danger, which, believe it or not wasn't the Spider CThree. It also wasn't the two close combat Tigers or the half-dozen Wolves milling about. It was the Raptor UAVs flying around with their line-of-sight laser weapons and machine reflexes. There were at least three of them, maybe four. Hard to tell, what with all the zooming about as they tried to shoot my Berkut.

One hovered in place for an extra long moment and I didn't hesitate. The SOCOM boomed and the Raptor was snatched from the sky like it was tied to a jet-powered getaway car.

Of course, the gun blast and the blown-out office window meant my element of surprise was gone. I switched targets to the Spider, but it was gone. Jamming the sight back down on the Tigers revealed both of them bounding at me in full, horrible glory. I put the reticle on the lead one and stroked the trigger, absorbing the recoil, then twisting and firing at its companion.

Tigers weigh over twice what I do. No regular rifle round, even as powerful as the .458, was going to physically stop them in mid-bound. But the cop whose rifle I had appropriated, had packed all his magazines with a carbide core bullet designed for extreme penetration. Actually, I think the bullet itself was made for .458 caliber elephant guns, to shoot, you know, elephants. Not much call for that these days, at least not here in New York.

Maybe out West in that Mammoth Park where they had lab-grown prehistoric pachyderms that might break out and go rogue, but otherwise no. But the product name of the ammo said exactly that, right on the ammo box. Extreme penetrators. They lived up to their billing.

The first round punched through the shoulder armor of the lead Tiger, right about where the killing bot's stabilizing gyro was. It crashed and sprawled, rolling up into a spastic, twitching mess of lethal legs and head.

The second Tiger caught the heavy bullet right in the head, an admittedly less damaging target, but Tigers, like Wolves, use their optic bands to gather essential environmental information just like flesh-and-blood tigers do. Loss of its vision caused it to veer slightly to one side, which gave me enough time and a decent-enough sight picture to put round three through its chest and deep into the ultracapacitor stored there. A new Tiger, fresh off the assembly line, would have been working on battery power. After ten years, most drones had cycled their batteries through too many recharges for them to be of use. Nowadays, most of the drones depended on their capacitors to store each day's electricity from solar chargers. My bullet ruined that big storage cell and the resulting flash of man-made lightning almost blinded me. It definitely ruined the Tiger's day.

A metal face filled the window as a Wolf hit the opening. I shot it out of the window frame with the SOCOM and then exchanged the rifle for the shorty shotgun. Two Wolves hit the side-by-side windows to the right of the first. Hardened buckshot might not be an instant kill, but two fast shots of it blasted the Wolves clean out of sight.

More drones were arriving by the second: Wolves, Leopards, Cranes on the street, Crabs on the buildings, and a whole swirling flock of hovering UAVs. I whistled, once, loud. A second went by, then another. Suddenly, Rikki came shooting in through the broken window, a couple smaller, slower aerial units right on his tail feathers. Buckshot does even better on flying drones, wreaks absolute hell with rotors and stuff.

The smoke from my three fast shots cleared as I stuffed more shells into the shotgun, the broken UAVs twitching on the ground. Reloaded with fresh ammo, I slung the shotgun behind my back and pulled the SOCOM AR to my shoulder. There had to be thirty ground units out on the road and unless I missed my guess, that had to be getting close to the right number. At least I hoped it was. My life depended right now on just how much provocation and temptation old Uncle Sam could take.

I lined up the ACOG on a Leopard, shot it in the chest, then shot a Crane right off its feet. The tall, skinny bipedal units are just a flechette gun on a metal neck with a small body and two long legs. Three more just like it came out of the streets feeding into FDR Drive.

There were still thousands of drones in the Zone, but you never see them in huge numbers and clusters, especially out in the open like this. The reason was the US Air Force.

"*Incoming Renders,*" Rikki announced. Yup, the right number was here.

A sharp sonic whistle started from far away, quickly becoming very loud. On the street, drones turned to run. Me, I chose to duck behind the counter and curl into a tight ball. Rikki joined me, both behind the counter and in choosing a ball shape.

Light flashed as I squeezed both eyelids tightly shut, hands over my ears as an angel roared and the ground bounced me like a basketball. The shockwave was massive, the blast overwhelming in sound and violence. Eventually it ended.

I was covered in debris and papers, bits of glass, and small pieces of particle board. Rikki had some junk on him too. I brushed us both off and stood up. The pointy head of a Crane drone was jammed into the wall above us.

Beyond the counter, the whole front of the terminal building was mostly gone. The street was blackened and smoking. Not a single drone was in sight. At least not a whole drone. Bits and pieces were everywhere. Stepping around the counter and to the wide open front, I glanced up at the sky. The only thing flying was a Render circling back through for a first glance at the damage. I stepped out and gave it a wave. Its big wings rocked side to side, then it was gone.

That had to be the biggest single kill strike by the Air Force in the last ten years. Between aerial and ground units, at minimum fifty drones had suddenly ceased to exist. Not sure what ordinance the Render had dropped, but it had been massively effective.

"Alright Rikki?"

"Systems nominal. No damage sustained."

"Let's get hoofing it," I said, turning left toward the Battery. The Johnson rig had likely exited via the Brooklyn Bridge. The building the Spider had been on (which was now almost completely windowless) was more in that direction. Never saw which way it ran, but it seemed likely it went north, so I figured south would be best. Wall Street was that way and my intention was to swing through on my way out and look for any sign of the ghost girl. Nothing to it but to do it.

Chapter 26

An hour later found me stuck inside another building. This one was at 11 Wall Street and used to be known as the New York Stock Exchange. My guess had been horribly wrong. I ended up going in *exactly* the same direction that the Spider had gone. I know that because it was now sitting right outside the Exchange, along with a small pack of Wolves, a Leopard, and a horde of fliers.

I *did* do one thing right. Before I left the helipad terminal, I went back up on the roof to retrieve the ammo cans. No weapons and no ammo left behind, lest it be used against you or others. The unwritten rule of Zone Salvage.

While I was up there, I spotted the dead Berkut and grabbed it. Spare parts for Rikki. But Rikki had other ideas. As soon as I brought it down the ladder, he descended upon it and extruded a connection arm. Plugged right into the dead drone.

"Ajaya suggested identity swap successful. Rikki Tikki Tavi is now Berkut Unit A7-134. Unit reported active. Old identity, A9-125, reported terminated. Probability of assumed identity holding up to handshake interrogation is 87 percent."

Suggested identity swap? Sure, we can go with that. Not that I thought it would be a good idea to have backup flight motors or anything. Of course I thought Rikki could change electronic identities with the dead flyer and plug back into the network... I mean, I'm brilliant, right? At least my drone thinks so.

So, sitting in the lobby of the Exchange, using a dental mirror from my pack to look out the window, I can stare at the Spider and not worry that it will detect Rikki and subvert him or attack us or what have you.

Instead, the Spider had already queried Rikki's sensors to ensure the building was empty of humans, particularly one pesky human sniper. In fact, Rikki reported that the Spider specifically was looking for a human named Ajaya Gurung, matching my description, which it, according to my drone, obtained from the Internet.

"Tell me again what image it conveyed?" I whispered.

"Time mark 3.21 of Zone War Interview with Cade Kallow, dated—"

"It watched that damned TV show?" I interrupted.

"Correct."

"Probability of other drones entering this building within the next two hours."

"Estimated at seventeen percent chance."

Good odds. I could live with that. Actually, I had to. That damned Spider was hunkered down, apparently directing the search for me.

"CThree unit designated Lotus is redirecting assets from FDR Drive toward 55 Broadway as a previously known location for target."

"Its name is Lotus?"

"Correct."

"What are the other two named?"

"Peony and Plum Blossom."

"The Chinese military named their deadliest drones after flowers?"

"Unknown. CThree units in Zone are so designated."

Must be some symbolic shit going on there. Maybe flowers are big in China. Not my thing.

"Well, they're not going to find me on Broadway."

"Aerial units have found equipment left in lobby. Contents of transport pack are consistent with operational methodology of target suspect. UGV Wolf unit dispatched to lowest levels of building to seek more data."

The bastards found my pack, the part I left behind before climbing all those frigging stairs to get that damned Rocon laptop computer. I didn't like that. Nevermind that I wasn't using it and hadn't been near it in at least a week. That level of forensic detection bothered me.

Here I was, less than half a kilometer from the Battery Park exit, and I was trapped by a deadly Chinese flower that *knew* my name and was now gathering information like some international assassin... or like those overly muscled killer robots in that old *Terminator* franchise. Actually, just like that movie.

Of course I'd seen all of them. Astrid and I watched them all one winter in sixth grade. They were funny. Who the hell would try to build the ultimate killing machine and pattern it after a human being?

Any of the machines out on the street was a more efficient design than a cybernetic copy of an Austrian bodybuilder. Four-legged machines were so much more stable than a bipedal design.

But it was the searching and researching that reminded me of the movie. Drone night was indiscriminate slaughter... horrifying, but not personal. The drones killed everyone and anyone, even their own programmers, at least those on the ship.

This was personal... Lotus knew my name. Lotus was targeting me specifically. I shuddered involuntarily. Then I shook it off. So be it. Hunt me all you want, here in the Zone. Once I was out, I was safe. It made entering the Zone more daunting, but I could deal. I had Rikki and he was back in the drone net, listening from within. Like every action movie ever, where the hero, who's being hunted, gets a radio from one of the bad guys and then monitors their every move. Rikki was my radio... one with a gun of his own. So we'd keep moving, first through the Exchange, then out onto the streets beyond. Make it look like Rikki was sweeping first the building and then other areas where me, the hunted human, might be hiding.

I turned and moved deeper into the building, Rikki hovering along at my shoulder. We found the trading floor, empty and clean, as it had closed on the afternoon of Drone Night and never reopened. Smaller than it looked in the old news clips and photos. Certainly a lot less messy. All my trips into the Zone and this was my first into the Exchange. Not sure why. Maybe because the damage done to Wall Street and the whole US economy—hell, the whole world's economy—was so great that it left a scar on America's psyche second only to the actual loss of life. We circled the room, then headed toward the area that I think used to be called the Ramp. The IT area of the Exchange that fueled the massive exchange. I read once that it had been the largest exchange in the world by a massive measure—the capitalizations of its traded companies valued at over twenty-five trillion dollars at the time of Drone Night.

Not anymore. Three exchanges had replaced the one. The Hoboken Exchange in Jersey, the Connecticut Exchange, and the

DC Exchange (nicknamed Dice).   Each of the three was founded by the only people who came out of the Slump whole... more than whole... super wealthy, in fact. The only ones who were actively shorting the market at the time this entire Exchange rang its final closing bell. So weird. What were the odds of having the exact right bet in place at the exact wrong time for the rest of the country and the world?

A sound derailed my train of thought. Just a little scuff. Rikki didn't even react, but I did. I turned and looked at the far wall, where a door stood open under a long-dark EXIT sign. It had been closed a second ago. My rifle, the .458 SOCOM, came up, almost on its own. Something moved in the darkness of the doorframe. Rikki still didn't react.

A figure stepped out—a human figure. Feminine, small and curved, with long black hair and a silver shine on the side of her face.

Chapter 27

She wore designer jeans, calf-high boots, and a deep plum blouse, her clothing either ten years out of fashion, or, if she was one of the super rich who could afford to buy Zone-recovered fashions, right in the heart of style.

She looked directly at Rikki, almost like she expected to see him, but then she turned my way and her eyes widened in shock and... fear. She froze.

I stood there in a head-to-toe stealth suit with a heavy armored SWAT vest over it, the lethal .458 SOCOM aimed right at a girl maybe a bit younger than me, who was unarmed, dressed for success, and... cute.

Dark, almond-shaped eyes, olive skin, and full red lips—that were currently pressed flat in fear and worry—and a mesh of very fine silver metal that flowed over the left side of her face, from her temple to her jaw.

I glanced at Rikki. He was facing forty to fifty degrees away from the girl, but she was still in the arc of his sensors. Yet no reaction.

"Who are you?" I asked, lowering the rifle slightly but keeping the muzzle pointed at the floor between us.

She glanced from me to Rikki and back again. Swallowed nervously, then straightened up. "I'm Harper, and you owe me," she said, voice not as certain as her words.

"I probably do," I said, bringing the rifle back to patrol sling position. "Rikki, scan arc forty degrees to your right. Report all anomalies, thermal, optical, audio, and electronic."

He spun slowly in space and a scanning laser (my own, personal, addition to his suite of sensors) sent a flickering line over everything in the arc, including the girl, Harper. He paused.

"Detecting thermal, optical, and auditory presence consistent with human—female. Event log indicates anomaly detected earlier but rejected as false data," he said in his proper British voice. There was no inflection, but I know my drone. To me, he sounded almost puzzled.

"You blocked my Berkut," I said to her. It's possible my tone might have been accusatory.

"And you have a killer drone as a pet," she said back, arms coming up to cross in front of her chest.

"What is that on your face? Some kind of linking interface? You overrode Rikki's sensors?"

"You named the most efficient killer the Russians ever produced Ricky?" she asked back.

"Rikki Tikki Tavi. It's a story," I said, somehow feeling defensive even though I had the drone and the gun.

"Oh, the mongoose story. Why? Berkut means eagle," she said, her tone lecturing, her face frowning.

"I *know* what Berkut means. When I brought him online after rebuilding him, he made a series of ticking noises. Like the cartoon. He still does it when he's rebooted. So, I'm right, aren't I?" I asked, flicking a hand at her face.

She frowned again, this time in annoyance. "You rebuilt a killing drone and rebooted it?" she asked, her tone indicating I had the intelligence of a suicidal moron.

"I replaced his CPU chip and completely reprogrammed him. New machine, basically. So you roam around the Zone wearing some experimental interface?" I asked, making sure my own tone questioned her own intelligence. I had my suspicions regarding the silver net, but I also recognized her type. Highly intelligent, highly competitive, overachieving know-it-all. Challenge their expertise and watch them unfold.

"No you idiot, it's a highly refined cybernetic neuroprosthetic that makes your wind-up toy look like a paper airplane," she said. Hah, like I said. I dealt with her type all the time in school, both high school and in my technical college classes.

"Ah, so you what? Convince the drones that you're not really there? Override their network encryption protocols?"

Her head tilted to one side, maybe, possibly, considering. She was small, like my sisters' heights, maybe a hundred sixty-seven or sixty-eight centimeters, but much curvier.

"Why are you here?" she asked.

"Hiding from the Spider outside. Why are *you* here?" I challenged.

"I live here, genius," she said.

"Here, in the Zone? Or *here* in the Exchange?" I asked.

A new frown formed, right after a micro grimace. She had no poker face at all. Every emotion flashed across her pretty face as soon as she felt it. Cool. I felt like I needed every advantage I could get. She hadn't blinked at the word *Spider* but was seriously concerned about telling me she lived in this building.

"Downstairs? Upstairs? You live here—alone?"

More emotions flashed. Yes, yes, and no—at least the tiny hesitation at the end sure seemed like a no.

"Who else is here?" I asked. She froze, her mind working. It was like she had almost no experience talking face to face with living people.

I shifted my gun as if I was feeling concerned for my safety. I really wasn't but my instincts told me to act like it.

Fear. Worry for someone else. Eyes held too tight on me, but a micro flicker toward the door.

"Family? Who? Dad? Mom?" I asked, ending with the most likely target.

She blinked.

"Where is she? Downstairs?" I asked, stepping toward her and more importantly, the door she had come through. Instantly she squared off, hands coming up in warning, frown becoming fierce.

"I'll yell. They won't find me but you'll be dead as a doornail," she said. Doornail? Where had she learned to talk?

"Same as if I fired this gun," I said, hefting the rifle slightly, this time like it was a useless dead weight.

Realization. Damn, this was kinda neat. I can never get anything over on Astrid, but this girl was, at least for now, an open book. I had a feeling she was a quick learner.

"You're mean," she decided.

"Yeah, sorry about that. But you seem to have the advantages here and I've still got to get home. Like you said, I owe you. I'm not a threat to you or—your mother, is it?"

She frowned at me, fear gone, replaced with anger and, maybe, annoyance. Don't like being tricked, huh, smarty? I gave her a smile. "Why are you both here? Why not walk out of the Zone? Obviously you seem to be able to fool my drone and you must have done the same to that Tiger and Kite the other day."

She looked away. "We can't leave."

"Why not? It's not safe here," I said.

"No, it's not safe out there!" she said.

"What? This is the most dangerous place on Earth."

"Not for me. Not for… us. Out there is."

"Why? What's out there?"

She closed down, face going blank for the first time. Her head turned and she looked toward the front of the building. "The Spider is gone. Most of the drones have left too. They went west. You need to leave."

"Harper, I'm sorry if it I handled that badly, but you have to understand… that *I* can't understand how you're here or why you stay. Paranoia is a survival trait in the Zone."

"Yes it is, Ajaya Gurung," she said, arms crossed again, frowning heavily. She knew my name? How? "You need to leave now before that Spider swings back."

I thought about it. "Will you be alright?"

She tilted her head. "You just met me. I've lived here my whole life. *I'll* be fine. You're the one in danger. You should go."

"Listen, I'm sorry if I interrogated you. It's just I saw you that day you helped me and then when I investigated more, I found other people had seen you and you became this riddle, wrapped in a mystery, inside an enigma."

"Winston Churchill? And you just compared me to Russia," she said, arms still crossed, but her lips twitched a little, like she was fighting a smile, if only a little one.

"Well, it's a good quote."

"At least you got it right. So you investigated me?"

"Of course. I try to expect anything when I'm in the Zone, but a pretty, unarmed, dressed-up girl my age distracting Tiger drones is outside anything I could imagine."

She sniffed. "Not much imagination," she said, quirking a little smile. Then her head snapped around and she stared at the wall, not seeing it but obviously sensing something.

"You need to go."

"I'll come back. Do you need anything? Does your mom need anything? Stuff not here in the Zone?"

"I have all of Manhattan to ransack. What could I need? But there is something important," she said.

"What?"

"You can't tell anyone about me... us. Not if you're serious that you mean us no harm," she said, frowning.

"Okay. Sounds like you're in trouble."

"No, they think we're dead. That Spider's coming back, with all its troops. You have to go *now!*"

"Okay, okay. We're gone," I said, turning toward the front of the building. I looked back and she was gone. Then her voice echoed up from the stairwell as the door swung shut. "Bring back—" she yelled, the ending word too faint to hear.

"Spider unit approaching," Rikki said.

We bolted, clearing the street and moving at a fast clip toward the Battery. Five minutes later, I sent Rikki back on patrol and headed for the exit into the tunnel. Two blocks away, I turned to my Berkut. "Can you replay Harper's final sentence to me?"

Her voice immediately issued from Rikki's speakers. *"Bring back some methotrexate."*

Chapter 28

"Ah, Ajaya, that was quite a little skirmish you whipped up in there," Major Yoshida commented as I exited the tunnel. I hadn't been forced to my knees or had to put my weapon in a drawer either. Things must be looking up.

Sergeant Alonso stepped up and held out his hand. I gave him the SOCOM, but he only checked that the chamber was clear and the magazine was out of the gun before handing it back. Then he held out a hand for my pack.

"Uncle Sam got a hell of a shot on the drones today, Major," I said. "Did the Johnsons get out okay?"

"Every one of them, and quite a haul of drones, too. All of them already tagged by you. I must say, Ajaya, you're even more of a sniper than I thought," he said, watching as the sergeant went through my pack. "And... your pet made it back into the Zone somehow." His smile was wide and packed with even white teeth, but I didn't buy it for a second.

"Yeah, neat, huh? I was happy to see him, especially in that helicopter terminal," I agreed.

"Nice shooting there. Cool toys," he said, walking over to a table covered with a cloth. "The brass was interested to see that XM-25 put to good use. Lot of money went into that project, only to have it canceled." He pulled off the cloth and there was the XM-25 and the Barrett 82.

"So excited that they sent me in to retrieve it," he said, picking up the short weapon and pulling the bolt to check the chamber.

"Worked pretty well. Wouldn't carry it as my only weapon though," I said. "Not versatile enough."

"Good point. Not like, say that .458 SOCOM, right?"

"Exactly. But I'm guessing you didn't wait here for me just to chat about guns?" I asked.

"We're considering giving you back your Zone license, Ajaya, but we'd like to see some cooperation from you."

"Cooperation? I'm the very essence of cooperation," I said. Sergeant Alonso snorted at my words, just finishing his very thorough inspection of my gear.

"Yeah," Yoshida said dryly. "Since it looks like that nifty drone of yours is back inside the Zone, we thought you could help us with some of ours," he said. It wasn't a question.

"When and where?" I asked warily. It seemed too easy.

"Tomorrow, let's say ten o'clock? So you can sleep in. Go to the same building where we planned the rescue. Getting great buzz off of that, by the way. Our Public Relations folks rolled out an edited film of the whole thing. You're even in there, Ajaya, in your practice armor."

Somehow he made it sound like I was a child, running along with the adults. Interesting that they released any of the video though.

"Well, that's fun. I'll have to watch a replay of it."

"Yeah, you do that, but not too late. Need you bright as a button tomorrow."

"Un huh," I said, picking up my gear and heading toward the exit.

"See you tomorrow, Ajaya," he said, a smirk on his face.

"Yeah. Wouldn't miss it."

I called home from the self-driver, Gabby picking up so fast that I knew they were all waiting in the living room. "AJ?"

"Hi Gabby. I'm headed home; didn't have my AI with me."

"We know, brainiac. You left it with us, remember?" she asked. I could hear relief in her voice despite her words. "It's Ajaya, everyone," she yelled to the background.

"Well, with all the boys calling you and your evil sister, day and night, I figure it's hard for you to remember much of anything," I shot back, smiling to myself.

I wasn't lying. My sisters are beautiful... too attractive for their own good. Perfect brown skin, Mom's high cheekbones, and Aama's black eyes. I've seen grown adult men watch them with an interest that makes me reach for my kukri.

"Haha, my memory is perfect. Wait, everyone's trooping in now."

"Ajaya?" my mom asked from near the microphone.

"I'm fine, Mom. Just bruises, a few tears and burns on the old stealth suit, but fine."

"When they bombed the road, it was..." she trailed off.

"Yeah, pretty intense. I figured they couldn't resist that many drones, so we were all set when it hit."

"We?" Monique asked.

"You remember my drone? The Berkut?"

"You still have that horrid thing?"

"It saves my life at least once every trip," I said. They had never gotten past the fact that Rikki, in his previous life, had killed our father. Pretty hard to blame them for that.

"You're on your way?" Mom asked.

"Yup. Traffic is slow, but I'm getting there."

"Okay. We'll all be ready when you get here. Goodbye for now. Love you!"

"Love you too, Mom. I'll see you in a few."

We'll all? How many were there? Just the twins, Mom, and Aama, right?

Wrong. Way wrong. When the elevator doors opened to my floor, I found many of my neighbors standing in their doorways, looking down the hall. Looking at our door. Mrs. Radmo, the older lady who lived nearest the elevator, was the only one to turn and look at me. The others, also mostly oldsters, were pretty focused on our apartment.

"What's going on?" I asked Mrs. Radmo.

"You have visitors, Ajaya," she said. Most of the others finally turned to notice me. There was an odd sort of interest in their eyes. Curiosity of a type.

"Oh? Who?"

"Famous folk. Fancy folk," she said. "But then, you're famous now too."

"Bah, he's not really," Mrs. Snyderman said from two doors up and across the hall. Mrs. Snyderman was a bit of a crab. Aama said that *Mr.* Snyderman probably willed himself to death for some peace and quiet.

I moved past each door, marveling that none of them looked even slightly embarrassed at their out-and-out nosiness.

I got to our door and the lock let me in. Any pretense of sneaking was gone as Monique came barreling into the foyer and hugged me. Gabby was right behind her, both girls laughing and smiling.

"Who are you and what have you done with my sisters?"

Monique punched my shoulder. "Don't be an ass, AJ," she said.

"We *do* miss you and worry, a bit, you know," her twin said.

I hugged them back. "You only smell a little horrible," Gabby said. "Like burnt stuff." She took my pack and her sister took the rifle in the case that I'd "borrowed" from Zone Defense. Didn't feel like dropping off a gun at the precinct and dealing with an hour or more of paperwork for a new weapon.

Mom came in a straight line from the living room, and I could hear more voices behind her. The girls took my gear to my room, fast enough to still precede me into the main living area. Besides Aama, there was Astrid, her brother JJ, Trinity, and, low and behold, her father, Chester Flottercot. The media mogul was wearing his trademark bespoke striped suit and a fancy tie. The three younger visitors wore jeans and casual shirts.

"Ah, hi everyone?"

"We had to come wait with your family," Astrid said. "After that bombing run by the Renders, I think *we* needed *their* confidence that you'd be alright."

"Oh. Ah Mr. Flottercot, I'm Ajaya," I said, holding out my hand to Trinity's father. We had never formally met despite him being at Zone Defense the day of the rescue.

"I know who you are, son," he said in his thick British accent. "Plus you were the one to come up with that plan to rescue the Destroyer team. Brilliant, that."

"You never mentioned that you were part of that rescue," my mom said accusingly. Behind her, the twins folded their arms and gave me their best put out looks.

"Because it was impressed on me that it was on the secret side. Trying to get my license back and all that," I said.

"We saw the government clip. You're in it, although you don't do anything much," Gabby said.

Mom led me into the room and I could see that drinks and snacks had been laid out. Since I had taken the time to change out of my stealth suit and into a Zone Defense coverall that happened to be there when I snagged the rifle case, I didn't feel bad about dropping down into a chair and munching on cheese and crackers. "Please," I said around a mouthful. "I've got the full footage. I did a lot more than whatever edited crap they showed the world."

"You have it all?" Trinity asked, excited.

"Throw it up on the wall," JJ said, waving with his left hand at our wall while sticking out his huge right hand for me to shake. "And thanks for the overwatch. Haven't felt that safe in years," he said.

"AI, project recording from Zone Defense mission to recover Destroyer armored vehicle," I said, bemused that Thor was here, shaking my hand.

"From beginning?"

"Start with rope descent from Quad."

Three sets of individual views popped up on the viewing wall, side by side by side. One was the camera on my suit, showing my hand holding the rappelling rope, the next was from another soldier's suit camera on the ground, and the last was from a camera probably on the Quad itself.

We watched, me shoving more crackers and cheese into my mouth, as the rescue unfolded.

"How did you get this?" Trinity asked, fascinated.

"No one told me I couldn't bring my AI, and since we were sending out the motherlode of EM signals anyway, I thought, what the heck. But the other two views were fed to my AI by one of the soldiers. I'm not sure which. Came in after the mission. Some of my treatment was a little rough and maybe one of the troops felt I deserved some help."

"Damn, son!" JJ said, as the firefight got fully involved. The other suit's camera kept me in focus much of the time, showing Rikki fighting in team mode with me, back to back, as we cleared out some of the aerial attackers. The footage froze as I turned toward the first bounding Tiger, the angle of the shot telling me it might have been either Corporal Boyle or Jossom whose suit was recording.

"That looks more like what I witnessed in the command center," Chester Flottercot said.

"Okay, your shooting really has improved," Astrid said, looking at me like I had a new haircut and she kind of liked it.

"Speaking of which, how did you guys do with the container?"

"Zone Def is still tallying, but the LAV was packed to the ceiling. Should be a real good payday for what was for us an hour's work," JJ said.

"And things are okay with the other Johnsons?" I asked, looking between the two of them.

"Yeah. Martin, as usual had some wiseass comments, but when we opened the container, he shut up," JJ said.

"Dad didn't say much, but I saw his eyes when we were unpacking. I suspect he would do it again," Astrid said, giving me a raised eyebrow.

"That was the easiest to get to of the two. The other one will take more planning. A lot more planning," I said. "Plus I have to meet with Zone Def tomorrow and help them with some stuff before they'll give me back my license."

"You don't need your license if we do more episodes like that one," Trinity said.

"I have a feeling that General Davis would still insist on Ajaya's participation. He'll have to put his time in, I'm afraid," Chester said. "And speaking of time, I believe we need to get going," he added, looking at the old-fashioned wristwatch on his arm. "Congratulations on making it out safely yet again, young Mr. Gurung."

I shook his hand, shook JJ's again, got a hug from Trinity and then a real nice hug from Astrid, and then the whole contingent left. Gabby shut the door behind them and whirled around to stare at me, her sister doing the same.

"Trinity said that she wants to do another interview, this time including all the Johnsons and… us too," Gabby said.

"She said they got a lot of comments from fans that want to see more of *us*," Monique added, leaving no doubt who she was talking about.

"Sure, probably a whole bunch of pervy boys that I'll need to beat up."

"No. For your information, all the boys at school are scared of you after they saw your shooting," Monique said.

"Except Billy Newson. He says thinks you're pretty cool," Gabby added.

Movement on the wall caught my eye. A bug or fly or something. I rolled up a fashion magazine. "What do you think, Mom? Should the twins be on the show again?" I asked as I stalked the little crawly creature. Its wings buzzed but my swing was true and I could actually feel the crunch under the magazine.

"Eww, AJ, that's gross. Glad I read that one already," Gabby said.

"I didn't," Monique said in slightly disappointed voice.

"I think it would be okay as long as they keep up to date with homework and chores," Mom said.

"Okay, I'll talk to Trinity," I said and was instantly swarmed with super-excited sisters. They broke the sound barrier with just their voices, then raced out of the living room to contact their friends on whatever social media platform they favored today.

"I'm serious. They get too much attention just being in school. Putting them on the show is going to bring creepers like flies," I said to my mom, pulling the magazine from the wall.

"Is the way of the world. Men of all ages like pretty young girls. You must protect them, Ajaya," Aama said.

"No, that's not fair to Ajaya. That's the point he's making now. They need to learn to protect themselves," Mom said to Aama.

The short, super sharp utility knife was suddenly in my grandmother's hand. "They have learned their own lessons in being Ghurka," Aama said.

"True, but they can't go around knifing everyone who looks at them. There'd be bodies everywhere. Astrid deals with exactly the same thing. We'll have her work with them, Ajaya. Don't worry," Mom said.

My mouth was still open at the fact that my grandmother had been teaching them to use a knife to defend themselves. I closed it, opened it to speak, then closed it again. Mom patted my arm. "Go change, dear. Maybe a shower as well. I'll bring you a tuna sandwich," she said with a gleam in her eye.

"No! I have tarkari for the boy," Aama said, her tone brooking no argument. Mom winked at me in full view of Aama but my grandmother just mumbled in a dark tone and headed to the kitchen.

"She doesn't like tuna?" I asked in a whisper.

"Victorious fighters don't get fed second-rate meals," Mom said, smiling. "Go get clean."

I glanced at the magazine and froze. The bug glittered, like metal.

"Give me that picture!" Gabby suddenly yelled from just behind me. I turned just as Monique slammed into me, her one hand grabbing my arm and spinning me between her and her twin. Gabby jumped forward, pushing both hands on either side of me, trying to reach whatever incriminating thing Monique held. She missed and her doppelgänger ran around me and then back toward their room, Gabby following and yelling. I looked down. The bug was gone from the magazine. Five minutes of searching the floor revealed nothing. I finally put the magazine down and headed to my own room.

Twenty minutes later I was in sweatpants and a t-shirt, eating an excellent if somewhat nuclear-hot dal over tarkari, sitting at my desk.

"Look up methotrexate."

"Belongs to a class of drugs known as antimetabolites. Used to treat some cancers or control severe psoriasis and rheumatoid arthritis."

Harper's mom had cancer? Or arthritis? Couldn't she find it in the Zone?

"What's the shelf life?"

"One year."

So how was she getting it before? Did her mom just get sick? Or did the tricky smart girl with the neuroprothesis have a way to get drugs in the Zone? Or a way to get in and out of the Zone? Past Zone Defense? No... there couldn't be something like that... could there?

Chapter 29

"Right on time. Very military of you, Ajaya," Yoshida said. I was seated in a waiting area and he was standing in a now open door that said *RESTRICTED* across its front. "Well, come on then," he said with a wave.

I followed him through the doorway and into a long, white, sterile-looking hallway. "I've got some things to show you. I think you'll be interested," he said, leading us past four or five doors before stopping at one. There was no lock or pass swipe or tag reader. Just three cameras, all pointing at us from three different directions. The door clicked open by itself and he pushed on through.

Inside, a big open lab area greeted us, intriguing in and of itself but made more so by the glass wall at the end that opened out to what looked like a massive test space.

He led me to a big worktable, where three people in civilian clothes were hovering around what looked like a drone.

"Aaron, Eric, and Maya, this is Ajaya," he said. "Ajaya, this is the dream team of drone design. Aaron has a doctorate in applied robotics, Eric is a design engineer who worked for two of the FANG companies, and Maya is one of the leading lights in neural network and machine learning. And they all know who you are."

"You reprogrammed a Berkut. How did you get past the CPU limitations?" Eric asked. He was tall, bearded, with curly brown hair and a slightly pudgy stomach.

"No, more importantly, how did you circumvent its core directives?" Maya asked, shoving forward. Petite to the point of childlike, she was dressed in jeans and a light sweater, possibly against the air-conditioned chill in the room, with skin just a hair lighter than mine. She definitely had India in her lineage.

"How do you stand such a clunky machine?" Aaron asked. He had a superior air, like he knew everything important and we would all be coming to him for the answers.

"Put in a set of new chips," I said to Eric, then turned to Maya, "which I trained on a gaming console before installing them, and," turning to Aaron, "it's the best toy in the sandbox. You got better?"

Eric and Maya both spoke at once, stopped to look at each other, and Aaron spoke into the opening.

"This right here," he said with a wave at the table.

The others parted enough for me to see what was spread out on the table. I almost started salivating.

"Meet the Decimator," Yoshida said from just behind my right ear.

It was a third larger than a Berkut, but had much of the same sleek delta shape. Thicker from underside to its top, I could see it held more rotors than Rikki did.

"Six fans?" I asked.

"Ten. All capable of multi-vector thrust," Aaron said, pointing to the back of the v-swept wings. Two smaller fans lined the back of each wing.

"It can climb and dive faster, turn tighter, detect other units from further away, has a longer flight range, greater battery capacity, quicker recharge time, multiple charge technologies, and carries both a high efficiency e-mag weapon and onboard micro missiles that are capable of airburst or hard target penetration," Aaron said, like the proud parent of a *summa cum laude* college grad.

"So what the hell do you need me for?" I asked.

Aaron frowned and started to open his mouth but Major Yoshida slipped a brawny arm around his shoulders, startling the scientist. "One on one, it's been unbeatable in all simulations and tests. But in multi-opponent battles, it loses two-thirds of the time. When paired with another drone, including the same model, or with a soldier, it doesn't achieve anywhere near the efficiency ratios the computer simulations say it should," the spec op warrior said, frowning.

"How do you train it?" I asked, looking closely at the lethal beauty on the table.

"We use the highest level simulations from the most advanced systems on the planet," Maya said. "How did you train yours?"

"Well, after I replaced his chips with more modern AI-based commercial units, I plugged him into the family gaming unit for three months."

"You what?" Eric asked.

"I customized all our video games to have a Rikki avatar that would partner with whoever was playing a game."

"What game?" Maya asked.

"All of them," I said, touching the matte black outer shell of the Decimator.

"Like first person shooters?" Eric asked.

"Yes, but also all the others. Everything in the family library. Then when anyone, usually me or my sisters, but sometimes Mom, played, Rikki partnered with them. He seemed to learn a lot from partners tennis, but obviously the team play in online competitions worked wonders."

"You put your drone online?"

"Yes. How else was he going to get exposed to as many other players as possible? Mostly it was him and me, but sometimes my sisters would join us in team play on Bleak or Lost Honor 45. Near the end of his training, I put him out on his own for about a week of battle-royale-type competitions. Also used some flight simulation programs to let him explore what his capabilities were after I upgraded some of his features. Then I took his CPU back into the Zone, upgraded old hardware in his shell, and we started some careful recon trips."

They all looked at me like I had three heads, then Yoshida started laughing. A real, deep, almost uncontrolled laugh. He caught himself and slowed it down, but he still needed to wipe the tears from the corners of his eyes. "I love this kid. You all have a billion-dollar supercomputer to hook into your beyond state-of-the-art combat aircraft and he takes his into online gaming competitions. Unfreaking believable."

They mostly looked embarrassed, although in Aaron's case, that look crossed over to a flicker of anger. Maya's chagrin changed to thoughtfulness and Eric just looked stunned.

"In the flight simulators, how did you model his capabilities?" Maya asked.

"I had him input his airframe's specs and aerodynamic features. He knew them way better than I ever would. He already had all the experiences of his earlier life stored in his hard drive. It's where we first worked out that ammo catch. When I finally took him into the Zone, we practiced it for real during slow moments when no other drone was near us."

"But wait, your online gaming would teach him to battle humans, but not other drones?" Aaron asked, an edge in his tone.

"Yup, and there's no more inconsistent opponent than a human. He learned to adapt and alter strategies and tactics on the fly. Although I'd bet you a thousand dollars that he wasn't the only machine in there. These games can go on for days, and some of the higher-ranked players demonstrate too much performance endurance to not have a bit of occasional computer help. Rikki even indicated when he thought a player was too consistently logical to be a human."

"You've totally personified it. You have no objectivity," Aaron said, almost in an *I gotcha* tone.

"Why do I need objectivity about it? Rikki is the tool that I depend on most to stay alive and thrive in the Zone. You ever been in the Zone, Aaron? You have any idea what it's like?" I asked.

"No of course not. I'm not stupid enough to go in *there*," he said.

"Well the major and I are, apparently, that stupid. We use what works," I said with a nod at Yoshida, who was staring holes in Aaron.

Awkward doesn't begin to describe that little moment in time. Eric and Maya actually took a step back away from Aaron, as he flushed red and looked anywhere but at Yoshida.

Maya finally asked if I would show her what games and programs I used, taking me to a work desk where the resident

AI projected a list as I stated them. Eric was quick to follow, which left Aaron to get a short, brutal lecture from the major.

"You went about this all wrong, at least according to doctrine, and your results are absolutely spectacular. When I saw the footage of you two fighting Zone drones back to back, it was like a glimpse of perfection. Total synergy between man and machine, and the result beat just machine," Maya said.

"You also need to take into account the inherent skill of the human in that scenario," Yoshida said, having left a quivering Aaron behind. "Not many operators have that level of shooting skill. You were seeing genetics, honed from an early age, combined with fantastic software housed in a pretty solid airframe design."

"Well, finding and training the human operator side is your job. Ours is to create similar programming in a superior drone," Eric said, smiling a little uneasily.

"Superior, huh? Show me," I said with a wave at the Decimator.

"Unit 19, bring all systems online," Eric said, a proud smile on his face.

With the slightest of hums, the Decimator lifted ten centimeters into the air and hovered absolutely still.

"Push down on it," Aaron suggested, finally joining us.

"What?"

"Put your hand on it and push down," he said, touching the top himself.

With a shrug, I reached over and pressed down on the drone. It didn't budge. I pushed harder. Not a wiggle, shift, shimmy, or dip. It was like it was sitting on a pillar of stone rather than columns of air.

"It could hold your body weight and lift you into the air," Eric said. "Our flight programming is so tight, it instantly compensates for the pressure you exert on it, in all directions."

"Unit 19, proceed to the test area," Maya said and the big drone slid silently through the air, crossing the room in a fast, smooth flight that had it at the glass door in about two seconds. A red light above the sliding glass door turned green and the door opened on its own, probably at the drone's direction, as no one made any gestures, commands, or touched any controls. The design team led me across the lab to the glass window and I could now see that they were very thick panes of some kind of polycarbonate.

Out in the test area, the Decimator was hovering on station, waiting.

"Albert, release four opponent drones," Yoshida said, earning himself a look from the others.

"Ah, four, Major?" Aaron asked.

"Worth the expense for our newest consultant to see what we got here," the major said. "Albert, first drone, one on one."

"Who's Albert?"

"Lab AI," Maya said.

"Who's personifying now?" I asked.

Outside, a panel opened in the far wall and four sleek US Kestrels zipped out into the big test room. Three took up stations by the wall, but the fourth moved directly into attack mode.

The Kestrel was pretty much current top-of-the-line hardware, or at least I would have said so before seeing the Decimator. About the same size as Rikki, they are disk shaped, like the old flying saucer trope, but in miniature. Fast, agile, and well armed, they are more than a match for a Berkut in tight quarters. In wide open space, the Berkut's speed and climbing rate outperform, but then the Russian unit would find itself up against the big jet-powered Renders.

Unit 19 instantly reacted to the Kestrel's threatening approach, sliding sideways through the air while spinning to fire at the disk. The Kestrel zigged and zagged, avoiding the first two shots, but got tagged with the third. Bright, zombie green paint covered its surface, the other two paintball rounds patterning right on the glass in front of us.

"Kill shot scored," a voice said over the speakers.

"Assault, three on one," Yoshida said. What followed was a violent, swirling dogfight that ended after about twelve seconds with two green-splashed Kestrels and one blue-painted Decimator.

"See what I mean?" Yoshida asked.

"Rikki would have lost too," I said.

"Only because Kestrels have better close combat maneuverability. Unit 19 was designed to exceed Kestrels at close quarters and anything else in open airspace. Plug your software into that drone and I think it would have cleaned house," Yoshida said. "So how can we get from here to there?"

I spent the next four hours brainstorming with the team, studying what they had done to date and making suggestions. Then Yoshida released me to my own devices, leaving me with a whirling mind and a free afternoon.

Chapter 30

"What did you say you wanted this for?"

"I didn't. And I'd just as soon not," I said.

"You realize I could get in ginormous trouble for this, right?" Dr. Lynn Coffey asked, one eyebrow arched in mild disapproval. She leaned down for a facial recognition scan before sending the prescription.

"It's not like it's an opioid or something," I said.

She snorted. "You'd have to be signed up for a licensed monitoring program *before* I could even issue that prescription. No chance of getting your hands on any of that."

"What if I said this will help me survive the Zone?"

A double snort this time. "How? Removing psoriasis on your gun hand?"

"Haha. I wouldn't ask if it wasn't important."

She put a hand on her hip and studied me with a serious expression. "That one, I actually believe. Can't imagine any reason for it in the Zone, unless it's to treat Brad Johnson's perpetual scowl. Honestly, he's damned lucky you like his daughter or the whole family would be toast."

"Why does everyone keep saying that?" I griped. Dr. Coffey had asked my dad and me to retrieve a prototype treatment device from her old office at the Manhattan Eye, Ear, and Throat hospital. This was like seven years ago and she had credited the device with changing the lives of hundreds of people dealing with semi-circular canal dehiscence, which I didn't really know much about. She's been volunteering to do favors for me ever since. I haven't had much need of an ENT specialist, so this was maybe the first big thing I'd asked for.

She smirked at me. "Oh I don't know, maybe because you hang on her every word, follow her with your eyes, and focus on her like she's the only person in the world."

"You got all that from like two episodes?"

"Ajaya, there are whole discussion boards dedicated to the topic of you and Astrid. People rooting for you two to be a couple, some root against it, you know... typical fan crap."

"She has fans. No one even really knows me," I said.

"You don't keep up with current events much, do you?" she said. "Honestly, Ajaya, you gotta pay a little attention to this stuff. And you've been in *three* episodes and the government mentioned you were a consultant on the Destroyer rescue. I hope the Flottercots are paying you well, 'cause they're making money off you hand over fist. What's your agent say?"

"Agent?"

"Ajaya Gurung, tell me you have an agent!"

"Don't even know any."

"And they haven't been coming out of the woodwork trying to sign you?" she asked.

I shrugged. "AI, any queries from media agents?"

"Thirty-seven emails with agent listed in either subject line, signature line, or body of message."

"Oh."

Doc Coffey just lifted her light gray eyebrow again.

"Hey, I've been busy," I protested.

"And now dealing in elicit medications?"

"Oh, not elicit... I've got a prescription," I said triumphantly. She frowned. "Trust me. It's Zone stuff."

She sighed. "Alright. Don't make me regret this. And get an agent already, would you?"

I nodded, gave her my biggest smile, and headed out the door. A four-hour work day for the gubmint left me with lots of afternoon to get errands done.

Next, I headed to the surplus shop where I get my stealth suits. It's one of those stores where olive drab is the main decorative paint color and every thing is festooned with ammo cans, mannequins wearing military load-bearing gear and gas masks, camouflage netting hanging on the back wall, and in this case, a beat-to-shit Humvee parked out front. The proprietor is a short, surly guy whose family emigrated here from Greece sometime in the late nineties. The funny thing is I don't think he was ever in any branch of any military. He was leaning over his counter, talking to a heavily tattooed individual who was wearing Multicam cargo pants and an overly tight black tank top.

"Hey Egan," I said, glancing around at the merchandise.

"Well, well, well. If it isn't the celebrity his own self," Egan said with a frown. The customer he was talking to leaned back to take me in, no expression on his face.

I waved off his comment. "Eh, so I've had my fifteen seconds. That and ten dollars will be me a coffee at Starbucks."

He raised one bushy eyebrow, considering, but otherwise the owner of Egan's Army-Navy store was a blank. Mr. Camo-tattoo was even blanker.

"Whatcha need?" Egan finally asked.

"Another stealth suit."

"Already? You just got the last one like four months ago?" he protested.

I waved at the old plasma screen on one wall. "As I keep telling people... I've been busy. You got one my size? Otherwise I gotta order it and I hate drone deliveries."

"Yeah, yeah, you know I do. I'll start looking for the next one right after I sell you this one. Gotta tell you, Ajaya, they're getting harder to find. Sold all my other sizes within two days of your first episode," he said, pulling back from the counter.

I expected him to head in back, which is where he always kept them before. Instead, he came out around the counter and moved toward the middle of the room, behind a rack of mall ninja paintball gear. I followed and once I moved past the rack of facemasks and plastic bags of multicolored paint balls, I saw a new display, almost in the center of the room. A brown mannequin wore an older model stealth suit with a fake sniper rifle slung over one shoulder. Hanging from a string off the ceiling was a plastic kit model of a Berkut drone, suspended over the dummy's head.

"Really?" I asked.

255

"You like? My boy Basil put it together like a year ago. Took it out of his room last night and hung it up this morning," he said, pointing at the model drone.

"You put that whole display together after I was on *Zone War?*" I asked. Then I saw the sign, stuck to the mannequin's back. *Get your gear where the Zone Sniper shops!*

"Zone Sniper? And you *are* not going to try and sell me that outdated piece of shit, are you?"

"Hey, it's marketing, baby. Adapt or die, am I right?" he said with a grin. "And no, I'm not selling you that thing. Have some faith, would ya?"

There was a footlocker by the display dummy's legs, covered with a swatch of camo cloth and stacked with expensive hiking socks and several pairs of combat boots. He pulled all the stuff off the top, revealing a lock on the trunk, which he opened with a combination. Out came a plastic-wrapped bundle, which he handed over.

I pulled it out and inspected it, looking for defects and damage. It was brand new. Actually, it was one of the newest versions, current issue.

"Where'd you get this?" I asked, eyebrows high.

"I, ah, made new connections since you bought your last one. Got that special. Cost an arm and a leg though," he said, shooting a suddenly nervous glance at the other customer, who was watching us like we were Monday Night Football. Ah, connections. Buying straight from the military, or at least people who worked for the military.

"Alright. Great, let's tag it and bag it."

"What else do you need? Knives? Hey, you need a new kukri?"

"No Egan, just the suit," I said, making the gestures that instructed my AI to pay the bill.

"Come on, how about shooting glasses? Got the latest with built-in range finders and ballistic compensation systems."

"Nope. That stuff will get me killed in the Zone," I said. "Wait, you got any .458 SOCOM ammo?"

"I think I might," he said, not bothering to ask where I would have picked up such a gun.

We arrived back at the counter, where the tattooed dude was still observing us. Egan went behind the counter and stuffed my suit into a proper biodegradable shopping bag, then rooted around, finding a couple of boxes of ammo that he held up to me. I nodded.

Mr. Tattoo was staring at me, and it felt aggressive. "Can I help you with something?" I asked, turning to him.

Amused, he shook his head. "Just seeing what all the fuss is about," he said, pausing to look me up and down. I fought the urge to pull out my blade from its sheath hanging down my back.

"What fuss?" I said, turning away from him in dismissal.

"All this sniper crap. You weren't even in the military, so how can you be a *real* sniper?" the guy asked, eyebrow raised.

"Right? That's what *I* keep saying. But you make a bunch of shots, kill a few thousand drones all by yourself, without a tattoo in sight, and suddenly people label you," I said.

Egan froze in the act of handing over the bag, eyes flicking from mine to the guy standing a meter to my right. Tension radiated off the dude, who had to be ex-military, based on at least three of his tats. I kept my eyes on Egan, but I was hyper aware of the danger to my right.

"Hah!" the dude suddenly barked out, clearly half of a laugh. "Hahaha, you aren't what I expected. All business, no nonsense. And some backbone. I like him," he said to Egan, thumb pointed my way. "I'm Tony. You need anything that Egan can't get you, *anything* at all, you have him let me know. Got it?"

"Yeah, ah, great."

"I gotta run. I'll get more of those lined up, Egan," Tony said, pointing at the bag as he turned to leave.

"Yeah, great, Tony. See ya around," Egan said, smiling uncharacteristically.

Tony left and, after watching to see that the door had closed behind him, Egan turned back to me. "Whew! Didn't know how he was going to react to you. He's been a doubter. But I kept telling him, *Tony, this kid is the real deal. Not some actor type,* I says."

"One of your... suppliers?"

"Yeah. For tricky stuff. State-of-the-art stuff. He meant what he said. You need something special, something maybe not easily obtained, and he's the guy."

"Cool. Always good to know a guy, right?"

"Yeah. Especially going into the friggin' places you go."

An hour later, I was home, going over the new suit, adjusting its fit, transferring bits of gear from my beat-to-shit one, when my mom came home.

"Ajaya, I was hoping to catch you. Can we talk?"

"Sure, Mom. What's up? Is this why you're home early?"

"Yes, plus my boss gave me the afternoon. Seems our recent fame, mostly yours, has been a bit disruptive at work. Partly what I want to talk to you about," she said, sitting on the edge of my bed.

"Cool. What's up?"

"Ajaya, I want you to think about quitting the Zone," she said. I started to speak, but she held up a hand. "Before you go on about money, let's talk about the state of our finances. We're flush. Better than that, even. Between what you've been paid by the show and our part of the joint recovery, we have a real solid slug of money."

"But the twins will have college coming up?"

"I've been investing part of every month's income since, well, since you father and I got married. Grandpa's been advising me. We've done real well. College is paid for, and with this new money, you could take a year off. Plus, I think Trinity would hire you as an on-air consultant for the show. She said that fans loved the back and forth you had with Cade."

I didn't know what to say, my mind reeling. "I just got my license back," I said, although what that had to do with anything, I couldn't say. Then I thought of Harper and the bottle of drugs I had just picked up at the pharmacy. "Okay, let me think about it. I've got some things I have to clean up in there, some stuff to attend to. And I have to figure out what to do about Rikki. I couldn't just leave him in there."

A frown crossed her face, but a frown of worry. Then she smiled a sad little smile. "Think about it."

"Oh, I already am. I didn't know we were doing that well. You didn't really say."

"Well, I know you don't trust the stock market so I haven't exactly paraded the numbers, plus I don't want the girls getting ideas that we're wealthy or anything, because we're not. But we are, I think, independent. The sooner you stop going into that awful place, the better."

"Alright. Let me think about it and what I'd need to do to wrap up. Can I see the numbers?" I asked.

"I've already had my AI send them to yours," she said, patting my shoulder as she stood up. "It would be a huge burden off all of us not to have you go in anymore. Me, your grandmother, and your other grandparents, and the twins. They don't show it to you, but they are nervous wrecks every time you go in. They have to sleep with me when you're out overnight."

"What? They sleep in your bed? Nobody ever said anything."

"Because you already carry more pressure and responsibility than anyone your age should."

"Oh. I knew they stayed home from school, but I didn't realize it was that scary for them," I said.

"Ajaya, it's that scary for all of us. When you and your father failed to come home for two nights and then you finally made out but he was... gone, well, it about broke all of us. If they knew you were going in to get college money, they would both

260

refuse to go. When we watched the show the other day, when you went in with the Johnsons, well, both of them were so anxious they had to have their sleep blankets with them."

"What? Those tired old scraps of blanket are still around? I thought they got thrown out years ago."

"No, and they would kill me for letting you know, but those little crutches are still around, mostly, I think, because of the Zone."

Societal fear and anxiety reached incredible proportions after Drone Night, but articles I had read indicated it was gradually declining year by year. Yet my own family was suffering from it and I hadn't stopped to even consider the effect on my outwardly confident little sisters.

"Mom, like I said, I have some things I feel obligated to clean up in there, but maybe after that, I can stop going in," I said.

"You have immense talent and potential, Ajaya, not just for hunting the Zone, but for life outside that death trap. I've been waiting with little patience for this time to arrive. Please, please drop the Zone, for all of our sakes."

She bent down and hugged me where I sat, then, with a sad smile, slipped out the door, leaving me to my work and my thoughts.

Chapter 31

I inserted the next morning after the twins had gone to school, intending to be in and out in record time. True to his word, Yoshida had reinstated my credentials and I was able to draw my Five-Seven out of the local precinct house with no troubles. I left the MSR, opting to carry the .458 SOCOM, collapsed down to its smallest size and carried in the discreet case I had snagged from the Defense base.

I had been overusing the Battery Park entrance recently, a practice I had assiduously avoided till now. AIs are experts at pattern recognition, and the drone AIs were particularly skilled at hunting humans through predictable patterns, so I was really, really nervous when I exited, standing behind the armored door while I whistled my call.

But I didn't have to hide Rikki from Zone Defense anymore and, in fact, they were very interested to record my use of his senses and shooting skills inside the danger area. He dropped down from almost just to the west of the entrance, hovering over my head about three seconds after my whistle.

"No drones detected in immediate proximity, Ajaya," he said. I still wasn't ready for his casual use of my name. It made me want to check his coding, but now was very obviously not the time or place.

"Target is the Exchange. Monitor sensors for anomalies or holes in sensor data, specifically the female encountered last mission."

"Affirmative. Will watch for sensor-cloaked human named Harper."

Again with the names. Not like him at all.

262

"Any Spider CThree activity?"

"Unit Lotus has been active below Worth Street. Last activity logged was a directive to this unit's id to patrol Wall Street and Battery Park area. Status queries occur on average every forty-three minutes."

Handy that the Spider had assigned Rikki, in his other Berkut electronic disguise, as the only lookout for this part of the Zone. Of course, why allocate more resources when a single Berkut was as good as a half-dozen other models together?

We moved up the ramp from the tunnel and I was very conscious of the cameras watching our every move. Rikki swung out on sweep patterns of his own devising, essentially circling me but using elliptical arcs. From overhead, it would look like the petals of a symmetrical flower, or a kid's drawing using one of those spirograph toys.

Soon enough, we arrived at the Exchange and Rikki, after a final sweep, folded into his ball form, hovering down next to me while I eyeballed the doors.

"No anti-personnel units detected. No Harper anomalies detected."

"Let's do it," I said, pushing the door open, leading with the thick, stubby barrel of the .458. Dangerous entry was likely the exact reason that the gun's former owner had the weapon. And despite Rikki's assurances, some ground drones could put themselves into a form of airplane mode and not show up on his network. Granted, he was actively pinging them with IFF protocols and they should respond, but this was the Zone and you took nothing for granted.

The entry was empty and quiet, dim and gloomy, as the only light came from the cloudy sky outside. We moved through till we got to the door Harper had come out of before. Carefully, because if it had been *my* door, *I* sure would have booby-trapped the shit out of it, I went through. No trip wires, no pressure switches, no passive light sensors. Just stairs leading down and up. Personally, I'd live below grade every damned day in the Zone. Every apartment dweller on the island either rushed out or died in place. Windows were no deterrent at all to killer machines that could shoot, stab, or pound through body armor. And if you were hiding from aerial fliers, it might be wise to take a page from rabbits and groundhogs and live in holes. There's probably a primordial reason why humans had once used caves.

I cracked a chemical light stick and loaded it into a chest-mounted holder that let me control how much of the pale green light shone by twisting a knob on top. Like a modern day shuttered lantern of cold light. Bought it at Egan's. Probably should have bought more light sticks when I was there. Oh, well. Hopefully I wouldn't need so many in the near future if I got to retire from the Zone.

The downstairs seemed to have held a barbershop, among other things, but there were signs that someone had lived here for a while. A while in the past. A light dust covered the floor and the empty cots set up along one wall, and the same dust lay on the metal shelves that held plates, silverware, and cups, all clearly scavenged from one of the Exchange's restaurants or cafeterias. A few papers were scattered on the floor, most of which seemed to be hand-drawn circuit diagrams and notes in a tight, tiny script that I had trouble reading by the dim light of the chem stick.

Tracks of a smallish foot showed where Harper had come through the room on occasion, but wherever she and her mom lived now, it wasn't here.

"Harper anomaly detected. Approaching from far exit door, descending stairwell," Rikki said in very low volume. His machine whisper.

I placed my light stick holder on a shelf to light the room, then stepped back toward the corner, leaving Rikki hovering in full view. Rifle barrel pointed at the floor but weapon held ready. The door opened slowly and a now familiar face looked in, lit by her own light stick, although hers was an industrial-sized one. She spotted Rikki instantly, then turned till she found me in the shadows.

"You're scarier than the machines," she said.

"Hardly. I brought you some methotrexate."

She looked at me, clearly making an effort to control her expressions. I saw surprise and maybe something that was pleasure before she got blankness back in place.

"Well, that's... useful," she allowed.

"You moved?" I asked, waving around at the abandoned stuff.

"Six months ago."

I raised both eyebrows and waited.

She fidgeted, reluctance written all over her. Finally, "The Spiders got aggressive, started to come through with drone battle groups. We retreated to a deeper hideout."

"They were looking for you? Even with the neuroprothesis?"

"Normal drones can never find me, but the Spiders are different... more powerful. They noticed... something... when I

265

was around them. I don't try to redirect them like the lesser ones."

"You can actually direct a drone?"

"Not like giving it a command, but I can generally redirect its attention elsewhere."

"Can you do that with Rikki?"

"That's a stupid name for a killer drone."

"But can you redirect him?"

She crossed her arms over her chest and stared at me. Maybe glared. "No. No, I can't. Whatever the hell you did to it messed up the overrides I use. I was able to cloud him a bit, before. Doubt it now."

"Can you redirect a Spider?"

"Hell no! Are you crazy? It would be suicide to even try," she said, looking at me like she'd already answered her own question.

"Right, I get it. They have a lot more computing power," I said.

"No, they have orders of magnitude more power," she said, frowning like I was an idiot.

I frowned back. "I've read the specs forward and backward. No way are they *that* powerful."

"No, you read the specs for *the standard* model. These were customized prior to release."

"What? I never heard anything about that. Where are you getting this from?"

"My mother."

"And how would she know?"

"Because she's the one that customized them. Oh, and she wants to meet you. So come on," she said, uncrossing her arms and turning toward the door she'd come through. I was so startled by her little bombshell that I paused for a second to process. In that moment, she disappeared out the door and I had to hustle to catch up, following Rikki, who hadn't shown any hesitation.

Moving faster then I ever did in the Zone, she led us upstairs, through the building, out another door, and into the building next to the Exchange. She twisted and wove through the new building, moving with surety and a fascinating sort of grace. Manhattan buildings are really big and even though we stayed on the ground floor, we still had to twist through hallways and doors and long-abandoned offices that looked ready to open for the day's work. Finally, we came to a side door that led out onto Broad Street. Some of the ever-present city scaffolding greeted us like old friends, shielding us from the air. There was more across the street.

She stopped at the edge of the metal framework, looking at her watch intently.

I glanced at Rikki, who hovered two feet to my right and about four feet off the ground.

"Units present?" I asked him.

"*None,*" he said, as she said, "None," at exactly the same time.

"Then why are we waiting?"

" A Google satellite is passing over right now. They tap it for Zone images."

"Who does?"

She ignored the question, nodding at whatever time she now saw and heading across the street, ducking under the next layer of construction framework.

"So you can sense drones in the network?" I asked.

She gave me a quick, sour glance as if the answer was patently obvious. Which, in hindsight, it kinda was. She just told me that her mom had worked on the Spiders. She told me she could redirect drones. And she had known there was no drone activity at the same time as Rikki. Ergo—yes, she could sense them. Maybe I should just keep my mouth shut for the moment and try to preserve some illusion of intelligence.

Across the street, we entered the ground-level door of the massive building and immediately headed into the stairwell. She led me down into the basement and through two more doors. Big panels of wire mesh fencing lay down across the floor, with panels on both walls and even the ceiling forming a short, two-meter tunnel of metal. Heavy wires led off into the walls ahead of us. Nope, that wasn't standard building code for New York. Somebody had built a trap.

"How do you know it's safe?"

She pointed at a small green plastic light on the right wall. It was dark. Clever to use a normal all-clear signal as a danger telltale.

"Drones would sense the power if it was on. So when it's armed, there is just a very minimal charge flowing through it. But it triggers if anything comes near the fencing. You know... passive sensing like a high security fence at a military base. Soon as it senses any object, it turns up the juice and fries it."

On the other side of the mesh tunnel, we came to a heavy steel fire door that looked like someone had thoroughly reinforced it with more steel. The plates were bolted on, not welded. She walked to the left side of the door and pulled on the plastic switch plate. It opened, revealing an empty space bereft of a single wire. She reached her finger in and did something, which resulted in a clicking sound at the door itself. Her right hand gave the door a pull and it opened right up. Some kind of mechanical latch.

The other side of the door was a mini-wall of concrete blocks, cemented together, reaching a third of a meter off the floor. We had to step over it and our feet landed on a heavy cement backer board that had a cable running from its far end up to over the doorway above us. I paused to look at it, realizing that the room was lit with electric lights, twelve-volt version by the look of the string of them suspended overhead.

"Secondary defense. To give us more time. Cable is attached to a stretched garage door spring. Triggering it will yank the panels up into place against the cinder block frame I made around the door, and then that wooden beam drops down behind it, wedging it against the blocks," she said.

The concrete block wall was actually a frame all up both sides of the door. The top was headed with a heavy piece of steel that I wondered how she'd lifted. Against the inside wall, about a meter up, was a square beam of wood, a four by four, whose end had a bolt through it, and the top was held from falling by a rope. So the cement panels (and I now saw there were two of them together) would cover the block frame opening and then the four-by-four would drop into brackets.

"It won't hold for long, but it will buy us some time," a new voice said.

I turned and found myself looking at an older version of Harper, rolling up to us in a wheelchair. Same brown, upward tilted eyes, same dark hair, but streaked with gray and thinning to the point of exposing some of her scalp. All of her exposed skin was covered in blotchy patches of thick, hardened tissue.

"I'm Dr. Theodora Wilks."

I only paused for a heartbeat, then stepped forward with a hand out, holding the package of prescription drugs. "Nice to meet you, ma'am. I'm Ajaya Gurung."

"Of course you are. Not like you haven't been plastered all over the Internet these past few weeks. We have access to that, you know? What's that?" she asked, not making any move to reach for the drugs.

Harper stepped up and took the package from me.

"Fresh methotrexate, Mother," she said, holding the package up for her mother to read. "High dosage, too."

"Ah, Harper told you about the systemic scleroderma," Dr. Wilks said.

"No, Mother. He asked if he could bring us anything... I told him this," Harper said. "Didn't think he'd actually do it."

"Will it help? The medicine? Will it help your scleroderma?" I asked.

"It's a Band-Aid. Helps with the skin tightening, but there is no cure for what I have. I'm hardening from the inside out," she said, a fierce light in her eyes. "It's part of the reason we stay in here. Too hard to move me."

"We could get you out, ma'am. Harper and me. Or I could maybe arrange a lift in an LAV?"

She shook her head. "I can't move fast enough to evade my fate either outside or here." She waved a hand around at the room and I noticed it was decorated in a glitzy, gaudy manner. Red velvet and lots of gold paint, but all faded like it was that way from before the Zone. Like a high-class brothel.

"What does that mean, ma'am? Harper mentioned a *them*. Who would be out to get you?" I asked, putting the question of the garish room's purpose out of my mind.

"The people who caused all this," she said, her right hand moving slightly off the arm of the chair in what might have been a wave.

"The Gaia Group? They're all dead," I said.

She gave me a tight little smirk of a smile. "That old obfuscation? Garbage, rubbish, misdirection. A bunch of overzealous fanatics who got caught up in bigger plots."

I couldn't stop the frown that I felt form on my face. "You're saying the Gaia Group didn't release the drones?"

"Oh, they did. At least, a small faction of them did. But the bulk of the group had no part in it. They didn't have anywhere near the funding to purchase state-of-the-art autonomous combat units," she said. "And certainly not twenty-five thousand of them. Pull up a seat, young warrior, and listen to the truth of the matter."

I looked around for a stool or something, but Harper was already bringing over a couple of folding chairs. I sat down and Rikki hovered over and latched onto my shoulder, pausing his fans to conserve power.

Dr. Wilks' eyes zeroed in on him and she studied the Berkut with fierce focus. "An excellent choice for a guard dog. The Russians achieved a subtle blend of efficiency and art when they designed it. Most of their other stuff was meh. But the Berkut is surprisingly elegant. I would love to have you tell me about how and what you did to bring it into the light, so to speak. But there isn't time. Where was I?" she asked Harper.

"About to reveal the real people behind Drone Night," her daughter said.

"Right. So, Ajaya, I worked here on Wall Street, employed by the New York Stock Exchange. I'm an expert on machine learning and AI systems, and my job was to keep the Exchange up with the latest changes and advances in the field. Several of the Exchange members approached me after I had been here for several years. They had a side venture involving drone technology and offered me a ridiculous amount of money if I could upgrade four Chinese units."

"The Spider CThrees," I said.

"Yes, you know this part already," she said with a frown at her daughter. Harpers only shrugged, busy getting a glass of water and some of the new pills ready.

"It was a challenge, you see. Mostly theoretical, but they gave me the four units to work on, and I did. Harmless venture, with limitless applications, plus, you know, the money. Single mom with an eight-year-old daughter living in the expensive Big

Apple. Who wouldn't? Especially if you'd just been diagnosed with terminal systemic scleroderma."

"You had to provide for your daughter."

"Yes, and you can't really buy life insurance *after* you get that kind of diagnosis. So I needed to build assets quickly."

"You improved the Spiders beyond original specifications?"

"Oh, Ajaya, I improved them beyond anyone's wildest dreams. I'm the one who named them and built their neural nets."

"You named them for Chinese flowers?"

Her eyes widened. "You know their names?" Her eyes flicked to Rikki. "Ah, but your double agent there would have known them, wouldn't it?"

"It's how they designate themselves. I've only had run-ins with Lotus, but the other two are out there."

"Oh yes they are, and nasty pieces of work, like Lotus is. Anyway, I had all but finished the work, with just a bit to go when my employers came and demanded the drones. I needed more time. They wouldn't hear of it. I knew they were businessmen; I didn't know they were killers too. We argued, one of their goons hit me with a baton and knocked me out. Harper was here that day, her babysitter sick. She was playing in my office and they didn't know. I shudder to think how differently things could have gone if they had found her. Anyway, when I woke up, Harper was crying and trying to rouse me. I cleaned up the head wound and we almost left but, at the last minute, I decided to check the news for maybe some grand announcement about new technology or something. Imagine my surprise when I heard that Manhattan was under attack by drones."

"Why? And who were they?"

"I'll answer the second first. They were a mixture of the wealthy elite. Many Americans, but I think quite a few from all over the world. The point-one percent. Mega rich who wanted to be even richer."

"They shorted the market?" I guessed.

"They did. Society was having a lot of conversations at the time about income and wealth inequality. Socialists were making inroads on the Democrat side, mostly by talking about redistributing wealth, taxing the rich, breaking up the mega-techs, even bringing up the idea of government seizure of the biggest companies. Fringe groups popped up, talking about revolting against the new world order. So this group decided to pop the pimple themselves, knock the markets into the dirt, making money all the way down, then buying back in at the bottom."

"But weren't they already at the top? Why go through all that and kill hundreds of thousands of people?"

"This group was near the top, but not quite at the top. And they had a certain set of shared beliefs, followed a particular manifesto. Many had been in politics, many near the top of Fortune 500 companies, some in the military, and others in powerful positions in the intelligence arm of the government. They disagreed with the folks at the very top, were tired of waiting for their turn to take over. They hated the tech billionaires, although many of them had ridden the coattails of the Bezos, Jobs, and Zuckerbergs to gain their own wealth and power. At the time, I thought they were all just greedy, but over the last ten years, I've gotten more figured out. They saw their own core members as people vital to the continuation of their countries, and conversely saw many of their peers as bloated ticks sucking the lifeblood of the world. Disliked most immigrants and almost all Wall Street fat cats equally. So they wanted to do some redistributing of their own. Mostly to themselves, but also to the poor. Knock the ultra rich power center of America's biggest city on its ass, create a Super Recession, give the world a common enemy to band against, restructure an ailing political system that was too easy for outside forces to manipulate. Then they would step forward with ideas that had been thought out years in advance, with wealth preserved and created when the markets fell. Put themselves at the top."

"They created the Universal Basic Income," I guessed.

"Exactly. Paid for by the extra corporate tax on any company over five hundred billion dollars in market capitalization."

"And they would kill you?"

"In a New York second. They think I'm dead, knocked out and left for Drone Night to finish off. But I programmed those Spiders. I had backdoor access. I kept them away from this area long enough for us to create shelters, gather supplies, and fortify our positions. I had been working on cybernetic interface devices on my own time for years. With my condition, I needed a way for us, but mostly Harper, to be safe in the Zone. She's been wearing successive versions of that prosthesis for the last ten years."

"So the entire Attack was a false flag event, constructed by the people who should have prevented it. Wait, you said that you *had* backdoor codes to the Spiders? You don't anymore?"

"My adopted offspring are far too advanced to be put off by a little trick of coding. They self-corrected it within the first month. I only used it a couple of times, and even then I was ultra careful to avoid being blatant about it. Just some very,

very subtle suggestions to stay away from the Exchange. They still found the weak spot and eliminated it. Luckily I implanted a deep suggestion to ignore the wearer of the prosthesis so they don't see or sense Harper. No drones do."

"That one does," Harper said, pointing to Rikki. She had been quietly moving about the room, getting meds and water for her mother, picking up and putting away clutter. Now she was focused on the conversation.

"What do you mean?" Dr. Wilks asked, frowning.

"It was expecting me before I opened the door," Harper said, turning to me.

"I asked Rikki to look for any real-time data holes in his sensor information. He found missing data and quickly learned that it was Harper. So he tracks her by a complete lack of data, rather than too much data. Seemed like an obvious trick. Wonder why your super Spiders didn't figure it out?"

A massive explosion rocked the room, bulging the steel door inward till it clanged against the short cement block wall.

Chapter 32

Dust fell and at least two of the twelve-volt lights on the overhead string were broken.

"Spider unit Lotus has entered the building's ground floor. Sensors indicate six ground units in next room. None of them are on the network," Rikki said as Harper picked herself up and ran to the wall by the door. She hit a big lever and somewhere, a spring twanged. The cement panels lifted up and slapped into the block frame, the four-by-four falling down to brace it. She hit another switch and I heard a heavy motor start somewhere.

"The building generator still functions. There's enough natural gas in the lines to power the mesh tunnel for about ten minutes or so. We need to leave," Harper said, running across the room to a pair of small backpacks on a shelf.

"You two need to get out of here," Dr. Wilks said. Her daughter spun around to stare at her, eyes wide with disbelief and fear. "No, I cannot go with you. I will not go with you. You have a very limited chance as it is if Lotus has found us. I will stay here and delay them. You will take the escape tunnel."

"No, Mother. I won't leave you," Harper said.

"Harper darling, use your brain, not your heart. I didn't hang on to life this long just to ensure a chance for you to live and then have you throw it away. You have an ally, one who owes you a debt." Dr. Wilks looked me in the eye with a pointed stare, before turning back to Harper. "You *have* to seize this opportunity to live."

"No. No, I don't want to," Harper said, dropping the packs and rushing to her mother's wheelchair. "We'll either find a way to

fight or die trying. Ajaya has killed thousands of drones before,"
she said, hugging her mother.

Outside, a steady, rhythmic, mechanical pounding started on
the metal door.

*"A Tiger unit has succeeded in bypassing the electrocution
barrier,"* Rikki said.

Dr. Wilk's stiff, patchy face scrunched up with emotion as she
hugged Harper back. Then her right arm came up from a pouch
on the side of the chair and plunged a small hypodermic syringe
into her daughter's back. Harper had time to raise her head and
stare at her mother with shocked, betrayed eyes, which then
slipped shut as she collapsed across her mother's lap.

"Stubborn girl," Dr. Wilks said, trembling arms holding Harper
in a feeble clasp. "Now," she said, raising her face to look me in
the eye, "you must take her and put her in the escape pod."
She pointed at the far wall, which had an unassuming door in its
center.

"Pod?"

"That generator is also powering a pressure pump that's forcing
carbon dioxide into a rather large piston. When triggered, it will
push a wheeled sled of sorts through a one-block tunnel at an
estimated fifteen to twenty miles an hour. You will coast to a
stop just about directly under the Trump building."

"What?"

"The tunnel was built in secret for a rich man to come here for
clandestine assignations. I'll leave it to your imagination as to
what happened here. Now hurry. You don't have time," she
said.

"Dr. Wilks, I'm not in the habit of leaving people behind," I said.

"No, you are in the habit of surviving the most dangerous land on the planet. You *will* get Harper out of here, you *will* take her out of the Zone, and you *will* help her start her life. Please?" she asked, her self-assured confidence cracking at the end.

I heard steel tearing behind the cement panel.

"Tiger unit has breached the outer door, Ajaya. Additional units have entered behind it. Evacuation is advised," Rikki said.

"Go! I will wait and trigger a final defense. I promise you, and you can assure Harper when she wakes, that I won't feel a thing. She built the bomb, so she should understand. I have only a few weeks or maybe a month or two of this life at best anyway. Better to die fighting... protecting that which I love most, rather than fade away, soiling myself in a camp cot. Now hurry! Open that door!"

She still cradled her daughter in her weak arms as I crossed the room and pulled open the door. A battery-powered LED came on, casting a white light on a small tunnel. Maybe three feet tall, it was round except the floor, which was flat and embedded with a single piece of rail. The sled that waited was a very professional piece of work, looking like the bastard child of a bobsled and a giant kids' wagon. Constructed of carbon fiber, aluminum, and plastic, it was locked onto the monorail with a mutant set of wheels.

"Quickly. Take Harper, your stuff, and your drone. You'll have to lay down with her on top of you. The original design carried one large adult human in the compartment, using electrically powered motors to turn the wheels. Not enough power, nor will the generator last that long. Hence the piston. Now come get her."

I took the unconscious girl from her mother's still clinging arms, the crippled doctor giving her a last kiss on the top of her head. Tears streaked the woman's face but her eyes were hard and bright. She handed me a small data drive as I hefted the girl. "This is for later."

Carrying Harper in my arms, I got to the cart and awkwardly set her down, leaning her against the side of the thing. My rifle went into the partially protected space that was shaped like a human form. Then I climbed in, pulling the surprisingly heavy girl in on top of me. Rikki hovered nearby, carrying my pack in his extruded talons. Harper's gear was between my feet, leaving room for Rikki to settle on the girl's back while I held her warm body in my arms. Dr. Wilks had, in the meantime, somehow wheeled herself to a panel next to the tunnel door.

"Your cart can't come off the rail, but you *could* fall off, or worse, drop my daughter. Don't drop my daughter, Ajaya Gurung, or I *will* find a way to haunt you. The ride should be quick. The tunnel will be caved in by a small charge after the piston propels you. Then the main charge will go off. With luck, I'll take Lotus with me. Goodbye," she said, only now she wasn't looking at me but the form of her daughter in my arms. A single tear trickled out of the corner of her eye. Then her hand pushed sharply forward. A giant's hammer slammed into the sled, the lights went out, and we were rocketing through the darkness.

Chapter 33

The sled made a hell of a racket as it went, but not enough to drown out the boom behind us. Two seconds later, the ground *bounced*, the rail flexing under us as the ground shook and a much greater, much more serious thunder announced the doctor's trap had been sprung.

When we bounced, I felt like we might both get thrown off, but the slightly curving half walls of the sled's travel compartment gave my feet and elbows something to lever against. The wave of energy passed and we settled back down on the metal rail, our speed starting to drop off rapidly. Ten or twelve seconds later, we slowly rolled to a stop, still in complete Stygian blackness.

"Rikki," I said.

"*Lights—action,*" my drone said, a pair of LEDs on his front lighting up enough to show me my surroundings.

"What?"

"*Immediate vicinity is clear. Drone network access not available, likely due to depth below ground and thickness of building materials.*"

Carefully I sat up, straining my stomach muscles a little to shove up Harper's dead weight. Right arm now free, I pulled another chem-stick from my suit and cracked it into bright blue light.

This room which, according to Harper's mother, was under the Trump building, was more function than form. A polished cement floor and a door much like the one in Harper's hideout. Setting the unconscious girl back into the sled compartment, I tried the doorknob.

The space on the other side looked like something building management might use. A metal desk, a few filing cabinets, shelves with various cleaning supplies, a rack with what looked like maintenance tickets on it for repair jobs. Another door in another wall. I opened that one, looking out into a long hallway with a bank of closed elevator doors, and further down, an unlit EXIT sign above another closed door.

I ignored the stairwell for now. Too risky. On my way back in, I stopped at the rack of cleaning stuff and took stock. Two separate bottles caught my eye. A cleaner my sisters used on their fingernails all the time and a disinfectant that my mom used on all of our cuts and scrapes. Smallish bottles, the both of them, and they fit together inside the bottom of a cut-off empty bleach jug. I grabbed the lot and went back inside the secret tunnel room.

Harper was still out, so I looked in her pack first to see what useful stuff she might have. There was cash, a pair of data chips much like the one I now had in my pocket, clothes, makeup, a small electronics repair kit, a picture that showed a much younger Harper and her mother, a baggie of gold coins, a few platinum ones, some diamond jewelry, a good multi-tool, a flashlight, a folding knife, more chem sticks, water in a collapsible bottle, first aid kit, what looked like a do-it-yourself personal AI mocked up from commercial parts, and a small 9mm pistol with several magazines of ammo. Survival and relocation stuff. My kind of kit.

Then I went through my own pack. It was light on entry tools, having just one lightweight titanium pry bar and my lockpick set. My mini first aid kit, lots of chem sticks, a few Rikki repair parts, ammo for the rifle, ammo for Rikki, six flashbangs, trip cord, compressed ration bars, a boobytrap kit of my own design, and a plastic aerial flare gun with one flare. At the bottom of the pack was a wind-up, self-generator flashlight with charging ports. I put the jug and bottles inside the pack and pulled out the self-charging flashlight.

I glanced at Rikki. He was settled on the edge of the sled, in ball form, just a few lights lit on his front. Energy conservation mode.

"Battery status?"

"Twenty-one percent."

"Come over here and present a plug," I said, starting to wind up the foldout arm on the flashlight. It made a whirring noise that sounded especially loud in the quiet of the basement. Rikki hovered over, setting down on my pack, a plug extruding from his round form. I plugged it into the port on the flashlight and dug my detailed city map out of my stealth suit pocket, spreading it in front of me to review while I spun the handle of the light.

The quick answer was to head for the Battery Park tunnel. But it wasn't necessarily the best answer. Should I appear at Zone Defense with an unknown survivor of Drone Night, ten years after the fact, there would be government questions, huge media interest, and Harper's immediate exposure to the people who hired her mother. Not to mention the data drives. Dr. Wilks hadn't given one to me at the last moment because it held her family's cooking recipes. No, whatever was on that drive, as well as Harper's two drives, was likely a really big deal.

"Mmmm," sounded from the sled.

Harper was about to wake up, have to face the fact her mother, who had to be the very center of her world, was dead, and that her Zone defenses weren't going to protect her any longer. I won't pretend to understand the female of the species, despite living with four of them, but I had some experience with children grieving a lost parent. This was gonna suck.

I stopped charging and took Harper's bag over, setting it back between her feet. Still not awake, but moving a bit here and there. Back to my spot and back to charging while thinking things through. We needed to stay here a bit. I had no way of knowing how much damage the other building had sustained without poking my head above ground, but based on the shockwave that shook us like a rat in a terrier's mouth, it was significant.

"Estimated damage to building and living quarters just vacated?" I asked Rikki.

"Blast attributes suggestive of a fuel-air explosion. Living quarters have a high probability of complete destruction. Building structure likely still intact but with severe structural integrity issues."

"Probability of Unit Lotus calculating for no survivors?"

"Variables numerous and some unknown. If initial blast successfully erased exposure of evacuation tunnel, probability is estimated at over seventy percent. On face data, fifty-eight percent likely."

"Discoverability of Rikki unit and Harper through drone network sensors here in present location?"

"Approaching zero."

"Likelihood of Rikki-assumed drone identity remaining intact?"

"Zero. Rikki unit was queried by Lotus and commanded to kill human targets Harper, Ajaya, and Wilks. Command was refused."

How about that... he stood up to a direct command by a CThree.

"Which human target was assigned highest priority?"

"Human Wilks. Followed by Ajaya and Harper."

So the Spider considered me a lesser threat than a disabled scientist in a wheelchair. I pulled out the data drive and pondered what it could contain.

"Where... where's Mother?" a strained voice asked in a whisper. Harper was sitting up, one hand on the edge of the sled for support, the other on her head. I stopped winding the generator handle and plucked my first aid kit and water flask from my gear.

Harper saw my pack and instantly looked for her own, frantic till she spotted it between her feet. I handed her a pair of ibuprofen painkillers and my water bottle. She took them but looked at me, her question foremost on her expressive face.

I shook my head. Her eyes welled up with tears and she instantly dropped her face, short hair swinging forward. I backed away and went back to charging Rikki, leaving her to her grief.

When my dad died, everyone offered their condolences. Only natural and, I'm sure, heartfelt. Yet I was too deep in my own grieving to be able to process their words. My words would mean nothing to her, at least not yet. Better to give her room to begin to process.

The headache from whatever her mother had injected her with finally got the best of her, her hand coming up to her mouth and water bottle following. I watched her from the corner of my eye, trying to give her what privacy I could. With my sisters,

285

I would have hugged Monique and given Gabby room for a bit. I didn't know Harper at all and, more importantly, she didn't know me. And now she was dependent on me, maybe more than she realized. Grieving, world upturned, and soon to be leaving the borough of bones for the world of the living. In my opinion, that was a perfect combination to turn to anger. Anger that could be directed at the world, at the drones, at me. I heard sniffling.

The map was laid out before me, but it wasn't offering up answers. "She was very strong. Like she had steel in her spine instead of that disease," I said.

She was silent, except for some soft sniffles. I looked at the map and spun the crank on the flashlight generator. Rikki sat unmoving, with one lit LED the only indication that he was alert.

"Harper?" I asked a minute later. "How did you get out of the Zone to get your mother's medicine?"

More silence. The northern end of the island is heavily fortified, the river being very narrow. East, west, and south sides have wide water barriers with patrolling Coast Guard, Zone Defense drones, and automatic gun systems. But the island is over twenty-one kilometers long. Hell of a hike on foot in drone country, even with a cybernetic defense device. No, her passage in and out would most likely have to be near the south end.

"Methotrexate degrades after a year. So all the drugs here in the Zone would have been useless long ago. But you were using it, because you asked for it. And it's not easy for you to get... but you did. How, Harper?"

More silence. More minutes. More winding the handle to power up Rikki.

"Tunnels are out. Too congested. Brooklyn Bridge is too visible. Manhattan Bridge... hmm."

I was watching her from the corner of my eye. She twitched a little on that last one. The Manhattan Bridge had layers. Obviously not the upper car deck, but under that were four lanes of subway tracks and a pedestrian passage. All layers were heavily guarded.

"Top deck has troops, auto guns, tanks. But the subway level has armored anti-tank drones and more troops," I mused.

"Not many troops. Mostly drones. Especially at night. Zone Defense is short on troops these days. They know most activity drops at night, so they use more drones at night, mostly on the subway track level," she said.

"And you can voodoo your way past them?" I asked.

"It's not voodoo, you moron. It's a complicated cryptographic handshake protocol. It took me months to learn it and it's very hard to do."

I kinda of knew most of that but she seemed to be a lecture kind of girl so I thought she could use the distraction.

"But you're good at it, right?"

"Yes, I'm good at it. Do you ever stop asking questions?"

"Not when I'm trying to get us all out of here. We're going to be trying to exfiltrate around and past Lotus and its assets. If we get to the bridge, and that's a big if, *I* can walk out. You, on the other hand, and probably Rikki, will need to slip by Zone Defense. Sure, we could walk you out, but there's a lot of media coverage on me these days. You and your story will be front screen on every media feed in the world. How long till these Wall Street crasher bozos come looking to make you disappear?"

"They call themselves the New Hope. I hadn't thought about leaving the Zone. I've got more hiding places," she said.

"But Lotus is hip to your tricks. You aren't invisible to them anymore. And you don't have a stealth suit, Gurkha ninja training, or a Rikki. You're gonna need to come with us."

"And die as soon as my story gets out? You just explained that one."

"No, I explained what happens if you walk out with me. If you sneak out, while I'm distracting everyone else, then we can get you hidden away. There are some empty rooms in my building that we can get you situated in while we build you an identity."

She leaned forward and rummaged in her pack. "I have an identity. Right here," she said, holding up one of the data chips. "Mother and I built complete digital IDs. Everything I need is on here: documents, assets, backstory."

"How do you have assets?"

"Same way you do, hotshot. I looted cash registers, office safes, emptied pockets. Methotrexate costs money. So I funded a bank account. Dropped deposits in an ATM near the pharmacy whose prescription system we had hacked. There are still a few places to get rid of cash. I have resources," she sniffed.

"That's awesome. So was I right about Manhattan Bridge?"

"Not much of a leap of logic, but yes, you were correct. Not sure how it would work in daylight, though."

"We'll find out. But I'm gonna be a massive distraction on the upper level, so you'll have that to work with."

"Massive, huh?" she asked, clearly not seeing the big picture.

"Oh, just 'cause I have mad stealth skills, don't think I can't capture the limelight when I need to," I said, giving her a smile. "You wait. It'll be huge."

I was more right than either of us could possibly guess.

Chapter 34

I gave her a ration bar to choke down while I did the same, and then pushed her to drink lots of water. The same went for me. Get fueled up. We had some big shocks to our systems, her more than me, and we absolutely had to get geared up, mentally and physically, for the coming battle. And I was pretty sure there would be a fair amount of battling involved.

"Can you disrupt a drone? Interfere with its processing, even for a second?" I asked her. Keep her focused on the here and now, continue grieving later.

"I guess. I haven't done it, but I can sort of surge at the lesser ones. Shove data and protocol processes all at once. It might slow them down a bit. But I can fight, too. I have a gun."

"One, have you ever shot a drone before? And two, you have anything larger than a handgun? Armor-piercing ammo?"

"You went through my bag, I can see that, so you know the answer to the second question," she said, tone unhappy at the invasion. "And no, I haven't shot it out with one. Seems like a bad idea."

"You're exactly right. I did go through your bag... I've never been responsible for getting anyone out of the Zone before, and yes, it is monumental idiocy to fight it out. They were designed to kill armed soldiers on a battlefield. They are, almost all of them, armored to some degree, and very hard to kill. Add machine response time and computer aiming and it's bad. We avoid it," I said, pointing to Rikki, then back at myself. "But it happens, and when it does, it's a blur, all reflex action, no time for slow, human thought. One on one, I could hope for about fifty-fifty percent. With Rikki, we move to high seventies. If that happens, anything you can do to slow the opposition down, *without* slowing Rikki, will be a huge help. Oh, and you can't go out with your sensors or whatever you have, active. You and Rikki are both compromised. We have to go mostly blind."

If her face had been looking pale before she started eating, my words now washed away any color that had returned to her. "What? That's a recipe for death. They have all the advantages with their sensors."

"Correction, they have advantages over *us,* not *him.*" Again, I pointed at Rikki. "We've done this before. Again, it's not fun and we don't do it unless there's no other choice. There's no other choice."

She looked at Rikki, who was still sitting quiescent, but I could see her really look this time. "You've made changes?"

"Rikki has better processing and storage hardware, his batteries and capacitors are far beyond his originals and brand new, all of his high-wear parts are replaced with brand new ones regularly, and his sensor suite is completely upgraded," I said. "In contrast, unless a drone was held back in reserve some how, they've all taken enormous wear and tear over the last decade. They squeak, whistle, rattle, and whir very loudly to Rikki's auditory receptors, they give off more electromag signals than they used to, and their response times have been slowing steadily for the last few years. Freezing New York winters followed by hot, humid summers has beat them up something fierce. They're no cakewalk, but neither are we."

She looked at Rikki, her brow furrowed. "You charged him back up?"

"Power is at ninety-three percent of optimal. Current usage is minimal. Operating in airplane mode reduces active usage."

"Airplane mode?"

I didn't know if she'd ever been on an airplane, but her tone seemed more amused than curious.

"We had to call it something short and sweet. Seems to cover it."

She nodded. "I only flew once, back when Mom was first hired. We came from California. I thought airplane mode was the stupidest thing ever invented."

"I wasn't sure how much effect the strong ones, particularly the Spiders, could have on him. Airplane mode was a safety precaution."

"You say that as if the question has been answered."

"Lotus instructed him to kill all three of us when we were in your place. He said no."

She looked impressed, eyebrows raised. "Mom would have been interested to hear that. It would have both fascinated her and probably piqued her professional pride that your homespun job stood up to hers."

"Ten years is a lifetime in tech hardware. Rikki has the best chips money could buy."

"Still, one of the top AI experts in the world versus a rogue college kid," she said, holding hands up like balance scales. "No offense."

"None taken. You're right. I got tremendously lucky with Rikki. Somehow, everything went right. I like to think my dad was helping from the other side."

Her eyes went wide, then went moist in an alarming fashion. But other than a quick head drop to recover herself, she held it together. I started packing up my gear, putting stuff back into my pack or stealth suit.

"So what's the plan?"

"It has the benefit of being simple. We're going to sneak and peek. Lotus won't likely know if we survived the explosion. We won't tell it. But if we get found, we'll have to go from snail slow to all out. We need to get as close to the East Side Zone wall as possible without tripping anyone to the fact that you exist. We'll scoot along parallel to it, but if it goes to hell, we get right up on it. If everything goes to plan, we'll sneak all the way up to the Manhattan Bridge. You go your route through the subway section. I'll take the top deck. At this point, Rikki will go with you. I gotta sneak him out. He won't survive Lotus searching for him with all of its assets. He might also be a help to you getting through there, especially if Lotus sends any drones after you."

She stared at me. "That's... disturbingly simple. Can't we just stay here for a few days?"

"Lotus is looking for confirmation of our deaths. Wolves and Tiger drones will be burrowing through the wreckage looking for our bodies. When they don't find us, Lotus will go all out."

She nodded. "Lotus is a nasty bitch. She'd do exactly that."

"She?"

"You call that thing him," she said. "The Spiders have a female feeling to them. Probably some imprint or personality flavoring from my mom."

"Hmm, I agree. There is sort of an evil queen bee thing going on there. Anyway, we have a short window to haul ass. Let's get going. Rikki, recon please."

His fans instantly whirred to life and he shot up and out the door I had left propped open. I checked my rifle one more time and turned to Harper. She was staring at me with a new expression—surprise.

"What?"

"You used please with your order?"

"So?"

"He's a machine."

"Again, so? Should I treat machines like shit?"

She shook her head, then picked up her pack and swung it onto her back. I gave one more glance at her but she just looked back, alert and ready, even if her eyes were red and puffy.

Rikki shot into the blackness of the stairwell, the soft hum of his turbines the only thing I could hear. The sound rose up into the darkness, fading completely after a few moments. I waited, my rifle ready, chamber loaded and safety off, finger indexed above and along the trigger guard. Moments that felt like full minutes ticked by. Then I felt a breeze, soft and familiar. The sound returned next.

Lights lit up the space, my drone hovering in place, facing away to avoid blinding us.

"Stairwell clear to the fifth floor. No sensory input at all. No air currents, no EM leakage. Audio review of first floor resulted in no sounds observed."

I turned to Harper. She raised both eyebrows. "That's his 'coast is clear,'" I said. She nodded and followed me up the stair, Rikki's lights bright enough to avoid tripping.

At the first floor door, I listened for a second or two, then cracked the door. Two skeletons, splayed out all over the floor. No sounds. I pushed the door open and let Rikki out, then held the door for Harper. She glanced at my chivalry, eyebrows raised. I shook my head and then shut the door with careful precision, making not a single sound. My turn to raise my eyebrows at her. She blushed, then glared, hands on hips. She mouthed "*No duh.*"

Okay, so she already knew that doors must be shut with exacting care. Pardon me for not being used to moving through the Zone with someone I didn't know but who'd grown up here.

The lobby was dusty but the marble reception counter that occupied one wall still looked pristine. Too bad one of the monitors on top of it had three flechette holes through it.

Rikki hovered silently across the big open space, the small breeze from his fans fluttering clothing that held the skeletons of those who had died here. I stepped carefully over them, not bothering to check on Harper. This was her stomping grounds and she must have seen thousands of skeletons. These two, a man and woman by their clothes, weren't going to shock her.

Rikki froze in place ahead of me and I held up a closed fist, realizing even as I did so that I had not gone over hand signals with Harper. The fact that no sound came from behind me indicated she'd figured it out.

Slowly Rikki hovered back toward me, his motion so slow it almost didn't look like he was moving at all. Outside the glass doors, the sun shone brightly, shadows indicating afternoon. I suddenly saw motion. A Tiger, pacing with slow, lethal steps up the street. It disappeared from view but Rikki stayed motionless for another five heartbeats. Then he moved up to the doors, sweeping across the arc of the windows, round body turning to look and listen in every direction. Finally he hovered in place by a door, and that was my cue to let him out.

We three slid out of the building, Rikki leading. After a moment of scanning, he spun in place and four LEDs lit up on his front. Two close together on the left part of his *face,* two spread apart on the right side. I turned to a puzzled Harper. I held up four fingers, then waved my other hand around to indicate four drones around us. Two fingers close together toward the left side. Two far apart on the right. I led the way back into the building.

"Both sides covered. We'll go out a back door."

"How did you come up with the light thing?"

"We just did. I don't remember. Why? It's minor."

"Hmm," was all she said.

We headed through the ground floor and found a back exit onto Pine Street. Rikki went back out. This time, the way was clear. We crossed the street and cut through the next building rather than go up either Nassau Street or William Street. I had to pick the door lock, but it was pretty easy.

The four drones Rikki had detected would have pretty clear lines of sight. We couldn't go out on the side streets yet. We cut through the building behind as well. They were big buildings and it took at least twenty minutes to get through both of them.

Finally, we caught a break. A set of crashed cars at the corner of William and Liberty gave us cover to crouch low and move across William Street, heading east. We followed Liberty till it merged with Maiden, then followed that. Rikki stopped us and pulled back fast to a building we had just passed. I grabbed Harper's arm and hustled her after him. We ducked through the doorway, catching a break that it was unlocked, and dropped down low. Two lights lit up on Rikki's front, then went out as another two lit up. His symbol for two approaching. Then I heard them outside. Metal on stone, a whirring motor that was long past its tune-up date.

The sounds clinked and clanked past us. Then stopped. Something had tripped their sensors. Could have been a lingering infrared image from one of us touching something. Could have been drops of sweat. The sounds came back. I pulled Harper deeper into the building, Rikki hovering backward, gun pointed to cover us. The sound of a scraping door came from far behind us.

I pulled off my pack, put it into Harper's hands while we kept walking. Pulled out my booby trap kit, selected a precut tripwire attached to a collapsible beer koozie. Plucked a flashbang from the pack. Slid it into the koozie; it was a tight fit. Tied a cord to the top of the grenade. At the next door, I stopped. It was a pull-to-open kind of door. I tied the koozie to the door, tied the cord from the flashbang to a wall fixture. Checked the tension, then pulled the pin. The koozie kept the spoon from flying off... till it was pulled off the grenade.

We kept moving, through halls and doors, backtracking twice, before finally getting to the street. Rikki had time to check for drones. Then the flashbang went off behind us.

"Run!" I said, demonstrating proper technique from the front. Rikki sped up, still in his round shape, but easily able to leave us in the dust. Harper, I discovered, was not a runner.

She was sort of walk-running, like it was something to figure out. Faster than a walk but nowhere near fast enough. Probably hadn't really done any running her whole life. It wasn't a lack of coordination, just a lack of practice. You normally don't run in the Zone. Drones are generally faster and drawn to noise and commotion. You move slow and steady, sometimes snail slow.

I dropped back and grabbed her arm, pulling her along faster. Rikki turned up another street. I didn't see any street signs and we were moving too fast to really look around. We made it a block and turned right, onto another street, now back heading east. We came around that corner fast, then skidded to a stop, my left hand dropping Harper's arm and coming up to meet the forearm of my rifle as it rose on target.

Rikki fired first, twice, his bullets knocking the Kite UAV out of the air, then I fired, my heavy .458 caliber bullet smacking the Tiger that had turned our way the instant we had appeared. The bullet hit it right in its face as it crouched to spring. My immediate second round blew through its chest, putting it down and out of the game, if not dead.

We ran to the far left side of the road, far from the twitching, sputtering butcher machine, its aerial companion completely dead and silent on the street behind it. "Come on, run!" I yelled to Harper as I did a moving magazine swap on the rifle.

Chapter 35

"I am running," she protested.

"Well, run faster," I said, not wasting time by telling her that the awkward, shambling jog thing she was doing was not a run. Behind us, I couldn't hear anything, but that didn't matter at all. We were pegged with the first gunshot.

I remember reading about an early twenty-first century anti-sniper technology that triangulated gunshots using a system of microphones spread out across a town or city. It never took off because police drones instantly replaced it. A networked group of drones could triangulate gunfire faster and better than a static set of microphones. Each of them immediately moving toward the shot, communicating with each other and command central, each getting better data with each subsequent shot.

Two aerials units came zipping into our street from opposite corners in front of us, and a whirring sounded behind us. Rikki spun backward to engage the rear attacker. I shot the first of the forward drones even as all three opened fire. Something tugged on my left shoulder, but the recoil of my short, powerful, modern-day buffalo gun distracted me. My round swatted the Raptor from the sky even as I swung the barrel and fired another round at the other UAV. Missed. Its own flechette gun snapped out a sharp reply that I felt on my left forearm. Then I fired again and this time got to see the Indian Falcon unit basically explode in midair.

Another drone swung around the same corner as my first kill, and my gun was off-target to the left. Being right-handed, it is always easier to swing a barrel across my body from right to left than to swing from left to right. Body mechanics. I had practiced both a lot. I snapped around but was still way too slow. Half-seconds are lifetimes in drone wars. But the new Raptor was frozen in place, just hovering somewhat erratically, and I had lots of time to complete the sight picture and blast it from the air.

I turned to check on Harper and found her un-hit but breathing hard. She looked at me with a triumphant smile. "It worked," she said, then her eyes flicked to my shoulder and my left arm. "You're bleeding!"

"Inside," I said, leading the way into another building, keeping the SOCOM's barrel out in front. This door was locked. I pulled lockpick tools and dropped to a knee. Rikki hovered, sensors and gun barrel pointed out. "Do me a favor. Inside the outer pocket of my pack is a block of cartridges. Pull them out and toss them up in the air at Rikki," I instructed her, working the lock the whole time. I could feel her rummage in the pack on my back, then she stopped and I next heard the chunk of a partial block of ammo hit the ground.

"Whoa! How did you teach him that?" she asked from behind me. I felt her stuff something back in the pouch and then zip the pocket closed.

"That's the million dollar question. Zone Defense wants to know too. Mostly he taught himself."

"Target tags detected in flechettes. Neutralizing."

Some drones had little tracking tags that could lead it after a wounded target. Apparently a few were still around. Rikki flashed them with a burst of EM and killed them.

The last tumbler finally clicked and the torsion wrench spun the lock cylinder enough to unbolt the door. I pushed it open and held it while she ran in past me, followed by Rikki. Then I dove through and closed the door as softly as possible.

Rikki moved over in front of me, LEDs all across his front lighting up.

There was no need to explain the significance of that to Harper. Her wide eyes and pale face said it all. The drones were swarming.

I pulled off my pack and opened the main compartment. Pulling the empty jug, I quickly poured one bottle of cleaning chemicals into it, then carefully and as slowly as I could make myself, stirred the contents of the other bottle into it. The mixture started to thicken and I stopped all motion except to set the jug against the unlocked door.

I motioned her to follow and led the way into the building, putting as many turns and doors as possible between the jug and us. Dad had taught me a lot about improvising explosives and traps from common items found almost everywhere in the Zone. This one was a favorite although it didn't always work. It was also dangerous as shit.

We got to the back side of the building and started to carefully peer out the windows.

"Another bomb?" Harper asked.

"Hopefully, although it isn't always reliable, especially if you mix it as fast as I did. If I did it right, it makes a super unstable, impressively high-energy explosive."

"And opening the door will set it off?"

"That's the plan. Like I said, it may not go off, although it's generally so touchy that even looking at it wrong can set it off. Not my favorite thing to do," I said.

Rikki, having swept the door and windows for information, hovered down in front of us. *"Approximately sixteen various units in the street we left. More approaching,"* he said, his volume pitched soft. Then he suddenly tilted up at forty-five degrees, his sensors aimed at the roofline outside. *"Unit Lotus approaching."*

He hovered down to the floor so fast, it was like his strings were cut, but he landed without a sound and instantly cut all power to his fans and lights.

Harper stared at me, eyes tight with tension as we each held our breath. I wasn't sure what led Rikki to the conclusion that the Spider was coming our way, but I knew better than to second-guess him. Then I heard it... the distinctive metallic patter of metal claws on asphalt. Lots of claws. Six or seven maybe. It was an entirely different sound from a Wolf, Leopard, or Tiger. All of those moved on four feet, and the cadence of their steps was similar to each other. This was different. Tik, tik, tik... tik, tik, tik. Three feet at a time. Probably two on one side and one on the other. Then wash and repeat on the opposite side.

It moved past our building, then, I think, onto our building, the sound fading as it likely worked its way toward the front.

Harper held both hands out, palms up, mouthing, *"What do we do?"*

I made a waiting motion with my left hand, right still holding the grip of my rifle, finger indexed by the trigger guard. Always be ready to shoot... words of my father.

Harper tilted her head, then made an exploding motion with both hands, her eyebrows raised in question. I shrugged. She didn't look impressed. In fact, she looked a bit underwhelmed.

The floor suddenly jumped up a foot and the walls all shook as the world roared. Dust and pieces of ceiling material fell in clouds as we were thrown off our feet. I hit the hard floor and then something punched me in the stomach. When the dust cleared, I realized it was Harper's head, still resting on my bruised abs. She sat up, looking drunk. I had to use my left arm to lever myself upright.

Rikki came to life, his fans lifting him straight up, dust and particles bouncing off his carbon fiber shell.

"Exit is indicated at this time."

Hitting the crash bar on the rear door popped it right open, making a bit of a racket, but hell, after that explosion, stuff was falling all over the place. A little noise wouldn't add much.

Turns out we were on the side of the building, and a glance back down the street showed a cloud of smoke and dust filling the street at the front of the building.

A side street was almost right in front of us, heading east, and Rikki took off down it. I turned to grab Harper but she was already running and damned if her stride wasn't longer and smoother. Almost a full-out sprint. Fast learner.

Rikki stopped at the corner, spinning in place as he folded out into fighter mode. We hit the corner and turned left, heading north. Seagulls flew overhead and the smell of saltwater told me we were getting close.

It took a couple of blocks before I saw an intact street sign—Water Street. Rikki stayed low and just ahead of us. Suddenly he stopped and spun thirty degrees right, gun aimed at the right corner up ahead. Then he hovered straight up about a meter higher.

"Aimpoint: corner of closest building, same elevation as Rikki unit. Countdown to fire," he said, his tone very soft and quiet.

I put my aiming reticle on the brick corner just over the street sign that said *Beekman Street*, same level as Rikki was hovering. My trigger finger took up the slack.

"Three, two, one, Mark."

I started my squeeze at one and the sear let off exactly on the M in Mark. The gun thumped my shoulder but I kept the reticle on target and was rewarded by the sight of a gray and black camouflaged Indian Harpy drone that came around the corner just in time to meet my bullet. The bullet won. Little gun hit like a freight train.

"A faster pace is advised," Rikki said, zipping over to put a kill shot into the Harpy.

We ran again, Harper glancing my way several times.

"What," I asked, stopping to pull a wind-up gizmo out of my pack. I opened it, stuck the loaded flare pistol into it, wound it, and pulled back the hammer on the pistol. Set it on the ground behind me, the pistol barrel pointed up and at an angle to our path.

She was clearly winded, shaking her head and sucking air in big gasps. We cleared the intersection and were now running with buildings on our right and a parking lot of rusted cars on our left. I moved to her left side, judging the wide-open parking lot, the street on its far side, and the green space beyond that as more dangerous.

"He—ah—he directed your, ah, shot?" she huffed out, slowing out of necessity.

"Yeah, what of it?" I asked, scoping the far tree line.

"Do you have any idea how complex that process was?"

It was actually the first time he'd done that, but I sort of expected things like that from him these days. "I don't know? Freaking awesomely complex?"

"Beyond. The Harpy was too armored for his gun, so he directed your bigger weapon. He had to convey an aiming point, so he aligned his own position to give you a reference you could rapidly and visually understand. Then he counted you down precisely to have the bullet hit the drone at the exact right moment. Ajaya, that's problem solving and communication at human levels."

"Most humans wouldn't have thought of it that quickly," I said, checking our six o'clock.

"No, they wouldn't. What the hell did you do to that Berkut?"

"Hold on, we gotta get across this street and it's a wide one. Rikki—targets close?"

"Negative, Ajaya. Aerial units approaching from west and north. Both ground and aerial units approaching from south."

A full street behind us, the flare gun suddenly went off, the flare arcing over a building.

"Okay, Harper, more running, less talking," I said, grabbing her arm. She shook it off, glared at me, and sprinted across the street. Not gonna win any track meets, but she was much faster than before.

The Brooklyn Bridge was visible to our right, the on-ramp just ahead. It was tempting to take it, but that would expose Harper to those New Hope idiots. I led her under the overpass that crossed the bridge, Rikki circling us every few seconds like a ship in orbit. At least the sun was out and giving him back a portion of the power he was burning.

We moved over a block closer to FDR drive and the Zone fence, but stayed far enough away to avoid the cameras. The fence and its auto guns gave us a little bit of security on our right flank, but the way ahead was going to be hairy.

"Multiple units approaching from the north."

I pulled my last grenades from my pack and clipped them to my suit. One went into Rikk's talons with the pin pulled. He shot upward, disappearing from view in seconds.

"Where'd he go? Why isn't he here?"

"He's hunting. We do this. Now come over here," I said, leading her into a thick cluster of trees between buildings. Before the Attack, this section, between the two big bridges, had numerous green spaces. Ten years later, it was a thick, overgrown mini-forest.

We moved deeper into the vegetation. "I don't like this... it's too... thick," she said.

She just wasn't used to forest or plants or normal nature. "Relax and sit low. Catch your breath," I whispered. "These trees are a nightmare for the aerials. The ground units are slower, and the batch behind us is likely damaged to some degree. Most UGV hunters aren't overly fast anyway. They just never give up tracking prey and I've been dripping blood," I said, pulling off my pack again. I pulled out part of my booby trap stuff.

"What's that?" she whispered.

"Two layers of duct tape with nails, screws, and BBs stuck between them. A couple of wraps of this around the body of this flashbang, being careful to stay under the firing spoon, and viola, a shrapnel grenade," I said, demonstrating as I whispered, pulling the pin. "Now stay low and don't move."

A buzzing filled the air and suddenly a dozen mixed aerial drones entered the forest. I had Harper positioned so that my body, covered in adaptive stealth camouflage, was between her and the drones, an overgrown rhododendron plant at her back. I noticed that her 9mm was in her hand. She was going to fight to the end. Like mother, like daughter.

The drones hovered, starting to spread apart. That's when Rikki's grenade fell among them, blowing up just above them. The blast shook me, even though I was expecting it. No time for that. I threw my grenade hard and fast, then turned and crouched, covering Harper.

I saw, before I turned, that my throw was going to go under the reeling drones and I sensed, more than heard, nails, BBs, and screws zip by us, ripping through the vegetation. Ears ringing, even with the suit's earplugs, I stood and turned, slipping into shooting mode. Target—fire, target—fire, target—killed by Rikki, switch to next drone—fire.

Suddenly there were no more drones. I tossed Rikki his last full block of ammo. I now had two partials in my pack. I'd have to try to consolidate them if we had a chance. Then I reloaded my own weapon.

If I lived, I was going to be keeping this little rifle for sure. The heavy bullets swatted drones like flies, the tungsten carbide-cored bullets blew through ground unit armor like butter, and the small, handy AR-15 package was sooo much easier to carry than a sniper rifle.

"And it's time to run again," I said to Harper.

She was curled up, hands over her ears, but facing the action. Her eyes were really, really wide.

"That's not even remotely normal, you know," she said, standing and then starting to speed up as we headed toward the now visible Manhattan Bridge.

"What?"

"The way you two fight together. And the way you shoot."

"Oh? You an expert?"

"Actually, I am... at least with anything to do with the Zone. I've had a front row seat to more Zone battles than you could imagine. Well, maybe not *you*, but more than any normal person would believe. I've watched *Z War* teams come and go, live and die. I've seen entire squads of soldiers get wiped out."

"Yeah, well, we all have our childhood issues, right? Anyway, none of us will live if we don't get to that damned bridge. Run!"

The area we were running through used to be residential, with kind-of cross-shaped apartment buildings, parking lots, basketball courts, and just ahead at the base of the bridge ramp, a baseball diamond.

"No, head that way," Harper said, pointing at one of the bridge ramp support towers that was well on the land side of things. "There's a quicker way up onto the bridge."

We sprinted, almost all-out, at least for my neophyte runner. My adrenaline was running low and a dull ache had started in my shoulder and forearm. I fully expected a much sharper impact in the back of my head or the middle of my back at any moment.

But we made it, arriving at the brick structure, which she seemed very familiar with as she led us around to a closed metal door. She yanked it up then out, using both hands, and the door screeched open. Rikki went in first, then Harper, with me taking one last look behind us as I closed the door.

A cloud of drones was flying our way, hundreds of aerials, a mechanical storm cloud on the horizon, which meant almost as many ground units that I couldn't see. And while Wolves weren't overly fast, Tigers were. We were out of time.

Chapter 36

She thought I would leave her on the subway tracks, with Rikki hovering above her. "Here is the last of his ammo. I loaded this one full while we climbed the stairs, so throw it to him when he asks for it."

"You can't make it, Ajaya. Not with that many drones coming! And you're leaving your greatest weapon with me."

"Of course not. I have no intention of going toe to toe with Lotus's troops. My goal is to get the wall guns to do the heavy lifting. I just gotta get in gun sensor range. Plus, by now, there has be a dozen Renders on patrol, just waiting for an opportunity to hose those metal bastards. I'm going with you for at least half the bridge. It's much more protected down here."

It was, with the thick steel girder caging that protected both sides of the subway tracks, plus the thick car deck overhead.

"But we have more running to do."

She gave me an incredulous look but started jogging as I did. The storm cloud of drones was almost on us and we only got about fifty yards before the first wave hit. Harper was out in front, Rikki in the middle, and I was tail gunner. My drone started firing immediately, his body turned sideways but still flying right behind Harper.

I got my first target at about his fifth or sixth shot. The mag emptied too fast, ten rounds not enough for the mass of deadly bastards. The second to last flash bang jumped into my hand, almost of its own accord. Good idea, primitive brain stem. Explosives are almost always the correct answer. The pin clattered to the ground and I sort of punched the little grenade out an opening in the girders. It went off with a shock and blast that punched my chest. Harper wobbled on her feet but kept running. I pulled and threw my last grenade, reloaded the rifle as the bomb went off, then jumped to the cage of steel girders and pulled myself through. Now I was out of the bridge, hanging off the side. The water so far below was the least of my worries. Harper was still running for the other side of the bridge, not yet aware that I had left. I climbed.

Instantly, three spots on my body—my right calf, left butt cheek, and the back of my neck—felt like I had been stuck with a red-hot branding iron. I ground my teeth and kept climbing, more laser burns searing different parts as some of the drones lit me up. Then I was up top. I dove for the asphalt, rolling behind a car, lifting my gun and shoving the barrel straight up behind me as I did, pulling the trigger as my elbow reached full extension. That's the key: no hesitation. You just gotta go with instinct and do something, even the wrong thing, just as long as you do it instantly. My gun went off as one of the laser drones came over the roof of the car. The bullet only grazed it but it still fell from the sky.

Then I was up and running. I was just about the middle of the bridge, weaving and dodging around the wrecked vehicles that someone, likely Team Johnson, had shoved to the sides some time ago. Drones hunted me, and there were too many. Suddenly there was one more and it started to shoot the others out of the air. Rikki had abandoned Harper? Then another, bigger drone shot through the air overhead. The Decimator blew through, EM gun blasting a drone while little missiles launched themselves from under its wings.

Rikki killed three drones in two seconds, the Decimator blasted like eight. I got one. I put my head down and sprinted, leaving the shooting to the two killing machines that were on my side. Flechettes tugged at my suit, burning stings all up and down my back, ass, and legs. Ignore them. Keep running. Just over halfway. I could see rows of auto guns swinging up, and a few drones around us suddenly just fizzled out and dropped. Infrared lasers, invisible but line-of-sight deadly. More drones were dying as Zone Defense AI systems targeted them, and Rikki and his new, big pal blasted others.

Weaving in and around the wrecks, my flying protectors swooping around me, fighting off drones, I turned sideways to get between the edge of the bridge and a burnt-out food delivery truck. It was a bad spot, but I had to get past it to get into the safety of the gun arc.

A shadow over the railing caught my eye and I glanced over in time to see a massive black monster pull itself effortlessly over the side, its seventh leg swinging down at my head, the starred and half-broken optical band coming right at my face.

I shoved sideways, unable to get my rifle pointed at the Spider, but I did hit the descending leg with the barrel. The impact did nothing to the steel-clad Lotus, but my rifle got knocked out of my soft human hand. A front leg shot my way, my body jerking away, just enough for the sharp claws to scrape my side and punch a hole in the metal body of the food truck. I pulled my kukri and swung wildly at the broken black eyeband. Lotus jerked itself back and the big knife just clanged into the armored head, hardly scraping the paint. The number seven leg darted at me, so I dropped and rolled under the truck, lancets of pain shooting through me. A different leg probed after me but I kept desperately rolling. The leg banged up into the underside of the truck and then started to lift. The wheels closest to the bridge side and the Spider rose into the air. Flipping to my stomach, I low crawled toward the rear of the truck, back the way I had come. I switched my knife to my left hand and drew the Five-Seven. Flicked the full auto selector.

Another vehicle, a SUV of some kind, was crammed up against the delivery truck. I crawled under it and spotted my rifle, which lay between the SUV's tires and the railing of the bridge.

Behind me, the truck fell over on its side with a grinding crash. Pointing my pistol at the visible parts of the spider's legs, I hosed them with the full mag of little armor-piercing rounds. They just sparked off the heavy metal, but the Spider pulled back. I dropped the pistol and got my right hand on the .458 and dragged it to me. Another massive leg slipped under the front of the SUV and then it too started to lift.

I racked the charging handle, rolled to my back, and lifted the muzzle at the same pace that the car was lifted. As soon as I saw black armor, I pulled the trigger twice. Lotus screeched, dropped the SUV, its legs disappearing from my view as I flattened myself to the ground. The big car bounced on its suspension, the metal underside smashing into me hard enough to stun. The bouncing stopped and I rolled to my side, spinning around by pulling with my boots on the ground like I was running in a circle, rotating on my left shoulder. Six massive legs hit the pavement to the left of the SUV, toward the centerline of the road. Metal squealed and tore, the car rocking side to side. Then the seventh leg shot underneath the SUV, a car door in its claw, darting straight for me. Rolling away, I popped right out against the railing, pulled my feet under me, and jumped onto the hood. The SUV door slammed into the railing where I had just been. Lotus stood next to the car, its back even with the hood, two massive bullet gouges running lengthwise from its mouth back. I raised the rifle but whirring metal slammed into my side. Reflexes kicked in, my rifle butt stroking the aerial drone out of the air, my boot crunching it into the hood beneath us before kicking it off.

I brought the rifle back on Lotus but it had the car door out, swinging it like a shield, blocking my shot. The bullets would go right through the door, but they would need every bit of power to defeat the Spider's armor, and car metal would rob them of some speed and energy.

The monster reared back, a front leg grabbing the broken drone and flinging it at me. I hopped sideways and that car door jumped forward, punching me right off the SUV, right over the rail. I let go of the rifle to grab the railing. The gun fell, then clanged against the outside of the bridge as its carry sling caught on something. Lotus leaped onto the SUV and raised the car door to slam me into jelly.

There was a sharp whine and then a massive clanging sound as a close-range electromag round hit the Spider's side, the metal slug getting stuck partway through the armor. The Decimator swung around to take another shot but the Spider turned to it and the Decimator froze up, hovering in place.

Rikki was suddenly there, firing rounds at the Spider's eyeband and leg joints. Lotus scuttled itself around to follow Rikki's flight, the flailing SUV door missing the Berkut by centimeters. I took the opportunity to get my feet on the bridge structure and push myself up, then get one leg over the railing and drop to the blessed pavement. Rikki continued to fire and dodge, fire and dodge, his rounds pinging off the metal armor but gouging paint near the vulnerable eyeband, empty casings ejecting straight down.

His gun clicked empty. Lotus leaped for him but he swerved away, back from the bridge, over open water. The huge Spider landed on the SUV, its seventh leg throwing the car door at Rikki. He dodged it easily. The leg came down and slammed right through the roof of the car, somehow latching in place. Then Lotus crouched and sprang, its leap much, much further out, a thin line of metallic cable reeling out from the interior of that seventh leg.

Rikki dove and the Spider ceased reeling, the line going taut, slamming the Spider into a pendulum arc. I jumped back to the railing, leaning dangerously far over, my feet hooked into the gaps. The rifle strap was just there, just a little further, and I stretched, hooking it with a single finger. Back up, heaving the rifle up into space by its strap, grabbing the gun out of midair, turning and putting the muzzle to the cable. It fired, the metal cable shattering and snapping loose. Jumping up on the railing, I got one leg hooked around a massive bridge cable, then leaned out and down. Lotus was falling after Rikki, but my drone could accelerate and the Spider couldn't. Plus the anchor to the bridge was gone, Lotus falling straight rather than speeding at the end of an arc. Rikki pulled up and away as my crosshairs lined up. I pulled that trigger as fast as I could, emptying all the remaining rounds into the body of the falling Spider CThree. Holes appeared in armor as the massive black body got smaller and smaller before finally splashing into the water.

Then the sky darkened and I looked up to see a huge form blocking out the light. The giant Quad rotor hovered directly over me, the back ramp opening and familiar forms diving off the edge. Two armored soldiers shot past me, headed for the water, thin lines of their own trailing behind. They splashed into the East River right where Lotus had gone in, disappearing after it.

Metallic thunks sounded around me and I turned in time to see other troopers land, legs barely flexing to absorb the impacts like it was nothing. The closest soldier had boob bumps and the name tag read *K. Jossom*. A taller figure landed behind her, facing away to guard her back.

"Yo, Gurung, how's it hanging?" Jossom asked.

"There's a possibility it got shot off," I said.

"Oh, that's gonna disappoint your Viking girlfriend, but then maybe I'll have a shot at her, " Jossom said, looking me over. "Medic!"

The Quad was shooting the shit out of all the drones in the area, which, now that the command Spider was gone, were leaving toward Manhattan as fast as they could.

My legs got weak and I suddenly sat down hard. Jossom and her partner Boyle stood guard over me as another trooper, whose nametag said *T. Kendall*, started to look me over for wounds.

"Shit, son, you've got at least ten flechette wounds and seven laser burns," Kendall said after having me peel off the stealth suit. "Lots more that didn't make it through the stealth suit, though," he said, picking a bent piece of shiny metal out of the tough fabric. "What the hell is this? A sewing needle?"

"They scavenge anything they can that fits the bill," I said, taking a sip of the water he had handed me.

"Good thing for you. This improvised ammo isn't as efficient as true spec flechettes would have been."

"Am I gonna live?" I asked, half joking. I certainly felt pretty bad, but I was breathing and the medic didn't look very concerned.

"Some blood loss, dehydration, and some really deep, painful burns, but all very localized. You'll do."

"See that, Boyle? Kid tussles with a freaking Spider and gets away scot-free. Oh, Major's gonna be pissed at you, shooter boy. You fucked up the Spider he wanted," Jossom admonished.

"He should have wrestled with it himself," I said, lying back.

"Nope, no lying down yet. Come on, up ya go," Kendall said, suddenly hustling me. Boyle turned and gave the medic a cold look.

"What? I don't want him passing out till he's on the Quad. Sue me," Kendall said back. "Chief, get that stretcher down ASAP." I didn't know who he was talking to, or who the chief was for a solid ten seconds, till it hit me that he was talking to somebody, likely the crew chief, on the Quad.

"Alright, here we are. *Now* you can lie down. Feet inside," he said, holding an injector gun to my neck and pumping something cold that instantly turned warm.

"Where's my, my rif- rifle?" I asked, tongue going gummy.

"Here ya go, shooter," Jossom said, tucking my cleared and unloaded rifle alongside me, my bunched-up stealth suit at my feet.

I lay back and looked up at the cloud-free blue sky, thinking it was an absolutely beautiful day. Then I closed my eyes, just to give them a little rest.

Chapter 37

I opened my eyes after just a moment or two and discovered I was in a bed, in a building, with the sun setting out the windows.

"Ah, there he is. Let me get the doc," a voice said, my mind telling me a second later it was Corporal Jossom. I turned and caught a glimpse of her camouflage battle dress uniform heading out the door. Four seconds later, she was back, holding the door for a female doctor who bustled in, eyes locked on me.

"Mr. Gurung, how are you feeling?"

"Confused, sleepy," I said, shifting upward, only to lock up as sharp needles of pain hit me from a half dozen spots at once.

"Easy, let the bed do the work," the doctor said, smiling. "Bed, raise head thirty degrees."

The mattress lifted under me and even though there were little twinges of sharp pain, it was better than when I tried it.

"You've got lots of little holes in you, Ajaya. All the metal and shrapnel is out, but I think I could start a hardware store with the nails, needles, and bits of wire I pulled out of you," said the doctor, whose name tag read *Dr. Christie*. She was a petite brunette, pretty, too. I glanced at Jossom, who was giving the doctor's form a thorough appraisal till she caught my look. She winked and grinned.

"I don't have to stay here, do I? How long has it been?"

"Ah, you've been in here about an hour. Took us forty-five minutes to pluck the iron out of you. How long since he was on the transport, ah, Corporal?"

Jossom snapped out of her appraisal before the doc finished turning to her and came to attention. "It's been two hours, thirty-three minutes, ma'am."

"I'm a civilian, Corporal, not military. You don't have to salute or ma'am me."

"But can I buy you coffee?" Jossom asked, instantly changing posture to a more relaxed stance.

Doctor Christie looked surprised when she turned back to me, her professional face taking a second to flicker back into place. "You'll be going home as quick as I check you over. There's a waiting room of uncleared people waiting to haul you back, if my understanding is correct."

"That's true, ma'am. Your mom, sisters, and your Viking are all outside the restricted area. I volunteered to keep watch over you for them," Jossom said.

"Hah," I said. "You secretly pine for me, Jossom. Go ahead and admit it."

"Actually, Shooter, I took one look at that bevy of beauties and fell all over myself to help them out," Jossom said. "I'm hanging near you, kid. You're my new wingman. Beautiful women surround you like bees on a rose."

"Won't Boyle be hurt?" I asked, glancing at the bemused doctor with a grin.

"Boyle? Boyle's the worst. Old gloomy Gus drives women away left and right. He's my bud and all, but for a night on the town, you're my new bestie. Hell, look at the doctor they gave you. Like a movie star or something."

Dr. Christie ignored her, busying herself with checking my eyes with a penlight, but I saw a deep blush flow over her skin.

"You're gonna have to wait a few months, Jossom. I won't be twenty-one till November," I said.

"Aw, that's nothing. I could sleep till November. But hey, that means your Viking will be twenty-one before you, right? I read she's a little older than you."

"A month and a half. Hey, where did you read that?"

"You get this guy, Doc? Talk about clueless. Anyway, I'm going to go tell your clan of models that you're awake and due out soon. That's true, right, Doc?"

"Yup, his vitals all look fine. I'll have the duty nurse start his discharge."

"Okay, I'll be right back, Shooter," Jossom said, pushing out the door. "Don't fly away on me."

"She's kind of a bit extra, but she sure seems protective of you," Dr. Christie said after a glance at the door.

"She's a really good soldier. Elite. I think she took me under her wing when I helped her and her combat partner."

"From what I've seen, you've made a habit of helping people lately... at great risk to yourself."

"Seen?" I asked. She just raised one eyebrow and it hit me.

"Not you too Doc. Does everybody watch that stupid show?"

"Only three quarters of the planet, Ajaya. My *husband* would be thrilled to know I treated you, if I could tell him. Of course, I can't."

"Ah, sure. Go ahead. You have my permission Doc."

"AI did you record that?"

"Affirmative."

"Just being thorough," she apologized.

"No problem. No telling anyone what I look like in my underwear though. Gotta keep the mystery alive, you know."

"No? You sure? I bet they're gonna ask," she said.

I jerked my head around to look at her and caught her smirk.

"Dr. Christie, I'm not sure the military would approve of a sense of humor," I said as she pulled the IV needle. "And isn't that something most nurses do?" I added, nodding at the used IV kit she was disposing of.

"First, as I told that young soldier, I'm not military. And second, you're a special case. That Major Yoshida didn't want too many people near you. That's why you're in a restricted area. Now that's all done, I'll leave you to get dressed, then we'll get you to your family." She smiled and pushed the door open to leave.

I peeled back the covers and looked myself over. Lots of bandages over lots of places. The closet held a set of scrubs and some slippers as well as a plastic bag with my beat-to-shit stealth suit and old boots in it. My brand new stealth suit. It was bloody and burnt and smelled like a high school boys' locker room. My knife, pack, and ammo pouches were all in it as well, but no rifle or sidearm. I closed the bag, put on the scrubs and slippers, and turned toward the door.

It opened even as I looked its way, Major Yoshida filling the space. My .458 was slung over one shoulder and he held my Five-Seven in one hand.

"Ah, AJ. My Spider killer," he said mildly.

"Thanks for the use of your Decimator. It kicked freaking ass," I said.

"It did, didn't it... right up till that CThree unit overwhelmed its processors. But your Berkut ignored it. Out-flew every attack the Spider made, lured it off the bridge and right into your gunsights."

"Did you recover the Spider? Lotus?"

"Is that the thing's name?" he mused. "We dragged it out of the ocean, but it was fried. Something about six heavy caliber rounds punching big holes for the seawater to flow into. My drone team is dissecting the thing, so we'll learn something at least, but the programming is long gone."

"So... what's the current bounty on a Spider?"

His eyebrows went up. "You *are* a salty one aren't you? The going rate is a million point two... for everyone else. For you? About two hundred and fifty thousand."

"What?"

"Well, there's fees for a rescue like that. Those Quads cost like crazy to fly, then there's your medical bills, and, of course, a rental fee for the use of my drone."

"Rental? I oughta be charging you for beta testing that thing," I said.

He looked me in the eye for a moment, then laughed. "Be happy with a quarter million, Ajaya. And yes, you will get paid for consulting with us. I'll give you a few days to recuperate, plus the team will be knee-deep in Spider parts for the rest of the week, so let's see you back here on Monday."

Corporal Jossom appeared behind him in the hall and he spun around as soon as my eyes went to her. "Ah, Corporal. Kindly escort our Mr. Gurung to his family, if you will. You can hand over his weapons at the door to the building," he ordered, handing her my guns. He nodded at me and strolled away.

Kayla watched him till he was gone, then reached for my bag of gear.

"I can handle it," I said. She nodded once, then proceeded to snatch it out of my hand.

"When you're better. Plus, you're gonna need your arms free for all the hugs I sense coming your way. Come on," she said, leading me down the hall. She went a little fast and had to stop, as my pace was greatly reduced by the pulling of stitches, staples, and blistered tissue.

We went through a couple of halls and I started to feel winded.

"Isn't there like a wheelchair protocol or something?"

"Nah, that's civvy stuff. Here we march out, usually to a drill cadence."

"Oh, I guess I should count myself lucky," I said.

She laughed and pushed open the door in front of her. Suddenly there was a flood of Gurung women hugging me and fussing over me. Over Gabby's shoulder, I spotted Astrid smiling at me and I held out a hand to her. She grabbed it but Gabby turned and pulled her into the group hug.

Mom looked at me, eyes wet. "Your unfinished business finished?"

"Yup, at least as far as I know," I said, realizing I didn't know what became of Harper or Rikki.

"Well, let's get you home."

Chapter 38

Aama had a huge meal ready for me and I ate as much as I could, then rested in the armchair, Dad's old chair, in the living room. Trinity came to visit with JJ Johnson. But the real kicker was Brad Johnson and Martin walking in.

"Quite a day's work, Ajaya," Brad said, waving to the video playing on the wall. The military had released an edited video of me on the bridge with Rikki and the Decimator and Lotus. It cut out when Lotus fell into the East River, but there was some pretty violent footage of me and the two drones cutting through a veritable swarm of flyers, a handful of Wolves, a single Tiger, and two Leopards. I had some pretty good shots on flyers but I hadn't even seen the ground units, as the Decimator had killed them all by itself. Those little missiles it shot were hella powerful. "You killed a Spider CThree. I know there's bad blood between us but I gotta say... your old man would be bursting with pride right now."

Part of me wanted to tell him to go to hell, but my mother was watching anxiously and so was Astrid, so I nodded and smiled and thanked him.

"Listen, if you want to go for any of that other drone cache, we'd be real interested," he said.

I glanced at Mom again and saw her worried look. "You know, maybe we can work a deal. I supply the location, you take the risk, and I get a percentage."

The shine of greed lit up in his eyes, but he just nodded. "I'm sure we can work something out."

Brad and Martin left a little later, Martin never saying anything to me but I did get a nod as he left. Rather the snotty bastard kept his mouth shut anyway.

The building super, Lee Hudson, came in with someone behind him. He was about sixty, with deep brown skin and a short, cropped white beard and crew cut white hair. Always wore jeans, a button-up khaki shirt, and work boots. Didn't matter if it was summer or the dead of winter. Same uniform every day.

"Ajaya, I just wanted to tell you I got your friend situated in the studio apartment downstairs," he said, moving aside so I could see who was with him. Harper stood there, dressed in new black tights, a new button-up shirt, and flats, holding a string bag with something round inside it. She had a clear bandage on one cheek but otherwise looked fine. No prosthesis on her face though. Her skin tone was uneven.

"Oh hey, you made it," I said.

"Yup. Piece of cake."

"Ajaya, who is this?" Mom asked, coming up on us from the kitchen.

"Mom, this is… Harper," I said, realizing I didn't know if she was using her real name or not.

"Hi Mrs. Gurung, I'm Harper Leeds."

"That's really similar to the famous Harper," Mom pointed out. "Yeah, my mom had a pretty interesting sense of humor," she said, a little flash of pain crossing her face. She wasn't broadcasting her thoughts on her face as much, or maybe it was just that she was learning to control her expressions a bit.

"How do you two know each other?" Mom asked.

"We were in the same AI class in community college. Worked on a couple of projects together," Harper said smoothly. "When I told Ajaya I was moving to Brooklyn, he mentioned that this building had an unleased studio. So here I am."

I realized that the room was very quiet and glanced around. My sisters were studying Harper with thoughtful expressions, Aama was frowning as she brought out more food, Trinity and JJ seemed mildly curious, and Astrid—Astrid had her arms crossed and a slight frown on her face as she looked the newcomer over.

"Oh, here. It's the last of the robotics stuff from our lab. You said you could use it for something," Harper said, handing me the bag with a familiar orb-shaped object inside.

"Hi, I'm Monique," "I'm Gabby," said twins one and two, inserting themselves into the conversation.

"Oh, I saw you both on the television interview. Ajaya, your sisters are so beautiful," Harper said, shaking their hands.

The dangerous duo does like flattery, so it didn't hurt, but they were still oddly reserved. Then Gabby spun and pointed to Trinity and JJ.

"Have you met JJ Johnson? Or Trinity Flottercot? She's the producer of *Zone War,* you know?" Without hardly a pause, she spun the other way and waved a hand at Astrid. "Or AJ's best friend... Astrid Johnson?"

They all said hello, JJ and Trinity with bemused expressions on their faces.

That was a really odd way to introduce them all, I thought, studying my sisters.

"Wow, I was just going to pop up and say hi. I didn't realize I would be meeting so many celebrities," Harper said. "I also didn't realize you were all banged up like this, Ajaya. I should leave you all to get back to your gathering." She started to back away, her eyes cutting away like she was nervous.

"Oh nonsense," my mother said, frowning at Gabby. She smiled at Harper and led her over to the food. "You must be starving if you just moved in. Have some food." Mom's hostess instincts were kicking in.

"She didn't have hardly anything to move," Mr. Hudson said, almost to himself. "Just all those bags."

Harper glanced at him, eyes worried, then back to my mom. "That's very nice of you, Mrs. Gurung, but I feel like I'm intruding on family time."

Mom gave the room a frown, then smiled at Harper. "Not at all. I for one would like to hear how my son did in class. He got good grades but he never really shared many details."

"Well, he knew quite a bit from going into the Zone, but not as much as he thought, right, Ajaya?" Harper said, raising an eyebrow at me.

"That's true. Got schooled more than I want to admit," I said. The twins were kind of crowding near me, and I noticed that Astrid had moved up closer.

"AJ, you never mentioned your friend Harper?" Astrid asked.

"Well, Trid, we haven't had a lot of catch-up time lately. The show and the Zone and all," I said, trying to figure out what the new dynamic was. The pain meds I had swallowed weren't helping much either.

"Trid? What a cute nickname," Harper said, smiling, but it looked forced.

"Well, they've known each other *forever*," Monique said, reaching out to wrap an arm around Astrid's narrow waist.

"Yeah, that's great. Hey, thanks for the food and all, but I really have to get things settled downstairs. Thank you so much, Mrs. Gurung. Ajaya, I'll see you around," Harper said, looking around for a place to set her plate.

"Take it with you, dear. You can drop it by later. You live in the same building now," Mom said.

"Well, it's absolutely delicious, so if it's truly okay, I'll take you up on that."

"Well, Ajaya's grandmother is an amazing cook," Mom said, pointing out Aama, who had stayed out of the room for the introductions. "Her paneer marsala is legendary."

"It's the very best I've ever had, ma'am," Harper said sincerely. Aama smiled at the ring of absolute truth in her words. Harper wouldn't have had much opportunity for fine cuisine, growing up in the Zone. Probably her first Indian food of any kind.

"Take some nan too. It's fresh out of the oven," Aama said, putting a whole piece on Harper's plate.

"Okay, well, I've stayed too long. Nice to meet you all," Harper said, sliding out of the apartment as fast as she could. Mr. Hudson looked like he wanted to stay but ended up leaving too.

Mom had her arms folded and was staring at the twins with a dangerous frown on her face. A huge yawn hit me right then and my mother turned my way immediately, her frown changing to a worried one.

"You're exhausted, aren't you?"

"Yeah. I think, if it's okay, I might go to my room and call it a night," I said.

"Here, I'll help you," Astrid said, plucking the string bag from my hands before I could stop her. I said my goodbyes and then led Astrid down the little hallway to my room.

She closed the door mostly shut behind her, then looked at me as she hefted the bag gently, with both hands.

"Is this what I think it is?" she asked.

"Open it."

She loosened the drawstrings and held them wide open. Rikki floated up, spun in place, then hovered over to my desk and the induction power station there.

"AJ, who is that girl and why did she have Rikki?"

"That's a long, long story, Trid. I'm not sure I have the energy."

"Give me the condensed version. You didn't meet her in any class, did you?"

I shook my head. "Some of it's her story and not mine to tell, but I met her in the Zone."

"*In the Zone?*"

"Yeah, crazy right? Met her and her mother. Her mom didn't make it out. She snuck out on the lower level of the bridge while I was up top, creating a big distraction."

"Is that what you call that? Funny, I thought it was you almost getting killed a hundred times in ten minutes," she said, frowning at me, arms crossed, one hand waving at my wounded body.

"Well, I hadn't planned on the Spider."

"Really? Going toe to toe with a Spider CThree wasn't in your playbook?"

"Was it that bad to watch?"

"AJ, it was the most horrible thing I've ever seen. Only knowing I was seeing a replay and that Zone Defense had already announced you were alive and being treated made it watchable at all."

"Really? I'll have to take a look. Not right away though. Still too fresh."

She came closer, unfolding her arms and grabbing my right hand in both of hers. "AJ... Ajaya, I saw you almost die over and over again and something almost died inside me. Don't ever do that to me again, you hear me?"

She was very close now and I could smell strawberries again and feel the heat coming off her skin. My heart was pounding.

"I told Mom I would most likely stop going into the Zone after I finished up some business."

"Getting that girl out was the business?"

"Yeah. Pretty much. There's a bit more to add, but I don't see why I'd have to go back in."

"I'd prefer it if you didn't."

"But you're still going in? Right?"

"That's very much different. I have tons and tons of steel surrounding me, plus my brothers and my father. And even then, I think our future trips will be short and sweet. Maybe drone cache recovery for a potential new client," she said, smiling at me.

"Well, that's not a certainty."

"Oh, I don't know. Maybe if I do some schmoozing. Wine and dine the client. Think he could resist my charm?"

"You? He'd probably give you his lunch money if you asked," I said.

"Oh, he already did. Whenever I ran short of funds in middle school, I knew I could count on him."

"That only happened like four or five times," I said.

"Six, and I owe him thirty-seven dollars and forty-two cents, including interest at three percent."

"You'd owe most of it to his mom. She gave him extra money after the first time just so you'd be covered if you forgot your own."

She pulled back and blinked. "Really?"

"Absolutely. I told her... I mean *he* told her that your dad had forgotten to give you money and that he'd split his lunch with you. She insisted he always have a secret five dollar bill in his backpack for just such emergencies. Then she'd replace it if you needed it."

She swiped at her eyes but just managed to smear her tears all around.

"Hey, what's the matter?" I asked, getting alarmed despite the soft fuzz of the pain medication.

"It's just that your whole family has always been there for me, and my family hasn't been there for you."

"Well, we like *you*, irrespective of family. Plus, *you've* always been there for us. Look what you did for the twins with those shitty kids in their school. That was huge. To have a TV star show up? Big stuff. They'll love you forever."

"What about you?"

"Well, they're my sisters so I *think* they love me on *some* level, but probably not as much as you."

"No, you idiot. How do you feel about me?"

"Oh! I thought we already went over that?" I said. She just gave me a baffled look. "You know? The lunch money thing?"

"*That's* supposed to be some kind of declaration or something?" she asked, hands on hips.

It was distracting, but I kept my eyes on hers.

"Ah, hello? Teenage boy giving up food for teenage girl is maybe one of the biggest declarations possible!"

She tapped a red lip with one finger, thinking it over. "In many cases, that's just lust, but in this case I'll allow that it was pretty special." Then she leaned over, fast, and kissed me on the lips. The motion was fast, but the kiss was long. I tried to move her closer but my motion pulled on various wounds and I suddenly gasped in pain.

"Not the reaction I was expecting," she said, with a quick grin to let me know she was kidding. Then she frowned. "That's enough for you, Mister Catches Flechettes With His Bare Skin. You need to heal up."

"What about the music guy?" I asked.

She waved a hand. "That's been over for days. You *do* know that it was set up by our publicists, right?"

"Maybe to begin with, but I'm sure he's devastated. Probably got too needy, right?"

"No, his publicist got too needy. Wanted to find ways to include *you* in our photo ops."

"Me? Why me?"

"Poor clueless sniper boy. You're a hot ticket right now."

A bad thought occurred to me. She read my face before I could cover it up. "Don't you dare say what you're thinking. I'll slap you so hard, your whole family will feel it. I would *never* do that to you." Her arms were crossed again, so I'd fallen very far, very fast since the kiss.

"No, I know. I just wonder sometimes why you'd ever want to hang out with me when the whole world wants you."

"You'll find out how real that whole world thing is soon enough. They want the fiction they see on the screen. We both know how much reality is in reality shows, even if this one airs live."

"Well, I think my fame will be fleeting at best. After all, I'm out of the Zone business."

"I hope so, but I know you, AJ. It draws you like a bee to honey," she said with a sad smile. She kissed my lips, quick like, then pushed my head backward till I fell back on the pillow. "Rest. We'll be having that story from you in the very near future."

She stood up and walked to the door, turned, gave me a smile, and then clicked off the lights and stepped out into the hall, closing the door behind her.

I lay back in the darkness, just the soft hum of Rikki charging and the burble of background voices from the living room, thinking about the sudden vast changes in my life. The family suddenly had more money than we had ever had before, not rich, but at least secure for now. Rikki was out of the Zone and safe, for now. And Astrid seemed as into me as I was her. I hoped it wasn't just for now.

"Shit, Gurung! Things are the best they've ever been. Can't you stop worrying for a moment and just enjoy?" I asked myself in a whisper.

"The implications of being at the top are that there is only down," Rikki suddenly said, his volume as quiet as my whisper.

"Let's hope not, Rikki. Let's hope not."

Chapter 39

The thing about pain meds is that they wear off. This point was made abundantly clear when I rolled over sometime later and pulled hard on a stitch. Suddenly wide-awake and blinking in pain, I sat there in the dark for a few minutes, sucking in deep breaths. My motion alerted my AI, which helpfully projected the time onto the ceiling. Too soon for any more of the good stuff, which I probably wanted to avoid anyway. So ibuprofen was in order. None in my bedside table, but there's always some tucked in the pockets of my stealth suit, or in this case, what was left of it. I got out of bed and rummaged through till I found some, also finding the little data chip that Dr. Wilks had handed me.

Swallowing the pills, chased with lukewarm water from a glass that Mom must have left next to my bed, I contemplated the chip.

"AI, please scan this chip," I whispered, putting the chip on the reader/scanner surface.

"Just one file. Labeled Play Me.*"*

"Okay, play it, volume super low."

"Affirmative."

A video window appeared on my blank wall and opened to reveal Dr. Wilks staring into the camera.

"Whoever you are, the fact that you're watching this means that I am likely dead. My name is Dr. Theodora Wilks and I am the person responsible for programming the Spider CThrees that were released into Manhattan. I mean to say that I did not choose the direction of their programming, just that I was the

336

one who upgraded their CPU capabilities and coded their neural nets. When their purchasers... I won't say owners because nobody owns them now... gave them their initial instructions, I argued long and hard against it.

"But ultimately, it wasn't up to me and had I known what they would be used for, I would never have agreed to enhance them to the degree I did. But that's all behind us now. I'm sure if there is an afterlife, then I am already atoning for my actions even as you watch this.

"Here is the important part of this message. The Spiders that I finished were, at their time, the most advanced AI networks on the planet. That may sound like bragging, but it's the simple truth. Today, there are more powerful chips and more sophisticated systems out there, but none have been running... growing... learning, as long as the Spiders have. You need to know this. Their instructions were open-ended. The people who released them into Manhattan programmed them with one simple order—kill humans. With no other restriction, the Spiders will do everything in their considerable power to complete that order. Kill humans... all humans... everywhere. You should under no circumstances believe that just because they are momentarily contained on the island that they aren't actively pursuing their mission. They won't stop, they'll never stop, and my modifications will give them a viable lifespan far in excess of their original specifications.

"They have to be stopped. Even contained on the island, they have access to the internet via optic lines running through the city. They are unmatched for hacking power and experience. They already control more around you than you could imagine. Should they succeed in escaping the island, they will spread out and seek to fulfill their mission. Eradicate humans— everywhere. They must be stopped. They must be killed. If you have this message, you need to pass it on. Without any sense of overdramatics, the fate of the human race depends on your actions. A list of the improvements made follows."

"End video," I said.

I looked at the clock. My retirement from the Zone lasted all of five and a half hours. Shit, Mom was gonna be pissed.

Author's notes:

Thanks for reading *Zone War*. It's a new direction for me, a bit different from the Demon Accords (which I will be writing for a long time). Ajaya, Astrid, Harper and Rikki will all be back in the second book of the Zone War series, *Borough of Bones*. You can expect to see that book in 2019.

Before I thank the usual suspects, I would like to dedicate this book to my friend Gary Eggers, a true gentleman who loved the idea that a finance guy could also be a writer of fiction. I miss my weekly conversations with you, my friend.

Susan Helene Gottfried has helped coach readable sentences from my grammar challenged drafts and Gareth Otton has once again come through with a cover that captures my mind's eye.

My family is always behind me, urging me on, bucking me up and ready to bring me back to Earth when my imagination takes me too far away. Thank you Emilee, Alli and, of course, my lovely Robin. You three are the world I orbit.

I also want to thank Susmita Dhakal and Rohit Tha Shrestha for giving me words and insights into the Nepali culture (as well as Alli for introducing and sharing your wonderful friends with me). Any translation errors or misquotes are solely my own.

Please follow me at www.johnconroe.com or on Facebook at the Demon Accords page. Now please excuse me while I get back to work. There's so much more to write.

Made in United States
North Haven, CT
18 June 2023

37906014R00203